"Suppose I were to tell you that I meant to kiss you," Nicholas said.

Emma closed her eyes and said, "You may proceed, sir." A pause followed, but no kiss.

"You are very odd, Miss Drenville," Nicholas said, bemused. "Most young ladies behave as though they are shocked that a gentleman wishes to kiss them."

"Why?" Emma wondered.

Nicholas laughed. "I thought, being a young lady yourself, you might tell me."

"I fancy that some young ladies are offended by kisses," Emma ventured to guess. "Others, like myself, have been kissed and petted by their families since an early age and find it most pleasant."

"You are not only beautiful but wise as well," Nicholas declared, and taking her firmly by the shoulders, he pulled her to him and kissed her.

Emma was used to love from her family—but Nicholas's lips on hers gave the first hint of how dangerously little she knew of the love he was offering her . . .

DAUGHTER
OF THE
DREADFULS

by

Barbara Sherrod

A SIGNET BOOK

SIGNET
Published by the Penguin Group
Penguin Books USA Inc., 375 Hudson Street,
New York, New York 10014, U.S.A.
Penguin Books Ltd, 27 Wrights Lane,
London W8 5TZ, England
Penguin Books Australia Ltd, Ringwood,
Victoria, Australia
Penguin Books Canada Ltd, 10 Alcorn Avenue,
Toronto, Ontario, Canada M4V 3B2
Penguin Books (N.Z.) Ltd, 182–190 Wairau Road,
Auckland 10, New Zealand

Penguin Books Ltd, Registered Offices:
Harmondsworth, Middlesex, England

First published by Signet,
an imprint of Dutton Signet,
a division of Penguin Books USA Inc.

First Printing, January, 1994
10 9 8 7 6 5 4 3 2 1

 REGISTERED TRADEMARK—MARCA REGISTRADA

Printed in the United States of America

To my daughters, Nancy and Ruthie

CHAPTER ONE

A Perfect Loppet

Dear Lady Landsdowne,

In answer to your kind letter, I send you a basket of cress, which I believe you will find as crisp and peppery as that which you so admired Tuesday last at the Admiral's table. In addition to ornamenting your salade verte, it will provide excellent accompaniment to his lordship's cheese and biscuits. Or you may prefer, as my Aunt Fanny does, to dip a sprig in salt and eat it on warm bread with pink shrimps. The Admiral begs me to send his compliments to you and his lordship and urges you to quit the Castle before Sunday at dawn, as that is when the enemy will most certainly strike. In the event it does not, however, he asks if he may expect you to tea the following afternoon.

As ever, I am your ladyship's most obedient servant,

Emma Drenville

As Emma walked by the side of a ditch, she paused from time to time to pick a sprig of wild parsley. In the process of gathering herbs for her basket, she invariably slipped on the melting snow or stumbled into one of the many spring puddles that dotted the lane. Reaching for a curly leaf, she slid on a patch of ice. The result was that her charming green morning dress—like her charming bonnet, spencer, and nose—was spotted with mud, much to the vexation of her cousin George.

This young gentleman trailed after her, fastidiously avoiding the snares that had sullied Emma. She strode ahead at a pace so brisk and so heedless of the mud that it required all his energy to keep pace. "You have not answered me," he complained, neatly evading a splash from her boot.

Emma had been preoccupied with admiring the hint of yellow buds resplendent on the trees. It appeared to her that spring was about to burst forth with glorious fanfare. But when she heard George scolding her, she slowed and grew remorseful. "Dear me, I am afraid I have forgotten the question."

Exasperated, he hastened to catch up with her. "Blast it, Emma. When a gentleman proposes marriage, he expects a lady to listen with more than half an ear."

"You are right, of course," she apologized. "I ought to have paid closer attention. I do beg pardon." Here she stopped at the entrance to a wood and considered the path that led into the trees.

Her cousin stopped by her side, saying, "An apology is all very well, but it does not constitute a reply."

Emma did not hear, for she had turned onto the path and was following it toward a stream that wove into the hazy sunlight amidst alders and buckthorns. She was already kneeling on a stone surrounded by a pool of gurgling water when George found her. As she reached for a clump of watercress, he warned, "You shall wet your stockings."

She smiled, though the water was freezing cold on her hand. "I always wet my stockings. It would scarcely be a proper cressing if I did not. Indeed, you would scarcely know me, nor would I know myself, if I came away from this or any other adventure without wet stockings or a muddied hem or a bloodied finger or a torn petticoat or some catastrophe of that nature." During this speech, she succeeded in locating a likely specimen of delicately bronzed cress. Unable to resist a taste, she bit off a leaf. The plant, meanwhile, dripped onto her skirt.

It was not lost on George that his cousin was soaking her dress. "You want taking care of," he stated. Carefully, he employed his linen to dust off the bark of an alder so that he might lean against it. "It is a wonder to me that a young lady as sensible and beautiful as you are could have turned out so utterly lacking in grace."

"It is a wonder to me, too," she agreed. "I am a perfect loppet. But it is very amiable of you to say I am beautiful."

"I only speak the truth when I say you are beautiful. Everybody says so. I mean your hair, that gold color—it is the most remarkable thing, especially in our family, which is so undistinguished. And the curl of it. How do you contrive to look so divine and still be a loppet, as you say?"

In an effort to gather another clump of cress, Emma inadvertently dislodged the stone that supported her hand. It fell into the stream, sending up a splash that wet her face. Laughing, she licked a drop from her lips and held the watercress aloft for George to see. "I believe it is a Greek proverb that advises, 'Eat cress and gain more wit.' Perhaps if I have another taste, my gracelessness will improve." She chewed slowly, closing her eyes as she relished the piquancy of the ripe cress. Then abruptly, she stood tall with her arms spread wide, her basket dangling from her wrist, and while the rock under her feet shifted alarmingly, she declared, "I do believe that I am transformed. The cress has worked its magic. When I join you on the bank, dear cousin, I shall be as elegant as a statue." She held her hands up for him to see. "Look, George, look at my fingers. No longer shall they be all thumbs!"

Horrified at the sight of Emma poised precariously on the rock, he cried, "Do not move, Emma! I shall come and save you."

Gallantly he leaped toward her, pitching himself as well as her off balance, so that they both emerged from the bubbling water with wet stockings and boots.

Emma's laughter did little to mollify him. He scolded, "I hope it will also amuse you when I catch my death. Oh, how can you use me so! I had thought you were merely awkward. Now I come to find you are heartless as well."

This charge stung her. If there was one thing Emma Drenville cherished, it was seeing the people she loved smiling and contented. When they were not, she grieved, and in those instances when she was the cause of their discontent, she grieved most of all.

She had found it increasingly difficult of late to grieve for George, who was forever scolding her, and as it appeared that she could never please him, she had determined not to trouble herself by trying. But in this instance, she could not help feeling some compassion for him. His wet stockings and dull boots, she knew, would render him disconsolate for days. More important, regardless of how much he might scold and complain, he was a Drenville, a member of her family, and, as such, he held first claim on her loyalties.

"I expect I have gathered enough watercress to enliven both Lady Landsdowne's tea and ours," she said with a gentle smile, "so I shall take you home now, George, and you may give me a wigging as we go, for I know that is what will make you happy, though the entire calamity was your own fault, if I may say so. Had you left me to my own devices, we should never have got ourselves soaked. Or at least *you* would not have got soaked. No doubt *I* should have got soaked. I always do."

The young gentleman had been engaged in shaking the water from his feet. In answer to this speech, he grumbled, "I suppose you would have liked it better if I had let you drown."

With as much contriteness as she could feign, Emma said, "Well, you were very brave to come after me, and I thank you," after which she permitted herself to be led along the path to the lane and thence to the road to Cracklethorne. As soon as it appeared that George had calmed a bit, she ventured, "I hope this adventure teaches you that we must not marry. We are not at all suited, you know. I drive you quite distracted, though not with love. When you do choose a bride, I trust she will not be so maladroit as to cause you to ruin your hose and your Hessians."

"I have every intention of marrying you," he stated, "if I can keep from throttling you."

She smiled. "You are a sweet old thing and I am obliged

to you, but I cannot allow it. You would risk life and limb by such a union."

"I am already dished up. Marriage to you—though fraught with peril—will be the saving of me, the saving of us both, in point of fact."

"I was not aware that we wanted saving."

"The Admiral has said he will settle an income upon each of us when we marry. If we marry soon, and marry each other, we shall have enough to support an establishment of our own, one as far from Southampton as it is possible to get. We shall be free of the Drenvilles."

"But I do not wish to be free of the Drenvilles."

He regarded her skeptically as he steered her round a puddle on the path. "Then you have not considered your true position, Emma. You shall never be able to marry. I doubt there is an eligible prospect who has not heard of our family. If such a creature exists, it will not be long before he sees for himself what he is about to marry into, and when he does, you shall soon find yourself jilted. We have no choice but to marry each other if we are to escape the Admiral's household."

With genuine sorrow, she replied, "More than anything, I wish you could be happy at Cracklethorne."

"Happy! Happy! How can one be happy—condemned to live with a grandfather who insists that the French mean to invade England through the port of Southampton and that it is his duty and the duty of every member of his household to be on the watch so that we may have earliest tidings of the plunder and pillage?"

"Grandpapa does no harm," she said. "Surely you might indulge him in his little oddity. He has been so amiable as to give us a home where we have been coddled and fed and taught and fondled in the most affectionate manner. He has been the only parent we have known since our early years. Moreover, he has, as you say, settled an income on each of us."

"Which we cannot touch until we marry. Do you not see,

Emma? Until we marry, we cannot be independent. We are prisoners!"

"I wish you would not say such things. Grandpapa is the kindest creature who ever lived."

"I should find it infinitely preferable if the Admiral were less kind and more like other folk. They laugh at him everywhere he goes, and it reflects upon us, Emma. They point at us and say, 'What a pity. Such a beautiful young lady. Such a handsome young fellow. But with such a family, there is no hope of their ever being received in polite Society or of marrying well.'"

"I am glad they say you are handsome, George, for you are. You have the noble Drenville nose and the excellent pointed chin."

"Do not attempt to divert me from the subject. Noses and chins notwithstanding, I overheard Lady Landsdowne whisper to Mrs. George Austen Tuesday last that we were the most lamentable creatures who ever lived because we were doomed never to know connubial bliss. Nobody with a groat's worth of sense would have us, she said."

Gravely, Emma replied, "I had thought better of Lady Landsdowne. I did not think she was a gossip, and I do not know that I shall send her any cress after all."

"You cannot blame her ladyship. She speaks only the truth. Coming from such a family as we do, we are doomed to loneliness and woe. Why, consider Uncle Angus. Nobody makes more indecorous, mortifying observations than Uncle Angus. Do you recollect what he said at dinner? He had the face to ask Lord Landsdowne if he did not think he was too fat to wear a fitted waistcoat!"

Suppressing a smile, Emma replied, "Yes, he did say something to that effect, but he is very old, and his lordship was not discomposed in the least."

"And what of Aunt Fanny? I spend my days hiding in the stairwell to avoid her because whenever she spies me or any human creature, she launches into an account of her errands and activities, and so minutely that I think I shall go distracted. Only this morning, she told me of her visit to the draper's—the cloth she bought, its color, measurements, texture, and cost. I did my utmost to doze off, but there was no escaping her catalog."

Emma laughed. "Aunt Fanny does require a bit of patience, I will allow."

"Not as much patience as Aunt Harriet, however. When Miss Harriet Drenville suffers one of her periodic attacks of deafness, the entire world is required to shout at the top of its lungs. Poor Aunt Fanny has forgot how to speak in a civilized tone; she shouts at me and all the world as though we were as deaf as her sister. I have questioned Dr. Fortescue very nearly on Aunt Harriet's malady and he assures me there is no such thing as occasional deafness. One is either deaf or one is not. I believe, and he concurs, that she is deaf out of spite."

"Aunt Harriet does not like to be ignored. It therefore suits her at times to appear deaf. It does no great harm."

"It is perfectly insupportable—all that screeching—as though we were fishmongers instead of people of refinement and taste. If you care for me at all, Emma, or for yourself, you will accept my proposal so that we may be at liberty to live in a house where there is nobody who is tiresome excepting ourselves."

Shaking her head sadly, Emma acknowledged, "I was aware that their oddities plagued you, though I did not know until now how very desperate you were. But I am not like you, George. You are blessed with a tender sensibility, while I am oblivious to niceties. Perhaps that is why I am content to remain with my grandpapa and his brother and sisters. I am saddened to learn that there are those who whisper about us, and I wish they would not. But I cannot forget those I love and those who love me simply because others choose to whisper."

"They do not merely whisper. They snigger."

Emma put a soothing hand on her cousin's arm.

"Do you know what they call us?" he cried. "Do you know what our acquaintance in Southampton and even as far as London call us?"

She felt his distress so keenly that she spoke with great softness. "I did not know they called us anything at all."

He looked about, as though certain he would find a French spy, or what was worse, the Admiral, lurking behind the hawthorn hedge, ready to mount a surprise attack. "The Dreadfuls!" he said hoarsely. "Instead of the Drenvilles, they call us the Dreadfuls. Unless we escape that house full of rum touches and loose screws, we shall be outcasts for the rest of all eternity."

"We shall not be outcasts," Emma said resolutely. "We shall find a way out of this pickle, I promise you. Nobody shall mock our family. When you go to the Dolphin or Castle Square or the beach, the gossips shall not presume to pity you. They will say, 'There goes Mr. George Drenville, the most fortunate fellow this side of the Itchen.' That is what they shall say of you, George. And when you go up to Town, the ton will endeavour to outdo one another in courtesy and attention to you. We shall find the means to make it so. I give you my word."

Emma set her jaw in determination. She had just taken her oath to help her cousin, and she meant to spare no effort, no sacrifice, to see him happy.

George sighed. "I am not entirely selfish, you know. My wish to marry you is prompted by a conviction that your loyalty, while commendable in itself, renders you somewhat careless of your own best interest. I wish to love you and look out for you. I think I should make a creditable husband. At least, I should do my best."

This speech, spoken with emotion, moved Emma. "Oh, you would make a most creditable husband," she said, patting his cheek, "for you are a dear, and I adore you."

Hearing this, George felt more contentment than he had for some time, for as far as he was concerned, she had just agreed to bestow upon him her hand in marriage.

As soon as they returned to Cracklethorne, Emma deposited her basket of herbs with the cook and sought out her uncle Angus, whom she found on the terrace, swearing

and shaking his fists at a flock of crows, whose noisy cack-
ling had wakened him from a nap. Kissing him on the
cheek, Emma asked if she might have a moment with him.
She had an urgent matter to discuss.

"Where have you been?" he asked. "Did you go looking
for a husband? I hope so, Emma, my dear goosechild, for
you are twenty-two and no spring chicken."

Accustomed to her grand uncle's unorthodox style of
conversation, Emma ignored the question and led him to a
marble bench under a chestnut tree. When they had both
seated themselves, she took a breath for courage and asked,
"Uncle, I have heard a vile rumor that our family are called
'the Dreadfuls.' Is it true?"

He slapped his knee with laughter. "So you have heard
that, have you? No doubt that old sow Mrs. Dobbin has
been whispering. I shall be obliged to stomp on her daffodils by way of revenge." He chuckled, his eyes twinkling
with malice.

"Mrs. Dobbin has said nothing, and so I beg you not to
think of revenge." Angus's unbridled glee had unsettled
her. She could see how his singular manner, which she had
always smiled on indulgently, might strike one who did not
know him as dreadful. The more he chuckled, the more uneasy she grew. "Only tell me if it is true, and if it is, then
why."

"Now, now, daisytop, do not be in a pet. There is a very
good reason why we are the Dreadfuls."

"Perhaps there is a reason, but I cannot believe it is a
very good one." She blinked back tears.

"My dear flutterbelle," he said, beginning the tale, "the
first Drenville ever to trod English soil crossed over from
France with the conquering William. However, the family
achieved no distinction beyond a modest gentility until, in
the year 1806, your grandfather, my brother, Captain Francis Drenville, was exalted to the admiralty on account of
his boldness at Trafalgar. His sudden rise, and his capture
in the West Indies of three enemy privateers and their
booty, was the occasion for much whispering and wit in the

Town. You see, my brother will never mind his tongue and had made himself something of a laughingstock by proclaiming in speech and print that invasion by the French was imminent. Bonaparte meant to enter England through the small port of Southampton, he declared, and he took every opportunity to warn everybody within earshot to make preparations to meet an enemy so vicious that it would either relieve them of their heads or force them to learn a language fit only for coxcombs." He laughed uproariously at the absurdity of the notion.

"I am certain that Grandpapa merely wished to be of service to his country," she said glumly.

"Exactly so, but others did not view it in that light. They regarded him as odd. In consequence, he was the object of much jesting in the clubs and drawing rooms. One wag penned a couplet that circulated throughout London within hours of its inception:

> The gods have made him Admiral Drenville,
> But can they make him any less dreadful?

And from that day forward, he was Admiral Dreadful. The nickname also attached itself to the rest of us—myself, your doddering old Uncle Angus, two sisters, one an incessant prattler and the other deaf as a post; a grand nephew, George, who has taken up the profession of idleness with a zeal not often observed in young people; and finally, a granddaughter, you, my dear Emma, the dearest goosechild in all the world. Believe me, whatever they may say of the rest of us, the worst anybody can say of you is that you are handsome and exceedingly good-humored."

"How dare they speak of us at all!" Emma cried. In her indignation, she rose and paced before the bench.

"What do they say that isn't true?" Angus asked with a philosophical shrug. "Your grandfather will have it that the French mean to invade, I cannot seem to speak at all without uttering some foolishness, and as for Fanny and Harriet, they both have windmills in the head, which would be tolerable, given the faults of the rest of us, if only they were not such a pair of rattle-pated old blabs."

"Oh, Uncle Angus, this is appalling."

"Wait, you have not heard it all," he said cheerfully. "It may be worse than you think." After inducing her to sit once more, he continued, "There were those who, hearing the couplet, chose to shun the society of the Admiral and his family, principally great personages who value a man according to the vintage of his blood and the reputation of his tailor. I offered to waylay one or two of them on the street after dark, but my brother would not have it. I vow, he is too scrupulous by half."

"They would have put you in prison, Uncle Angus, and I should have missed you."

"Yes, but I should then have been at leisure to pen my memoirs. However, to return to the history of our family, your grandfather was fortunate in that his elevation excited the favorable notice of the Earl of Landsdowne. His lordship had lately built himself a mock-Gothic castle in the middle of Southampton, a city of eight thousand people, a castle situated among plain houses with cracked chimney pots, where, as you know, he now resides."

"It is certainly an extraordinary house. And Lord Landsdowne is certainly an extraordinary gentleman."

"Do not mince words, flutterbelle. His lordship is a queer fish, a case if there ever was one."

"Perhaps that is why he appreciates a high degree of eccentricity in Grandfather."

"I would not doubt it, for Lord Landsdowne took it upon himself to persuade the Admiral to settle near him in Southampton. Because he had long anticipated meeting Villeneuve and his invading forces on the beaches of this serene city, my brother was easily persuaded to make his home here. Immediately upon his separation from the navy, he purchased Cracklethorne."

"And we could not wish for a more charming house. It is

the prettiest sand-colored villa, and I love the garden, for it is directly on the Itchen."

"It isn't domestic charm which keeps your grandfather at Cracklethorne, dear daisytop. It is the French. Watching the water has always been a favorite occupation of Southampton's citizenry, and nobody has become more devoted to that pursuit than the Admiral. Indeed, he can be observed at any hour, gazing through his glass from the highest points of the city, keeping vigilant watch for the enemy. In fair weather, he walks from Cracklethorne to Windwhistle Tower and looks down on West Port, from which, as he informs me daily, Harry of England sailed to meet the French at Agincourt."

Emma felt as though a leaden weight had settled on her. She could see now that many of the events of recent years—the separation from the navy, the remove to Southampton, the purchase of Cracklethorne—had served to fix the Admiral's obsession with invasion more firmly than ever in his mind. After one of their frequent visits to Lord Landsdowne, she and her grandfather typically climbed the flight of steps leading from Castle Square to Catchcold Tower, and holding fast to their hats in the bright wind, they gazed for hours out to sea. When the tide was in, the two watched the waves lap the foundation walls of the old city. Passersby who stopped to chat noted that young Miss Drenville cherished almost as great an affection for the bounding main as the Admiral. He invariably replied that it was thanks to vigilance such as his and Emma's that Bonaparte would soon think better of picking a quarrel with the glorious British Navy. This pronouncement was always greeted with startled grimaces and hasty leavetakings. Emma ached to think that her grandfather's innocent pastime was cause for sneering and sniggering.

"And there you have the story," declared Angus. "It's a tedious tale, now I think of it, not half so amusing as the story of that old sow Mrs. Dobbin and her cicisbeo. You are shocked, I expect, to hear that a woman of her advanced years has been spied stealing into the tailor's shop at midnight, but I have witnesses who will swear to it, and, if she means to speak of our family in a manner that offends you, dear flutterbelle, then I shall broadcast word of her indiscretion to all my acquaintance."

While Angus proceeded to recount the details of Mrs. Dobbin's sordid liaison with the tailor, a seventy-eight-year-old man who was lame, bald, and dyspeptic, Emma wiped away tears. What roused her passion was the injustice of it all. If they knew her grandfather, really knew him for the sweet, generous old thing he was, the wags and gossips would be ashamed of their vile prattling. They would never be so cruel as to whisper behind her family's back, ridicule them, and dub them all "the Dreadfuls."

Well, she could not keep the world from its prattling and cruelty. But she could—and she would—know who her friends were. They were those who refrained from sneering and laughing, those who judged a man by his goodness of heart and not what he dressed it in. As for the others, the ones who did sneer and laugh, they were, quite simply, the enemy.

CHAPTER TWO

Captain Hale

To the Earl of Stonewood,

Dear Father, I am obliged to inform you that business keeps me in Southampton longer than anticipated. Please extend my compliments to my mother and be assured that I shall pay them to her in person as soon as I may.

Your dutiful and affectionate son,

Nicholas Hale

The view from the hack window struck Captain Hale as so charming that he called out to the driver to stop. As soon as the horses halted, he got out, instructed the driver to take his valises to the Dolphin, and tossed him a coin. When the hack had gone on its way, the captain looked about him and breathed in the agreeable air of early spring in Southampton. The street was close, narrow, and medieval, with overhanging buildings of dark timber crisscrossing cream-colored walls. It offered such a stark contrast to the open sea, which had been his home for eight months past, that he decided to walk to his hotel.

It amused him to notice as he walked that he had yet to find his land legs. As usual, he would require adjustment to terra firma. He had been wise, he thought, to promote his adjustment by packing his uniform and wearing instead his blue coat and fawn pantaloons.

Turning onto the elegant tree-lined esplanade, he found himself continually surprised by the steadiness of the street. After a time, during which he took in the ruins, the beach, the quay, and the picturesque banks of the rivers Itchen and Test, he turned north into the High Street. In leisurely fashion, he paused to admire the trim brick-built shops and to peer at the tarts in the baker's window and the lockets in the jeweler's. At the china shop, he stopped to consider whether he might find a gift for his mother inside. The Countess of Stonewood, though she possessed every trinket and gew-gaw known to man or woman, liked to receive gifts, especially from one of her sons, and whimpered quite pathetically if he came before her emptyhanded.

A bell tinkled prettily as he opened the door and stepped inside. Carefully, he made his way among the linen-covered tables on which stood samples of teapots, crockery, and platters of every design. One table in particular caught his eye, but not favorably. In the middle of it, propped on a stand, was a plate bearing the likeness of Admiral Horatio Nelson. Captain Hale stared at the image of his hero-mentor for many moments, overcome with revulsion. Nelson was portrayed as smiling into an unnaturally blue sky, wearing an expression of dotty beatitude. While Nelson himself would have hooted with laughter at such a nonsensical depiction, the captain abhorred its tawdry sentimentality, and as he had not only admired the great hero but loved him as well, the image on the plate roused his disgust.

Though it had been three years since the admiral had died in battle, Captain Hale still mourned him, not only because he did not think England would ever see his like again, but also because it was Nelson who had given him the opportunity to prove himself. His orders had been to sail with the *Mercury,* which was headed for Gibraltar in quest of supplies and water. Unwilling to leave either the admiral or the action, he had had the temerity to exhort Nelson in the most manly and earnest manner to permit him to stay. Amused at the young officer's determination and ardor, Nelson had relented.

"So, you wish to stick where you are, do you?" Nelson had laughed. "You prefer to see battle? Well, you are a fool and I am prodigiously fortunate to be surrounded by such fools."

Thus, Lieutenant Hale had fought on the deck of the *Victory.* He had sustained a wound to his shoulder and seen his admiral fall, fatally wounded. With Nelson's death, he had lost the kindest and most esteemed friend he had known. So deep had his sorrow been that he had scarcely mustered a smile when news came that he had won a medal and his own ship.

Those momentous events, still fresh and sore, had now been reduced to a grinning portrait on a bit of crockery. Captain Hale felt his neck grow hot and his eyes sting at the sight of it. Suddenly he wished he had never debarked from his ship. On the open sea, he was protected from abuses such as this plate represented to him—the exploitation of the memory of one of the greatest Britons who ever lived, the vulgarity and folly of public taste, the reduction of genuine patriotism to vile commercial enterprise. As he held the plate in his hand, he experienced an impulse to heave it against the wall with all his force, smashing it to pieces.

He was saved the trouble, however. At that moment, his elbow was jostled and he saw the plate fly into the air and come crashing to the floor in a scattering of porcelain splinters.

"Oh, I do apologize," he heard a gentle sweet voice exclaim. "I am such a loppet!"

He looked into a pair of eyes the color of the Caribbean on a sultry summer afternoon. Her hair was fine gold, curled round her ears and forehead. Framing her rosy complexion was a straw bonnet, tied with a vermillion ribbon. She stood nearly as tall as he did and presented a face of such pretty remorse, that he no longer wished to be back on the high seas. Indeed, he had no wish to be anywhere but where he was.

"I shall pay for the plate, of course," said the young lady.

If she had not worn an enchanting smile and two flaming cheeks, he would have thought she was a vision, a siren sent to lure lonely sailors to be dashed against the rocks.

"I shall not hear of your paying for it," he said with every appearance of calm. He hoped that by drawing her into a dispute, he might prevent her from going away.

"It is nothing," she said amiably. "I am always breaking the crockery in Mr. Dennis's shop. He is quite accustomed to it and is kind enough to add the sums to my account."

Her smile was disarming, so that he was obliged to remind himself to dispute further. "I cannot permit you to pay for the plate," he insisted. "You did me a great favor by breaking it, and therefore, it is my duty and pleasure to pay."

Her blue eyes went bright with curiosity. "I do not understand," she said. "How could you possibly benefit from the breaking of a plate?"

"I should like to break every plate which bears the likeness of Lord Nelson. If there are cups and saucers of the same ilk, I should be delighted to break those as well."

"You did not admire Lord Nelson, I collect."

"On the contrary. I admired him fervently."

She nodded. "I see. My grandfather was also devoted to his lordship, and like you, he cannot abide to see his face on trinkets and teacups."

"Your grandfather is clearly a gentleman of great discernment and taste."

She smiled archly. "Because he agrees with you?"

"No, because he has the wisdom to have a beautiful and charming granddaughter."

He quite expected the young lady to blush at this compliment. In his time, he had seen countless fashionable maidens produce studied blushes at such moments. It always amused him to see how cleverly a knowing and calculating female could contrive to seem innocent. His companion surprised him, however, by looking at him directly and saying, "I suppose that was flummery. You do it very well."

"Why do you call it flummery? Has nobody ever told you that you are beautiful and charming?"

"My grandfather says that gentlemen are in the habit of paying young ladies compliments which grossly exaggerate their attractions, and it is nothing but flummery."

"Surely he does not condemn the whole species of gentlemen. Surely there are some gentlemen who, upon occasion, speak sincerely, as, I take my oath, I am doing now."

"My grandfather says that none of them speak sincerely, excepting sailors."

He found that exception highly interesting, not to say pertinent. "Why sailors, if I may ask?"

"Because," she laughed, "Grandpapa is a sailor."

Captain Hale was on the point of confessing that he, too, belonged to that sincerest of professions, but an interruption occurred. An older lady trimmed out in laces, ribbons, powder, and beads approached in a flurry. "Oh, dear," she cried, "you have not broken another plate! I must go and tell Mr. Dennis." Instead of going away to tell him, however, she called loudly to the proprietor, who stood in another corner, and informed him, in a voice which summoned the attention of everybody in the shop, that he must fetch the broom at once.

Then, without looking at Captain Hale or, indeed, acknowledging his existence, she turned to the young lady and said, "Come, Emma, we must hurry. Mrs. Frank Austen expects us, and if we are to find you a new shawl for the assembly on Thursday, we must have her opinion. We must go to the chemist's for Angus's cough elixir and to the baker's for the tart I ordered for your grandfather. Afterward we are off to find a watch fob for your cousin George. I do not know how we shall contrive to do it all in a single day."

Captain Hale heard none of this itinerary. *Emma,* he said to himself. The young lady's name was Emma. It was a fine, plain, forthright, gentle, adorable English name, and though he had not thought about it before, it now occurred to him that it had always been one of his favorites.

The young lady glanced at him from time to time as she listened to the schedule being set out for her. He was pleased to see that at no time did she lower her lashes or pretend she was not glancing his way. These glances might have been taken for brazenness in another woman; in this one, they were clearly the product of a curious mind wholly incapable of dissembling. Her open looks told him much—she found him interesting to look at, she would have liked to continue their conversation, and she was not looking forward to an afternoon of shopping. At her next glance, he smiled at her, and instead of looking haughty and missish, as he had seen other young ladies do, she smiled warmly in return.

"Come, Emma," the flurried woman cried on her way to the door.

After throwing him an apologetic look, she followed the lady from the shop. He watched her go, oblivious to the shop boy who swept up the shards of porcelain by his feet. When he had collected himself enough to get out of the way, he located Mr. Dennis to pay him for the broken plate.

"It is unnecessary, sir," said the proprietor. "The ladies have an account and expressly wished the plate to be added to it."

"Oblige me by letting me pay for it," said Captain Hale. "At one hundred times the cost, it would still be worth it to have met the delightful Miss Emma."

Leaving the china shop, Captain Hale continued along the High Street until he reached the Dolphin Hotel. As soon as he was settled comfortably, he sent a note to his longtime friend, Lieutenant Dibdin Bentworthy, then seated himself by a tall window overlooking the dock to await a reply. Instead of a note, he had the pleasure of receiving Lieutenant Bentworthy himself, leaning heavily on a walking stick but wreathed in smiles.

"Why, you are walking," Captain Hale declared heartily. "I expected the French shot had done your business for you, but you have foiled the enemy, and splendidly."

"Walked the entire way myself," said the lieutenant with shy pride.

The captain saw that his friend was still breathless from the exercise and steered him toward a chair.

"Glad you have come," said the lieutenant, repressing a surge of emotion. "Very glad. Thank you."

"You will oblige me, Dib, by not thanking me. If you recollect, I promised I would come and see you that day when you lay on the deck, bleeding on my epaulettes. I swore then you would buy me a new pair, and I mean to hold you to it. That is why I no sooner arrived in port than I made my way here." He clapped the man affectionately on the shoulder. "Besides, one cannot forget a promise sealed in blood."

"Sorry about the stains. Not a proper way to repay the fellow who's just saved your skin, is it?"

"Let us not speak of it. Let us speak only of the present." Captain Hale invited his friend to sit and called to the host to serve them up some refreshment. Together, the gentleman looked out at the dock, where a graceful sloop was moored, her bare masts rising and falling lightly with the water.

"How long do you stay in Southampton?" Dib asked.

"Now that I see you are well, I shall set off for London tomorrow. I have written to my parents, but after eight months they will wish to see for themselves that I am still alive and reasonably whole."

The lieutenant's disappointment was evident. "Can you not stay longer, at least until the assembly?"

Ordinarily, Captain Hale took little interest in dancing parties of any kind. He had had his fills of balls, simpering misses and their rapacious mothers on the hunt for a son-in-law. But at the mention of the assembly, the captain recalled that the young lady who had assisted him in destroying the offensive plate had been preparing to attend it, a fact which rendered it uncommonly interesting. Accordingly, he inquired, "Are you acquainted, by any chance, with an exquisite damsel with golden hair and blue eyes who goes by the name of Emma?"

Dib smiled. "You sly dog, Hale. You have been on dry land less than half a day and already you have made a conquest."

The captain laughed. "No such thing. Indeed, the lady regards all my prettiest speeches as just so much flummery."

"Sounds a sensible girl, I vow."

"She appears sensible enough. I might add she is also good-humored, good-natured, and handsome."

"Unfortunately, there are a vast deal of young ladies hereabouts by the name of Emma. Can you give me any further clue to her identity?"

"She has a grandfather. That ought to help." He laughed.

Dib shook his head. "Be serious. I cannot ascertain the name of your lady love unless you tell me everything you know."

"I know that she associates with a chatterbox who hurries her hither and thither in quest of elixirs and watch fobs. I know that her grandfather is a sailor, and, therefore, an excellent fellow. I know that Miss Emma is so enchanting a creature that even if I had not been too long at sea I should still wish to know more of her."

A dreamy looked filled Dib's eyes. "I should like to see you fall in love with her. It would do you a world of good."

The captain's brows went up. "When did you become such a champion of love, my friend? Did that bullet take you in the brain as well as the leg?"

"It would make you quite perfect, you know. That is the only thing wanting in your character—a young lady to love."

Captain Hale regarded his friend ironically. "Love does not suit me. Despite what poets say in its favor, it is merely a commercial enterprise. A lady trades her virtue for a fortune and connections. A gentleman trades his fortune and his reason for her virtue."

"You are cynical. Where did you come by such notions?"

"The ladies I have known have taught me by their own illustrious example."

"Well, I have the pleasure to inform you that there are women of a superior nature who have tender hearts and good souls and men who contrive somehow to deserve them."

His suspicion roused, the captain said, "Tell me the lady's name, Dib."

The lieutenant blushed. "Which lady?"

"The one who has transformed you into this rhapsodizer."

Looking deep into his tankard, Dib confessed, "Her name is Clarissa Merkle, and she is an angel."

"Naturally. They are always angels, at the beginning, at any rate."

Rising to the lady's defense, Dib cried, "But she *is* an angel, I assure you. She has helped to nurse me these many months. If not for her ministrations, I daresay, I should have lost my leg altogether, and I certainly should have been incapable of walking here to see you today."

Captain Hale called for another draught for his friend. "I am prodigiously grateful to this Miss Merkle of yours."

"She is not mine, not yet, but she has promised to be, as soon as I am able to throw away this blasted walking stick. I depend upon you to attend the wedding."

Amused, the captain said, "So, this angel has persuaded you to marry, which, if I recall, you swore you would never do, not upon pain of death on the rack."

"It is true, I swore I should never marry, but if you knew Miss Merkle, you would know why I have changed my mind."

"You call her an angel, but I think she is a sorceress. She has cast a spell upon you, like a West Indian man of medicine. I am perishing to meet her."

"You may meet her at the assembly, if you will stay. Furthermore, you may have my permission to dance with her, as I am unable to perform so much as a turn in my present state."

Captain Hale considered this invitation. The longer he remained in Southampton, the longer he might put off the odious duty of visiting his parents' house. Further, he might not only meet the angelic Miss Merkle at the assembly, but there was every promise that he would encounter the interesting Miss Emma as well. In that event, he would have a dance with her and put her to the test, for, despite what experience, logic, and caution told him, he hoped that such innocent, forthright charm was capable of outlasting a single meeting.

CHAPTER THREE

Up to London

Dear Lady Landsdowne,

The Admiral, who has just come from Castle Square, informs me that his lordship is feeling poorly, and I am instructed to send you these chops suitable for preparing Invalid Lamb Cutlets. If you will have Mrs. Bloodbane trim the fat closely, add a few peas, and wrap the cutlets securely in paper before steaming, Lord Landsdowne will have a mild dish full of salutary juices. As to your kind hope of seeing me at the assembly on Friday, I am delighted to say you will. Unfortunately, an injury to the foot will prevent my dancing.

Yours, etc.,

Emma Drenville

Lady Landsdowne ascended her phaeton and pointed its six dainty ponies in the direction of Cracklethorne. When she alighted in the drive and was handed down by the footman at the door, she saw that she would not be permitted to speak privately with Emma or her grandfather without having first to run the gauntlet. The gauntlet, in the persons of Miss Fanny Drenville and her brother Angus, appeared in the door, smiles of welcome on their round, ruddy faces. The Admiral's youngest sister was turned out fetchingly in a lace cap and a yellow walking suit. The brother wore a coat and breeches in the style fashionable in the previous century. They made their way down the steps to greet the visitor, murmuring words of welcome.

"What did you pay for that equipage?" Angus inquired. "I'll wager it set his lordship back a pretty penny."

Ignoring Angus's impertinence, Miss Fanny said, "How kind of you to call, my lady. I am afraid I am unable to stay to welcome you properly. You will understand, I daresay. I am to take Angus's boots to the cobbler. He is most anxious for me to hurry, for he says nobody understands the mending of a boot better than myself, and therefore he insists upon my going at once. Indeed, he is so importunate that one would almost think he wished to be rid of me!"

"I do wish to be rid of you," Angus put in.

"Well, it is no bother, for I must stop at the silversmith's and the haberdasher's as well. Then I am to meet Mrs. Frank Austen at the Dolphin for tea, and we are to see whether her bombazine gown may be made fit for the assembly on Friday."

Her ladyship endured a recitation of Miss Fanny's errands with suppressed impatience, and as soon as she paused for breath, interjected, "Do not let me keep you. I see that you have pressing business, as do I. I must speak with the Admiral."

"Oh, you are most kind to excuse my running off," Miss Fanny cried, making no move to go. "Be assured that I would gladly have put off my errands in the High Street if I had not taken my oath to my sister Harriet that I would not stay but would go and get her a pound of green tea. She says there is nothing like green tea to alleviate her deafness, and I must hasten to purchase it before the price rises again, which she says it does every half hour. I daresay, she is as anxious to see me gone as my brother!" She punctuated this last with a titter.

"She could not possibly be more anxious to see you gone than I am," Old Angus remarked.

"Why thank you, Brother!" Fanny beamed while he rolled his eyes.

With supreme civility, Lady Landsdowne said, "I, too, am anxious to see you gone, for the longer you keep me in conversation—out of your too scrupulous wish to be hospitable—the longer your brother and sister go without their boots and their tea. And so I take my leave of you and wish you good day."

Before Miss Fanny could utter another apology or another catalog, her ladyship entered the house, where she informed the butler that she was to be announced to Admiral Drenville, but that Miss Emma was not to be told of her arrival until such time as she gave the word.

Accustomed to her ladyship's high-handedness, the butler bowed and led her to the deer parlor, so called because its wallpaper depicted bucks and does in various pleasant attitudes of grazing.

Admiral Drenville was seated in a straight-backed, thronelike chair, while his older sister, Miss Harriet, sat on a delicate stool, netting what resembled a shawl for a whale. Seeing who had entered, Miss Harriet put her trumpet to her ear, while her brother rose to greet her ladyship with genuine goodwill. He entreated her to sit on the rose brocade sofa, a place of honor in which the family never sat as it was reserved for her ladyship and her esteemed husband.

"It is Lady Landsdowne!" Miss Harriet shouted to her brother. Her deafness often resulted in her speaking at top volume so that she would not miss a syllable of what she was saying.

Her ladyship perceived that Miss Harriet was not in a hearing humor that day and would prove as difficult as Miss Fanny and Old Angus.

"It is indeed!" boomed the Admiral into his sister's trumpet.

Though Lady Landsdowne winced at the blasts of noisy conversation that passed between the brother and sister, the thrust of which was to inform each other again and again that Lady Landsdowne had come to visit, she composed herself enough to say, "Admiral, I have come to speak to you of your granddaughter."

"What did she say?" Miss Harriet demanded.

"She has come to speak of Emma!" he obligingly thundered.

"I see," the lady shouted in return. "She has come to speak to us of Emma. Such a dear girl, our Emma."

"Very dear indeed!"

"What I have to say, I must say to you in private," Lady Landsdowne whispered to the Admiral.

"What did she say?" Miss Harriet cried.

"She wishes to speak to me in private!"

Offended, Miss Harriet rose and with all stateliness, moved to the door, dragging with her her netting and her trumpet. "I should like to know what could be more private than to speak in my presence!" she sniffed. With a toss of her head, she made her exit.

"You must offer my apologies to Miss Harriet," said her ladyship. "If this matter were not so important, I should never have been obliged to speak with you alone."

"What is it?" the Admiral inquired with concern.

"As I said earlier, I wish to speak with you of Emma."

"A very dear girl, our Emma. So good-humored."

"And so deserving of happiness. Do you not agree?"

"Certainly I agree. Have I not seen to her happiness?"

"No, my good friend, you have not."

He sat bold upright, gaping. Nobody, with the exception of his brother Angus, had ever spoken to him so bluntly.

"Though your intentions are the best in the world, the fact is you have kept her confined to this house and a small circle of acquaintance. She is twenty-two years old and has had no experience of the world. Believe me, Admiral, I know whereof I speak. I myself was bred in virtual isolation. It was a life as tedious and lonely as your granddaughter's. The only relief was a single Season in London. Thanks to that opportunity to meet eligible young gentlemen, I met the one who was destined to become my husband. I should like to see Emma afforded the same opportunity."

Aghast, he cried, "What the deuce does Emma want with a husband?"

"For one thing, she will come into her money when she marries. You have settled it so. And for another, she may wish to have a life's companion, children, a house and garden of her very own."

"Nonsense. She has never indicated a wish for anything but what she may enjoy here, with her family."

Incensed at this shortsightedness, her ladyship said, "Of course she has never expressed such a wish! How could she? She has no notion of what the world offers. Before coming to Southampton, you kept her in that cottage in Lyme, with no society but that of her uncle and aunts, and no companion but her cousin, that bloodless prig George. Having brought her here, you have kept her too ignorant and secluded to comprehend that there is more to the world than what she knows at Cracklethorne."

"By Jove, you make it sound as though I've kept her locked in the brig. She goes to the assemblies at the Dolphin, does she not? She bathes in the sea, shops in the shops, and travels with me to Portsmouth when I go to observe the building of the frigates. What more could she wish for?" His breath came quickly as pique reddened his leathery cheeks.

"I am aware, Admiral, that you do not wish to part with her. You fear that if she were to go where she might experience something of the world, as every girl ought, you should miss her. But, speaking as one who has suffered as Emma suffers, I beg you to think of her and not yourself. You must look to her future."

Sheepishly, he allowed, "Cracklethorne would be the very devil without her—I hope you will excuse my salty language, my lady. We should all be at sixes and sevens if we did not have our dear Emma about. Why, it is Emma who prepares our broth and our pudding. She is not above visiting the kitchen, you know, and she quite likes baking my plum cake and burnt almonds. I'm afraid we could not possibly do without her."

"You could, Admiral, if you knew, as you must know, that you were providing for her happiness. You would make the sacrifice with a very good grace in that case, for

you are as good-hearted a gentleman as ever lived. If you
were not, my husband would not esteem you so greatly."

Pathetically, he sighed. "What would you have me do?"

"Permit me to send her up to London to my sister. There
she may be taught those things that only a Town education
can impart. She may be introduced into Society. She may
converse with young ladies and gentlemen of her own age
and of knowledge and manners superior to what she is able
to meet with in Southampton."

He shook his head. "I do not think she will like it. Even
if I did wish her to go, even if I were perfectly willing to do
without her, she would not wish it."

Her ladyship had to acknowledge that Emma was so
fond of her grandfather that she might be reluctant to leave
him. "It is true," she allowed, "she is dreadfully fond of her
family, but she is too sensible not to know her own best interest."

"She will refuse to leave us. I am certain of it."

Sighing, her ladyship replied, "You may well be right.
However, there is only one way to find out. We must ask
her."

Emma was in the garden, inspecting a number of old and
worn gooseberry bushes, thinking about the stranger she
had met in the china shop. That he was a stranger she was
certain, for if he had lived in Southampton, she would have
known. He was too fine-looking to have escaped her notice.
Indeed, one would have to have been made of pure granite
to have failed to notice such a handsome countenance and
charming manner. His smile contained so much electricity
that she could see it now, as she contemplated the goose-
berries. The vivid recollection made her sigh.

Abruptly, she tore her mind from the interesting stranger,
telling herself that she must think of George. Some days
had passed since she had vowed to help him, and she had
done nothing toward keeping that promise. It was one thing
to make declarations of one's noble intentions, she told herself, quite another to take action. The difficulty was that she

had not known what action to take. If she had known, she would not have hesitated. The only action that came to mind was tearing out the old gooseberry bushes and replacing them with young, healthy, fruitful ones. That would do much to improve the garden; it would do nothing, however, to cure George of his blue devils. Such were her musings when she was interrupted by the servant who had come to say that she was wanted at the house.

As soon as she entered, she stopped. Lady Landsdowne wore an expression of anticipation, while her grandfather looked as grave as if he had just spotted a French tricolor waving beneath his window.

"I bring an invitation," her ladyship said to her with a smile.

"Thank you, my lady."

"An invitation to visit London."

Alarmed, Emma paused. "I do not know anybody in London."

"My sister, Lady Chitting, would be obliged if you would visit her. She has no daughter, you know, only sons, and would like nothing better than to show you the Town."

Emma's eyes darted to her grandfather, who avoided her confused look. "But your sister does not know me."

"I have written to her all about you, and she is certain she will be charmed to know you."

"Of course, she will be charmed!" the Admiral cried as loudly as though he had been endeavoring to communicate with his deaf sister. "Anybody with a groat's worth of sense would be charmed!" To her ladyship, he said, "I hope you will pardon the saltiness of my language, my lady."

Because Emma was unwilling to leave the only home and family she had ever known, she was on the point of declining outright when it struck her that here, thanks to Lady Landsdowne's invitation, was the means she had been seeking to help her cousin. If he could go to London in her place, all would be well—she would please him and herself at the same time. With that in mind, she replied, "Perhaps your sister would like to welcome my cousin George. If she has sons, he would prove a valuable companion to them, and if she likes showing visitors the Town, nobody would be more delighted to be shown than George."

An expression of distaste spread across her ladyship's face. "Your cousin George?"

"I am certain we could spare George," said the Admiral eagerly. "You might have George as long as you liked!"

Her ladyship was adamant. "My sister quite depends on having a young lady to visit. She is heartily sick of young gentlemen. She has four sons."

"I could not possibly go without George," said Emma, who could be equally adamant when she chose.

"There, you see!" said the Admiral. "She will not go."

"Perhaps she would go," Lady Landsdowne replied, "if her cousin were to accompany her. While my nephews entertained the young gentleman, my sister would have the pleasure of entertaining Miss Drenville."

"Do you think George wishes to go to London?" her grandfather asked.

"I think he would like it above anything," Emma answered.

"But you would not like it above anything, would you?"

Seeing his sorrowful expression, she went to him and bussed his cheek. "What I should like above anything is to stay here always with you, Grandpapa, but for George's sake, I think I must go to London."

"Well, if it is only for George's sake . . . ," he murmured, resigned to parting with his favorite human creature in all the world as long as she did not truly wish to leave him.

Lady Landsdowne clapped her hands together. "I shall write my sister and tell her to expect two visitors." To Emma, she exclaimed warmly. "You shall be lionized in London. The ton will know how to appreciate such beauty and good humor. And I shall have the pleasure of seeing both you and my sister happy." Squeezing Emma's hand, her ladyship whispered, "You shall see, my dear. It will be the making of you."

Emma bowed her head and modestly thanked her lady-ship.

"I suppose it is just as well you are going to London," the Admiral sighed. "At least there you may be safe when the enemy strikes."

"I am the bearer of excellent tidings," Emma announced to George. After a search through the garden, the riverbank, and the library, she had found him at last in his dressing parlor, having his hair curled.

He could not move to look at her, lest he disturb the valet, who was wrapping a strand of hair in paper. Emma moved round so that he would not be obliged to inconvenience himself in order to look at her.

"As you see," George said, "I am occupied."

Emma peered into his pouting face. "Not too occupied to listen, I daresay, especially when the news is so likely to please you."

"Very well," he said, eyeing the hot iron the valet applied to his head. "But get on with it."

"What would please you most in all the world?"

"If we were to marry and be gone from this place."

"Stop teasing, George. Be serious. If I could grant you one wish, what would you wish for?"

"I detest riddles and conundrums."

"I shall not leave you in peace until you answer."

"Very well—to go up to London, I suppose. If a magician knocked on my door and offered to grant me a wish, that is what I would wish for."

"Granted!"

"Eh?"

"The magician has knocked, disguised as Lady Landsdowne, and she means to send us to her sister in London. We shall be in Town the rest of the Season. Is it not famous!"

He shooed his valet away, though only half his head was curled. Then he stood and approached Emma. "You are not

hoaxing me, are you? You could not be so cruel as to hoax
me on such a delicate subject."

"I take my oath, it is the truth."

Incredulous, he shook his head.

Emma smiled archly. "Of course, if you do not wish to
go, I shall tell her ladyship at once. You see, I took the liberty of accepting the invitation on your behalf."

"Not wish to go?" He embraced her. "It is the best news
you could have brought me." He stepped back, holding her
at arm's length. "You have made me the happiest of men.
How may I repay you, dear cousin?"

Emma exulted, returning his fond smile. "You may repay
me by remaining happy."

"When may we go? Shall I go and pack my valise this
instant?"

"We are to go following the assembly at the Dolphin."

His face fell, and he was as castdown as ever.

"Do not be so gloomy, George. The assembly is only
Thursday next. That is not so very long to wait."

"I had hoped we might quit this place before the assembly. Nothing is so hateful to me as those assemblies."

"I am aware that you regard a private assembly as more
refined than a public one, but we shall be with our family
and neighbors and have their company to amuse us."

Throwing himself into his chair, he slumped in an attitude of despair. "You shall be amused. You always are. I,
on the other hand, shall be mortified. I shall spend the entire time trying not to observe the behavior of my family,
endeavoring not to hear the whispers and insults from our
good neighbors."

Emma patted his hand. "Perhaps we may persuade one or
two of our relations not to attend. The Admiral would much
prefer to keep the night watch, and Aunt Harriet would
much prefer his company to that of anybody else. Aunt
Fanny is so obliging that if we suggested she stay at home,
she surely would, and Uncle Angus makes himself content
wherever he is."

He shook his head bleakly. "I wish that were all that was required to make the assembly endurable."

"What more can be wanting?" Emma asked.

Sitting up, he said, "You."

"You wish me to stay at home, too? George, you are an ungrateful toad and I have no opinion of you!"

Heedless of the destruction he wreaked, he raked his hand through his hair. "I am a perfect wretch, I know, but as one who loves you with all his heart, I am obliged to tell you the truth. The truth is, whenever you dance, I am put to the blush for you."

She put her hands on her hips. "What is wrong with the way I dance?"

"In your own words, you are a perfect loppet."

"Lord Landsdowne says I dance with great energy."

"With energy yes, but with skill and grace, I am afraid not."

"Well, I do not intend to stay at home merely because you are too pigeon-hearted to witness my dancing."

"I do not wish you to stay at home. There is nobody I would rather have at my side than you."

"Then what do you wish—besides the opportunity to wound my feelings?"

He raised her hand to his lips. "I am sorry I have wounded your feelings. It is very hard to have to tell the truth. What I should like is for you to come with me to the assembly but to refrain from dancing."

"Unlike you, George, I do not find it hard in the least to have to tell the truth, and the truth is that you are a selfish toad and I am sorry I told Lady Landsdowne I would go to London with you. The only thing which prevents me from planting you a facer this minute is that you are right—I cannot dance. I have never caught the knack of it. Moreover, I never shall catch it, being as graceless as a goose. My only comfort is that as soon as Lady Chitting sees how awkward I am, she will bundle me back to Southampton straightaway and you shall be left in London to fend for yourself."

"I hope she does not send you away, for I shall miss you."

"You think too much of yourself to miss anybody else."

"If you can be so magnanious as to confess you cannot dance, I can be so magnanimous as to allow that I am a selfish toad, just as you say. There, you see, we are well-suited after all. We are both magnanimous and shall make a handsome married pair."

"I shall not forgive you so easily as that, George."

"What would you have me do?"

"You must go and do the pretty to Aunt Fanny and Aunt Harriet. You must sit with Uncle Angus for ten minutes and smile at whatever he says. And you must go down to the West Gate with the Admiral and look out for ships in the bay."

He groaned.

"And if you are very very good and do exactly as I say, your reward will be that I shall send Lady Landsdowne a note saying that I cannot dance at the assembly as I have injured my foot."

CHAPTER FOUR

Carried Away

Dear Lady Chitting,

Lady Landsdowne informs me that Lord Chitting has been
taken with a cold, and as her ladyship and Lord Landsdowne have been so good as to praise the medicinal bene-
fits of my cinnamon sticks, I here take the liberty, at their
urging, of sending you the receipt. You need only mix an
ounce of powdered cinnamon with a lump of gum arabic,
melt the mixture in a boiling rose water and fill with sugar
and cinnamon. Work the whole and beat it out flat on a
slab. As it hardens, cut it into ribbons and roll them into
neat little sticks. If you do not wish to go to the trouble of
making the sweetmeats, I shall be happy to do so myself
when I arrive in London. I do thank you for your kind invitation and think it best to apprise you in advance that I am
accounted awkward. I shall not take it amiss if you do not
wish to have me as your guest for very long, but I am
pleased to be able to assure you that you may have the pleasure of my cousin George's company the entire Season.

I am very truly yours,

Emma Drenville

Emma entered the assembly room leaning heavily on the arm
of her cousin. Although her right foot was wrapped thickly
and conspicuously in a bandage, she did not wear the woeful
expression of an invalid. Indeed, she inhaled with delight as
she looked about her.

"How festive everything looks, George," she said. Just
then the violins struck up the notes of a reel, and while the

dancers formed their lines on the floor, she smiled and admired.

As George shared none of her pleasure, he snapped, "I do not see what you are so cheerful about. Your foot looks as though it had sprouted a monstrous boil. It is ridiculous."

Emma turned to him in dismay. "I wore the bandage solely in order to please you, George. You might at least have the good grace to be kind."

"I am in too foul a humor to be kind."

"Look about you. How pretty the hall is, draped in yellow and green, and the table spilling over with the best dishes. I have it from Aunt Fanny that we are to have apricot jam ice. What more could a human creature desire?"

"A human creature could desire that the Admiral had stayed at home, and that when Old Angus and his sisters asked to be allowed to beg off, he had given them their way. Instead, they are all here, each and every one of them. They have stopped outside to shout at each other and make themselves conspicuous, but I expect them presently, whereupon they shall lose no time in plaguing me." He looked behind him at the curtained door with an expression of dread.

"At least you shall be spared the mortification of seeing me dance. Can you not be grateful for that?"

"No, for my conscience plagues me whenever I look at your foot. I count myself as the wretch who deprived you of your amusement, in addition to being the object of ridicule, thanks to my less obliging relations."

"Permit me to remind you, cousin, that our friends are too generous to ridicule us, and the others are unworthy of our notice. Moreover, you have not deprived me, for I intend to be very much amused. I mean to begin by seeing you smile, with the corners of your mouth turned up, like so," and here she produced a bright smile for him to imitate.

"Oh, Emma! Why do you tease me so?"

With spirits too high to be dampened by her cousin's sulks, she replied, "Because if I am not to have a single dance, then I require recompense, in the form of a single smile. Besides, it will do you good to bestir yourself instead of indulging your blue devils."

To oblige her, George bared his teeth.

She laughed. "That is the sorriest grin I have ever beheld. You have made up your mind to be a grumbletonian tonight, I see. Well, I shall not try and talk you out of it. If it makes you happy to be unhappy, then by all means, scowl to your heart's content."

Before George could object to her characterization of him, a young woman approached, putting forth her hand and saying gently, "Why, Miss Drenville, how delightful to meet with you again."

Emma was pleased to see Miss Clarissa Merkle, whose acquaintance she had formed on her very first day in Southampton. Her pleasure deepened when she set eyes on the two gentlemen who stood beside her. One was a stranger, but the other was the gentleman she had accidentally jostled in the china shop, causing him to break a plate. He regarded her with the most engaging expression.

Once Miss Merkle had performed the introductions, Emma began to look forward to a conversation with Captain Nicholas Hale, whose blue coat and shiny naval buttons gave him an even handsomer air than he had worn in Mr. Dennis's shop, where he had not appeared in uniform. She was thinking complacently of that rencontre when all at once, she observed that the two gentleman exchanged glances.

"Did you say Miss *Emma* Drenville?" the stranger, Lieutenant Bentworthy, asked.

Emma saw him throw a questioning look at Captain Hale, and she saw the captain nod in answer, upon which both gentlemen laughed. She could not help wonder what they found so entertaining. It might be, she thought, that something was amiss with her appearance—it would not be the first time—and so she glanced down to see whether she had torn or muddied her hem.

"You must pardon us, Miss Drenville," said the lieutenant. "It is only that Captain Hale told me the unusual circumstances of your meeting. I must tell you, I heartily approve of whatever succeeds in bringing together a charming young lady and a noble seafaring gentleman."

It occurred to Emma that when Captain Hale had told his friend of the misadventure in the china chop, he had been obliged to report clumsiness of the young woman who had caused it. For the first time in her life, she blushed for her lack of grace, and when the captain asked her if he might have a dance, she was relieved to be able to point to her bandaged foot.

On the lieutenant's urging, Captain Hale engaged to dance with Miss Merkle, while George and Emma sat with Lieutenant Bentworthy by the window, far from the musicians, whose violins lilted rather loudly for conversation. George, restless with anticipation of his relations' imminent entrance, could not sit long. Abruptly he rose, and offering the excuse that he wished to look for Lord and Lady Landsdowne in the card room, took himself off.

As soon as they were alone, Emma said to Lieutenant Bentworthy, "I was surprised to learn that Captain Hale had spoken to you of our meeting. It was such a trifling encounter."

Dib shook his head. "It was not trifling in the least. It was memorable, in fact, for I met him soon afterward and he asked me if I knew of a delightful young lady in Southampton by the name of Emma. He did not know your surname."

She inhaled and smiled. "Did he truly speak of me?"

"In truth, he said a good deal, but you must grow conceited if I tell you all. Suffice it to say, it had to do with your blue eyes, your golden hair, and your good sense."

The aforementioned blue eyes searched the line of dancers until they came to rest on Captain Hale, who happened at that moment to glance in her direction. Immediately, he smiled, a full, generous smile which rendered his wind-tanned face inordinately handsome.

She could not help smiling in return. "I do not know," she said to the lieutenant, though she continued to watch the captain, "how he can have any idea of my good sense. We scarcely spoke."

"He said you charged him with speaking flummery. That bespeaks good sense, in my view."

"Is the captain in the habit of speaking flummery to young ladies?"

"Only if he likes them, which he rarely does."

Tearing her eyes from Captain Hale, Emma regarded her companion. "Is this more flummery, Lieutenant?"

Dib folded his arms and said, "Miss Drenville, I can assure you that Captain Hale is the best fellow in the world. Nobody is a greater authority on the subject than myself. You see, he saved my life."

Alive with curiosity, Emma pressed him for details.

"We were boarded on the open sea, two days out of Barbados. During the fray, a barrel was thrown at my head and I found myself knocked to the deck. My assailant pursued me and would have plunged his blade into my throat if our mutual acquaintance had not intervened. The point was deflected and went into my leg—this poor leg you see before you now, which, I am happy to report, is mending quite nicely, thanks to Captain Hale, who, seeing a flagon of rum lying on the deck, broken open its neck and poured it over the wound, which he then bound with his cravat. Without a thought to his own safety, he pulled me to where I could be concealed under a canvas. The next I knew, he was waking me and announcing that the enemy had been driven off."

Once more, Emma glanced at Captain Hale. It took no great stretch of imagination to envision him as the courageous defender of another man's life. He looked uncommonly dashing and danced with admirable grace. Moreover, he was again looking her way, and with an intentness that produced a catch in her throat.

Emma's family entered at that moment. They did not see her, secluded as she was with the lieutenant in an obscure corner of the hall, but she saw them. Aunt Fanny stopped to chat with poor George, who had just emerged from the card room. She pinned him helplessly to the wall with her chatter. The other three—the Admiral, Old Angus, and Aunt Harriet—walked in a line, inspecting the dancers and paying their respects to them in turn. Emma saw Miss Merkle pause, step out of the set, and present Captain Hale to the three Drenvilles. It gave her pleasure to know that her beloved grandfather and the attractive captain might have the uncommon pleasure of one another's acquaintance.

Before the introductions could be completed, Angus demanded of the captain, "Are you married?"

Surprised though he was at the bluntness of the question, Captain Hale replied cordially, "No, sir, I am not, much to the despair of my mother. She urges me to marry without delay."

Angus waved his hand in dismissal. "A son will never marry if his mother tells him to. Tell your mother she must learn to hold her tongue."

He smiled at this outspokenness, for he had often wished his mother would hold her tongue, and not merely on the subject of matrimony. "I beg your pardon, sir," he said. "I did not catch your name."

"Where do you keep your bird?" Angus enquired.

"What did he say?" Aunt Harriet asked the Admiral in a loud, quizzical voice that caused others in the room to look their way.

Her brother, in his customary obliging manner, boomed, "He asked the gentleman where he keeps his bird."

"His what?" she asked Angus.

Exasperated with his sister's deafness, Angus shouted, "His bird—his petticoat, his dasher, his high flyer, his bit of muslin! Deuce take me, woman, put that trumpet in your ear where I can speak into it! Why do you carry it everywhere if you do not mean to put it to its proper use?"

"It is most improper to inquire about a man's mistress on first meeting," Harriet scolded Angus. "You must mind your manners, or I shall be ashamed of you."

"I merely wish to know if the fellow keeps a bird in Southampton. He looks the sort to keep one in London."

Smiling at this unconventional exchange, Captain Hale glanced at Miss Merkle, who had taken on the coloring of a rutabaga—half red and half white. It was evident the young lady would have distanced herself at once from such unseemly companions had she known how to do so.

While Angus and Harriet sniped at one another, the Admiral took the opportunity to ask the captain, "What is your ship, if I may inquire, sir?"

"*The Ambuscade*."

"Indeed! I saw her once, and a lovely sight she was, standing in the Channel with every stitch of sail full in the breeze. But that was some years ago. How does she go on?"

"I fear she is pretty battered. Her fore-topsail, maintopsail, driver, and bootsails have taken such a pounding that she is crazy to handle in a wind."

"The Fleet must see to it. They must not let her sail out again lacking repairs."

"I have every assurance the repairs will be made."

"You must refuse to sail on her until the masts are replaced. How, I ask you, is invasion to be staved off if we do not look to our ships?"

"Did you say 'invasion'?" Captain Hale asked. He was finding these strangers more amusing every minute.

"What did he say?" Harriet demanded.

"He said 'invasion,'" Angus bellowed irritably.

"Oh," Harriet sighed, "is my brother on his hobby horse again?"

"I know what you will say, sir," the Admiral went on, as oblivious to his siblings as he was to the crowd, which stared at the odd trio with sneers and sniggers. "You will argue that the shortage of oak makes replacing the masts impossible. But I tell you, sir, this cannot be permitted. It sinks the morale of the men to have a crumbling ship for a berth. They have few enough amenities as it is, cooped up as they are for months at sea. The navy must not weaken. The French can taste weakness. It is what comes of eating a prodigious deal of sauce instead of good plain beef and pudding."

Captain Hale endeavored to soothe the Admiral's alarms. "There was a time," he said, "when it was feared that the French would invade at Kent, but it is some years now since this fear has been allayed. We have proved to Bonaparte that he cannot hope to vanquish the British Navy and he has set his sights on Europe instead. You may rest easy, sir."

"Rest easy! That is precisely what Bonaparte wishes us to do. He knows that once the young girls no longer fear a night attack and put away their Napolean blankets, he may unleash his landing forces upon an unwary, unprepared, undisciplined nation."

Seeing that Miss Merkle squirmed under the stares and whispers of the crowd, the captain did his best to take his leave, but the Admiral was too incensed to let him go. "I know what you will say. All the young sailors say it. This talk of invasion is nothing but Whiggish humbug. I suppose that is what you will say, sir."

"What did he say?" Harriet asked.

"He did not say anything," the Admiral replied. "He has not had the opportunity."

"You interrupted," Angus put in. "You always interrupt, Harriet."

"What did you say? I could not hear you."

"Deuce take me, woman! What is the good of a trumpet if you never put it to an ear?"

To the captain's amusement, the sister and two brothers launched into a dispute which ignored him entirely. In the midst of this hullaballoo, he looked to where Dib sat with Miss Emma Drenville. He noticed that they were immersed in conversation, so much so that if he had not known of the lieutenant's violent affection for Miss Merkle, he might have experienced a pang of jealousy. He looked for an opportunity to make a polite excuse on behalf of himself and his companion, but found none, for the disputants had forgotten his very existence. With a philosophical shrug, he offered his arm to the uneasy Miss Merkle and made his way toward Emma.

When the lieutenant rose suddenly, Emma looked round to see Captain Hale. Miss Merkle, who had let go his arm, looked peevish and pale. "Oh, Dib," she said breathlessly, "I think I must have a drink of lemonade."

Solicitously, Lieutenant Bentworthy suggested they go in

search of one, for she looked quite done up. Leaning on his walking stick, he took his lady love away, so that Emma was left alone with Captain Hale. He seemed not at all discomposed at the exchange of partners as he seated himself beside her.

Before Emma could question him on his conversation with her family, he inquired with some intensity, "What did my good friend Dib have to say that was so fascinating?"

Puzzled, she inspected his fine countenance.

"I saw you, Miss Drenville. You were hanging on his lips as though pearls dropped from them. What did he say that rendered you so spellbound?"

She smiled directly into his eyes. "He was speaking of you. He told me how you saved his life."

He shook his head self-deprecatingly, giving Emma another facet of his character to admire—modesty.

"Oh, is that all." He sounded relieved. "Dib likes to make me out a hero, but the sad truth is, I merely did for him what he would not have hesitated to do for me."

"If he does make you out a hero, it may be because you are."

The way his eyes glowed caused her to hold her breath. "Do you like heroes?" he asked.

"Everybody likes heroes."

"If you like them, then I shall be content to be one, as long as you do not paint my face on a plate."

The word *flummery* leapt to her lips but died there, for she saw him regarding her with an intensity that banished all wish for raillery. She searched her mind for something to say. He saved her the trouble, however, by remarking, "It is too bad your foot prevents you from dancing. You have had an accident, I am sorry to see, since our fortuitous meeting in the china shop."

Coloring, she said, "It was nothing, the merest trifle. Please, do not say another word about it. I do not mind it very much."

"But I do mind very much. I had promised myself a dance with you and now I am disappointed."

She blushed. No gentleman, excepting her grandfather, had ever expressed, in words and manner, such pointed pleasure in her company. With every appearance of calm, she said, "If my poor foot is an inconvenience, it is only because it prevents us from walking out to see the *Philomela,* which is docked just outside. She is a bit the worse for a pummeling near Cadiz, but she looks fair under the moon."

The captain glanced out the window. In the bay, the glimmer of a bobbing masthead caught his eye. "Permit me to offer you my arm, Miss Drenville. If you will accept it, I shall assist you to the dock." Here he rose, bowed, and proffered his elbow with an elaborate sweep of the hand.

Unable to resist, she stood, placed her hand upon his arm, and moved with him toward the door, making certain to limp pathetically.

They came out into the brisk spring air and strolled the walkway. Bulging clouds overhead were illumined by the full moon sailing swiftly behind them. Emma searched for stars so as to read the morrow's weather, and when she glanced at the captain, she saw that he was similarly engaged. She savored the pleasure of the shared moment.

When they reached the top of the steps which led to the dock, they stopped and looked down. The *Philomela* rocked prettily in the water below, her sails neatly furled, her decks alive with shadows playing over rope coils, canvas, and barrels.

"I am afraid," the captain said, "that your foot will not permit you to go further."

Emma considered whether she ought to seize this moment to tell him the truth about her foot. She did not wish to continue to deceive him. At the same time, she did not wish to cast her cousin George, or herself, in an unfavorable light. In the end, all she could think to say was, "We have come so far. It seems a pity not to reach our destination."

"Yes, a great pity. But do not despair. Granting the wishes of beautiful young ladies is my metier. Permit me." On that, he lifted her in one swift motion into his arms.

She gasped, not only because she could feel the warmth of

his hold upon her but also because he had said she was beautiful. As he carried her down the steps, she did not know where to look. How awkward it would be when she told him that her foot was not injured at all, that it had merely been a hoax. Where would she find the courage to tell him? She was too conscious of the strength of his arms around her to compose the words.

He set her down. "You may proceed to rebuke me now."

A little dazed, she asked. "Why should I rebuke you?"

"I behaved very improperly just now."

"Yes, but it was very pleasant."

In his laughter, she read surprise. "Miss Drenville, you are remarkably direct. Did nobody ever teach you that ladies must pretend to be offended by a gentleman's improper behavior, especially if they find it pleasant?"

His expression, illumined by the moon moving out of the clouds, was so magnetic that she could scarcely comprehend the question. When it did penetrate, she answered plainly, "No, nobody ever taught me."

He contemplated her a moment. "Suppose I were to tell you I meant to kiss you?"

She closed her eyes and said, "You may proceed, sir." A pause followed, but no kiss. She opened her eyes, curious as to what had caused the delay, and found him studying her.

"You are very odd, Miss Drenville."

"Oh, dear. I suppose you have changed your mind about the kiss, then."

"Not at all. It is only that whenever I mean to kiss a young lady, she insists upon preliminaries."

"If you will be so good as to tell me what they are, I shall insist upon them, too."

"You misunderstand. Most young ladies behave as though they are shocked that a gentleman wishes to kiss them. They pretend to be offended."

"Why?"

He laughed. "I thought, being a young lady yourself, you might tell me."

She thought long and hard, but having had no female companionship throughout her life, except that of two eccentric aunts, she knew no more what to answer than if she had been asked why the grass was green and the sky blue.

"I fancy that some young ladies are offended by kisses," she ventured uncertainly. "Others, like myself, have been kissed and petted by their family since an early age and find it most pleasant. I suppose your best course, Captain, is to refrain from kissing the ladies who would be offended and confine yourself to the others."

"You are not only beautiful but wise as well," he declared, and taking her firmly by the shoulders, he pulled her to him and kissed her.

Emma was dismayed to find that the touch of his lips roused many sensations, none of which resembled the effects of a kiss from her family. Their kisses never stopped her breath or accelerated her pulse as this one did. Kisses from her aunts, uncle, cousin, and grandfather consisted exclusively of lips brushed across a cheek or brow. This kiss, however, encompassed a great deal more. The grip of the captain's arm on her shoulders loosened and she was aware that his hands glided to her waist. She felt herself pressed to him so closely that his buttons were cool against her breast. Most of all, she was aware of his lips, for they did not stop at hers. He moved them to her eyes and then her neck. He said something in her ear, something she could not make out, but it was not at all like one of Angus's endearments— "goosechild" or "flutterbelle" or "daisytop"; it was tender and urgent. She felt the sensation of his mouth on her shoulder long after his lips had moved to caress her hair.

It occurred to her that at her age she ought to have known better what to expect. The kiss ought not to have taken her by surprise. At twenty-two, she ought to have known more of the world. Although she had never found anything to complain of in her sheltered, isolated life, she now saw that it had rendered her abysmally ignorant, particularly in regard to gentlemen and their kisses. Perhaps it would have helped if she had made it a point these past years to read more novels.

Slowly, he released her and peered into her face. Knowing

that he was endeavoring to read her response, she grew warm and said, "That was vastly pleasant. I only wish I knew what one is supposed to do next."

He took her hand. "I shall prolong my stay in Southampton, with your permission."

Stricken, she said, "I am going to London."

"Then I shall go to London."

"Do you mean to follow me?" she exclaimed thankfully.

"I mean that I shall not let you out of my sight."

"I cannot imagine anything more pleasant."

Throwing his head back, he laughed and spread out his arms to embrace the beauty of the night. "What an enchanted land Southampton is!" he announced. "The citizens are the oddest, most delightful creatures."

"Are we?" She laughed.

"Oh, yes. I had given up hope of ever meeting a young lady who was devoid of arts and airs and simperings. Yet here you are, and here I am, and we are both about to embark on a London adventure."

She was delighted with his delight. "You cannot assume that all the citizens of Southampton are as odd as I am."

"Oh, but I can, for before I came to the dock with you, I was engaged in conversation with the oddest creatures imaginable. They were every bit as astonishing as you, my adorable Miss Drenville."

As he raised her hand and pressed it to his breast, she stared ahead. "Astonishing?" she repeated.

"There was one old fellow who warned me that invasion from France was imminent. There was no talking him out of it, though I am certain Bonaparte means to disappoint him in the end."

Emma froze. Slowly she pulled her hand away. "What was the gentleman's name?"

"I do not know. Everybody began speaking before introductions were made in form."

"You did not like the gentleman, I collect."

"He was quite absurd, but not as absurd as his sister. Apparently, she is deaf, and, thus, it was necessary to repeat, in a voice which commanded the attention of everybody in the hall, each word which was uttered. Did you not hear them?"

Blushing fiercely, Emma said, "How very trying."

"Trying was scarcely the word. You see, the old sailor's brother asked me a highly indecorous question and was obliged to repeat it at the top of his lungs for the benefit of his sister."

"What question?"

He smiled gently. "I do not wish to repeat it. It really is quite unsuitable."

Restless with mortification, she insisted. "Captain Hale, you have carried me down the stairs and kissed me. I do not think you ought to be stopped by a few meager words."

Instantly he caught the tension in her tone. His smile faded. Carefully, he said, "Perhaps we ought to talk of something else."

"No, I should very much like to hear the question. Please."

After an uneasy pause, he said stiffly, "Very well. He asked me where I keep my bird."

Emma was mystified. Old Angus had never in his life evinced the least interest in ornithology. Why he should speak of birds to a naval captain she could not imagine, except that he was always making remarks apropos of nothing and disconcerting others with outlandish remarks. She recalled Angus's conduct toward Lord and Lady Landsdowne, among others, and for the first time in her life, she was ashamed of him. She was ashamed of all her relations, of their clamor and impropriety and disregard for the sensibilities of others. No longer did she find their eccentricity endearing; George's objections suddenly began to make a glimmer of sense. And as shame for them rose in her breast, she grew ashamed of herself. "What did you answer?" she inquired, trying to mask her high state of emotion.

"Naturally, I did not answer."

She collected herself and said with lofty dignity, "And where *do* you keep your bird, sir?"

Stepping back, he studied her, evidently uncertain that he had heard what he had heard.

"I should like to be able to tell my granduncle Angus your answer to his question," she explained.

"Your granduncle?"

"Yes, Angus is my granduncle. His brother, the Admiral, the absurd fellow who has his hopes on an invasion, is my grandfather. Their sister is my Aunt Harriet."

He closed his eyes an instant and let out a breath. "I have spoken carelessly. I did not intend to wound you. Forgive me."

Affecting lightness, she said, "You merely spoke the truth. My family are entirely ridiculous. Do you know what they call us? The Dreadfuls! It is a pun, you see. *Dreadful* instead of *Drenville*. Clever, is it not?"

When he reached for her hand, she pulled away.

"It is not important," he said. "We are not to blame for our relations. What is important is that I kissed you and you found it very pleasant. We both did."

Her eyes stinging, she shook her head. "Oh, but relations are important. You see, I am one of them. I am a Drenville. Their blood is my blood. I am as absurd and difficult as they. If you do not believe me, you may ask my cousin George. I shall never be anything but what I am—every inch a Dreadful!"

On that, she whirled around and dashed up the steps, leaving him to ponder how it was that a young lady who was so pitifully lame could be so remarkably fleet of foot.

CHAPTER FIVE

Denied

Dear Lady Landsdowne,

All is arranged for my journey to London on the morrow. I thank you for sending Mrs. Bloodbane to assist with the packing of my trunks. I must impose on your generosity yet again and ask you to look after my grandfather and my aunts and uncle during my stay in London. They are so good as to say that nobody prepares their favorite delicacies as I do. As they are especially fond of my Banbury negus, I entrust to you the receipt herewith: To your mixture of lemon juice, lemon slices, sweetened calves-foot jelly, spices, and boiling water, add, instead of ordinary wine, a bottle of silvery yellow cowslip wine and broken clear sugar candy. The Admiral never fails to be amused by the chimes sounded as the candy splinters in the hot brew. I hope it will remind him of me when I am gone. I do not know how well my family will bear up in my absence, but I take solace in knowing that I have commended them to the care of a kind friend. I shall miss them more than I can say.

Yours, etc.

Emma Drenville

Every stitch Emma owned bedecked the furniture of her bed chamber. Lady Landsdowne's housekeeper, Mrs. Bloodbane, oversaw the packing with a sharp eye and a tongue to match. That formidable lady took one look at Emma's halfhearted efforts and announced succinctly, "It will not do." She then proceeded to empty the trunks of everything Emma had folded and tucked inside and was in

the throes of organizing the young lady's belongings so
that, in her words, "nothing could possibly offend sense or
seemliness." To that end, she packed from inside to out.
Stockings, chemises, and shifts were first, along with dressing gowns, nightgowns, and caps. Next came dresses and
gowns, of which there were far too few, in Mrs. Bloodbane's humble opinion. The instant Miss Drenville arrived
in Town, said the housekeeper, she must insist upon being
taken to Bond Street.

Outerwear came next—cloak, spencer, and shawls—
and then footwear, consisting of shoes, slippers, nankin
boots, half boots, and pattens for muddy weather, though
when she got to Town, Mrs. Bloodbane prophesied, she
would probably think herself too fine to go clinking
about in the latter. The good woman then packed para-
sols, muffs and gloves, fans, purses, and jewelry, wrapping them tenderly in tissue, despite their being
decidedly worn and out of fashion, in her view. Finally,
she found niches for lavender water, a bottle of Gow-
land's lotion to prevent freckling, and bits of velvet for
Emma's gold curls.

It was well, Emma thought, that Mrs. Bloodbane was
on hand, for she could not seem to attend to the packing
herself. Indeed, she could scarcely attend to anything for
longer than thirty seconds. Her thoughts drifted to the
events of the previous evening, and each time she re-
played the scene on the dock in her mind she felt more
oppressed than before. Although she was ordinarily a
young woman of cheerful disposition, although she was
capable of the strict self-discipline befitting a naval officer's granddaughter, and although she strove again and
again to fix her thoughts on the adventures which lay
ahead of her in London, her mind—as though it had a
mind of its own—insisted upon returning to thoughts of
Captain Hale.

He had appeared remarkably attractive at the Dolphin. A
wisp of his brown hair had fallen onto his forehead. It had
been all she could do to keep from smoothing it into place.

His earth brown eyes were shadowed by thick lashes which must have been the envy of every female he met. The suntan which overspread his complexion gave it an appearance of ruggedness, the very same appearance she had always admired in the Admiral. On the whole, his air was that of a man who preferred looking at the sea to looking in his glass, who was more accustomed to reading the clouds and the stars than a hand of cards, who was as candid in his likes and dislikes as he was handsome and well-formed. She sighed. Why, she asked herself, did she persist in cataloging his manifold charms? Was she determined to make herself miserable?

George came to her relief, scratching on the door and begging for a word with her. She directed a questioning look at Mrs. Bloodbane, who had, to her horror, discovered that a scent bottle and a handkerchief had somehow got in amongst the bonnets. She was now tearing everything out of the trunks, preparing to begin again from the beginning. When Emma said that she would step out a moment to have a word with her cousin, the housekeeper waved her away impatiently, saying, "You are only in the way here, miss. I shall have it all in order when you return. Lady Landsdowne said I must take you in hand, and take you in hand I shall."

Closing the door behind her, Emma stepped into the corridor. Immediately, George took her elbow and steered her to a blue-and-cream-colored sitting room. As soon as they entered, he announced, "Emma, I cannot go to London. You shall have to travel by yourself."

Emma's eyes grew wide. She could not imagine what had caused such a turnabout. Her cousin had longed to go to Town. He had spoken of it in terms generally reserved for the Holy Land, and he had regarded their projected visit with rapture.

"I thought you wished above anything to go to London."

"I did. I do. But I have changed my mind."

"Why?"

"I am dished up. I haven't the face to go into Society."

"Oh, George, do not abandon me, please. If you do, I do not know what is to become of me."

"You will do well enough. You always do."

"No, no. I shall not do well. I am such a loppet. You said so yourself. Therefore, I had counted on you to advise and assist me, to be there as a companion I might trust, as the one Drenville amongst strangers."

Glumly, he regarded her. "Poor Emma," he said. "You will be very unhappy, I know. You are not as anxious as I am to distance yourself from the Drenvilles, and you will miss everybody excessively. Well, there is only one thing for it."

"What is that?"

"You must stay in Southampton with me."

"I cannot stay," she cried. "You are wrong, very wrong. I do wish to distance myself from the Drenvilles. That is to say, I do not precisely wish to, but I am forced to. I must."

He eyed her with interest. "You have had a change of heart, I collect."

She bowed her head. "A change of heart, yes."

"But why, Emma? This is sudden, is it not?"

"I suppose it is, but the fact is that I have seen what I had not seen before, that you are right, you have been right all along, the Drenvilles are a—a difficult family."

Seizing her hands, he cried, "This is delightful! You have had your eyes opened."

Blinking back tears, she stated, "It is not delightful in the least. It is perfectly dismal. It pains me to watch them all. They are so sweet, so well-meaning, so fond of me. If they knew how they mortified me, I could not bear it."

"You have no reason to feel mortified, dear cousin. It is they who make fools of themselves at every turn, not you."

"I am ashamed of feeling ashamed. If I had any courage, I should be more loyal, more steady than I am. I am a coward, George."

"Nonsense, you have a great deal of good sense, so much so that you have made me recollect why I was so set on

going to London in the first place. I shall not change my
mind, after all. That is to say, I have changed my mind
about changing my mind. You and I are to go to London tomorrow, and nothing shall stop us."

Emma broke into smiles and clasped her hands together.
"You are the kindest cousin in all the world. Thank you."

He blushed. "Do not thank me. I do what I do for the
most selfish of reasons. Your ease and comfort weighed not
at all in my decision."

"I see," she said archly.

Sidelong, he looked at her. "Well, perhaps they did a little."

She laughed, "You cannot play the fribble all the time,
my dear cousin. Every so often, the gentleman in you will
out, and when he does, he will do something sweet, in spite
of himself."

"*Sweet!*" he groaned.

"Yes, you are sweet and shall simply have to endure it."

"By all that's holy, Emma, do not repeat that word." He
shuddered. "I am doing everything in my power to be elegant, stylish, tonnish. And now you call me—you call me
by that epithet!"

She drew a ring from her finger. "I shall not employ it
again, as I see it mortifies you, and I shall not need to, for
when you look at this ring, it will tell you exactly what I
think of you—that you are most dear and precious to me."
She folded the ring into his hand.

Emotion made him blink.

"And very *sweet*," she added mischievously.

"My dear Emma, I have nothing to give you in return."

"Well, some day you may present me with a newly
curled lock of your hair and I shall be duly recompensed. In
the meanwhile, I hope you mean to tell me what suddenly
possessed you to stay in Southampton instead of going to
London as planned."

The scowl he had worn earlier now reappeared. "My cravats," he said darkly.

"Your cravats?"

"The silks are spotted, the lawns are worn, and the muslins are yellowed. I cannot appear in Society in such cravats."

She smiled indulgently. "Then you must have new ones. You shall buy them in London, where you will find the most fashionable cravats ever stitched."

His expression brightened. "Why, yes. I must have all new cravats, and new gloves, new waistcoats, and new beavers as well."

"Exactly so. You see how fortune smiles on us, George. You must go to London at just the instant when you are in need of new cravats, and I must go to London at just the instant when—," and here she left off and glanced down at the carpet.

"Just the instant when what?"

She cleared her throat.

"I know what you are attempting to say."

"You do?"

"Yes, you are grateful to be leaving Southampton at the very instant when you have discovered the truth about our family, that we are indeed the Dreadfuls."

It was impossible for her to reply, for to mention Captain Hale and his influence upon her decision was to open a wound that was too fresh to be exposed to the air.

Seeing her difficulty, he took her hand. "I thank you for the ring, cousin. I shall keep it always, just here, next to my heart." He put the ring to his lips, then in the pocket of his coat.

"You must excuse me now," she said, avoiding his eyes, lest he see that she was on the verge of weeping.

"Yes, of course. Go and finish your packing."

As she hurried away, he saw her dab at her eyes. He had never before seen his cousin teary, never heard her voice quiver. It gave him a pang to know that she was unhappy. When they were married, he vowed, he would see to it that she was never unhappy, even if it meant keeping her as far from the Drenvilles as it was possible to get.

Captain Hale breakfasted with Lieutenant Bentworthy, who let the upstairs rooms in a neat house not far from the Bargate. Though the rooms were small, they were well lit, clean, and perfectly suited to a gentleman of limited means. As they sat together in a parlor overlooking the ancient street, a servant brought them coffee and rolls and then left them to their conversation.

"I trust you are full of yourself this morning," Dib said. "You are feeling all the triumph of having made a worthy conquest. Miss Emma Drenville is an admirable young lady. I like her. You have my leave to gloat at your success."

Wryly, the captain replied, "If success may be defined as offending a lady beyond forgiveness, then I suppose I may count myself as a conquering hero."

Dib frowned. "I do not understand. At last sighting, you and the young lady were navigating toward the dock, which, if I recollect, stood under a fair, starry sky and bright moon."

"You have the weather right, old friend. It was the 'success' which you misconstrued. You see, I mismanaged the entire business."

"Ah, she did not wish to go down to the dock with you. Yes, of course, I remember now, her foot was injured."

"She very much wished to go down, and her foot was no obstacle, for I carried her."

Dib's eyes went wide. He cleared his throat as he imagined the romantic picture just presented. "Well, then, the delightful Miss Emma took offense when you offered to salute her."

"Not at all. She offered up her lips in return."

If Dib's tender leg had not prevented him, he would have jumped from his chair. "By Jupiter, Hale, I've never yet kissed Miss Merkle, and I have known her these six months! Meanwhile, you have kissed your lady fair on second meeting. I call that success, even if you do not."

"Yes, well, if I had contented myself with kissing, my

lips might have kept free of trouble. Unfortunately, I also spoke."

"Good heavens, you did not offer to make her your mistress! No wonder she was offended."

"What do you take me for, Dib? Miss Drenville is not the sort of young lady one asks to be one's mistress, no matter how much one would like to. She is the sort one marries."

"Ah, you proposed marriage and she did not like it because you had known each other scarcely two hours."

"I wish that were the difficulty, for it would be a mere trifle. No, I spoke unkindly about her family, before I knew that they were her family, and she was justly insulted on their behalf. I confess, I am not proud of having conducted myself like a gossip."

Waving his hand in dismissal, Dib replied, "Nonsense. You have never gossiped in your life."

"I did not intend to ridicule them, you know. It was just that they were so prodigiously entertaining.. I thought it would be harmless to mention their oddities. But perhaps you are acquainted with them—the Drenvilles, Admiral Drenville and his brother and sisters."

"Having been confined to these rooms until a mere fortnight ago, I cannot be said to have met anybody, but I believe I have heard of Admiral Drenville. It appears he is an intimate of Lord Landsdowne's. Have you heard of his lordship? He is reputed to be a great eccentric."

Captain Hale set down his coffee cup and stood. With a flash of anger, he said, "There is no excuse for my speaking as I did. I vow, I have never been sorrier for a few careless words."

"When one courts a lady, it is recommended that one refrain from casting aspersions on her family, at least until after the wedding. Even if she despises them herself, she cannot allow others to do so."

"Miss Drenville does not despise them. She is completely devoted to them, eccentricities and all."

With a sigh, Dib pronounced, "Well, it is done and cannot be undone. We shall simply have to find you another young lady who is as interesting as Miss Drenville. I shall enlist Miss Merkle's help. She is acquainted with everybody in Southampton."

"I have no intention of abandoning ship, Dib."

"You don't mean to persist, not after what has passed between you?"

"I mean to give chase, Dib, though she have all her sails unfurled and steer an elusive course. That is to say, I mean to visit her and apologize, and I mean to make her hear me out. After that, I shall heave about and make with all due speed for London."

Dib shook his head. "See here, Hale, if you mean to give chase, at least go after a prize you have a chance of winning. This ship's hold is empty, I fear, at least where you are concerned."

"You may be right. Still, I must make the attempt."

Mrs. Bloodbane surveyed the trunks and informed the footman that they might be locked. She and Emma sat on them so that their lids could be closed. When at last the footman had managed to find all the proper keys and fasten all the clasps, Mrs. Bloodbane rose with a start from the last of the trunks, clapped her hand to her mouth, and cried, "Where is puss?"

The footman and Emma glanced at one another.

"Your tabby," the housekeeper cried. "Where is she?"

They looked about the chamber, and not finding her, Emma said, "She must have slipped out the door and gone to find grandpapa. His lap is her favorite bed."

'I shall go and see," Mrs. Bloodbane panted and was out the door like a shot.

Emma could not imagine what had provoked this sudden interest in her cat, but she shrugged, excused the footman, and prepared herself to take leave of Cracklethorne and the bed chamber she had come to love. Before she could begin to adjust her thoughts, a maid entered bringing a note. She tore it open to read:

My dear Miss Drenville,

Will you be so kind as to receive me in an hour? I cannot in conscience quit Southampton without making the apologies which are your due.

I am your most obedient and humble servant,

Nicholas Hale

The words washed over her like hot steam. Captain Hale to visit her! She could not permit it. The last thing she wished to do was see his handsome sailor's face, hear his soft baritone, feel his powerful presence. For the sake of her family and her peace of mind, she must refuse to see him. For his own sake, she must end their acquaintance before it went further. At all costs, he must not be permitted to see her dance. He must not know that her awkwardness was of a piece with what he had found so droll in her family's conduct. If he ever laughed at her the way he had laughed at her grandfather and the others, she would not recover. No, she and the captain must never be more to each other than they were at this moment, else what lay in store for them both was an endless series of mortifications.

Only by putting their acquaintance at an end could she begin to salvage something of her self-respect, which rested upon her ability to feel genuinely indulgent toward her family's idiosyncrasies. She must put behind her the memory of the captain's laughter. More important, she must cease to feel ashamed of those who were lovingly devoted to her.

London was the answer to all these dilemmas. A few months in Town would lend her perspective. Her appreciation of what was good and dear and kind and well-meaning would be renewed. Sojourning among the affected, the false, the shallow, and the devious—for such was the reputation she had heard of the ton—would send her running back to the open arms of her family, purified of her wretched thoughts.

Thus, she wrote in answer to the note:

Dear Captain Hale,

I am unable to receive you today and assure you that it is not necessary for you to apologize.

I am most sincerely yours,

Emma Drenville

Scarcely had the servant left with the note when Mrs. Bloodbane returned in a frenzy, shouting, "Puss is nowhere to be found. The Admiral has not seen her, and neither has anybody else!"

As puss often took herself off for a moment of solitude, especially when her surroundings were in an uproar, Emma did not see any cause for concern, until Mrs. Bloodbane added, in a gurgle of apprehension, "I believe we have packed her in one of the trunks."

At once, the servant was summoned, the keys brought forth again, the clasps unlocked, and the clothes thrown on the bed and tabletops without thought to organization from inside to out or to anything else except what havoc might be wreaked by four cat claws in a trunk full of ladies' finery.

In the midst of this tumult, another note arrived for Emma, which read:

Dear Miss Drenville,

If you will not permit me to come for my own sake, will you do so for the sake of Lord Nelson? I invoke him because he was generous, even to the undeserving, and because I would gladly give you my head on a plate, as well as my face on one, to smash with my blessing, if it would persuade you to receive me. I take my oath I will make my apologies and be gone, never to trouble you again. I must see you, Miss Drenville. You are too intelligent and feeling not to know why.

Yours, etc.

Nicholas Hale

Emma did know why. She knew that a man of his sensibility would feel himself bound to do what was right, regardless of how much it might mortify him. His impulse to make reparations and his determination to follow that impulse nearly dissolved her. He was even more admirable then she had known. Still, it was impossible to receive him. She could not rely on herself to hear him with equanimity. She would collapse, metaphorically speaking, into a heap of confused emotion. Just as she was obliged to distance herself from the Drenvilles, she must avoid Captain Hale. Accordingly, she answered:

Dear Captain Hale,

Please believe that I bear you no ill will. I accept your apology without your saying another word on a subject which is too painful for me to mention, and, consequently, you had best not come to Cracklethorne. Accept my good wishes for your health and happiness.

I am, as before,

Emma Drenville

Mrs. Bloodbane seethed upon the discovery that puss had lain in the window seat the whole time and had never consorted with the packing at all. Beginning from the beginning yet again, she sorted, folded, and replaced each item in its trunk, taking a moment to exile the tabby from the chamber and warn her that if she did not mend her behavior in future, she would certainly fall afoul of a pack of hounds, which would be no less than she deserved.

Meanwhile, Emma received another note. This one read:

Dear Miss Drenville,

I am coming.

N.H.

There was no use answering, Emma saw. The only thing left to do was find a way to avoid meeting him. To that end, she slipped out of the bedchamber and hid herself in the garden, which though chilly and not yet in leaf, was easier to endure than the devastating smile of her imminent visitor.

Not surprisingly, Miss Drenville was denied to him. Captain Hale had prepared for that eventuality and, thus, followed his first inquiry at the door with, "Is Admiral Drenville at home, by any chance?"

The Admiral was indeed at home and the captain was requested to attend him in the saloon.

When he entered in the wake of the servant, he found the Admiral gathered with Old Angus, Miss Harriet Drenville, and the powdery lady whose breathless effusions he had witnessed in the china shop. The Admiral boomed a greeting and introduced the gentleman to his sister Fanny. He could not help finding them all a likable company, for they beamed at him benignly and made no secret of their welcome.

"So ye've turned up again, have you?" Angus greeted him. He fingered the captain's lapel as though to estimate the fineness of the cloth. "What did you pay for that watch ye're wearing?" he asked. "Is it gold or merely gilt?"

"What did he say?" Harriet cried, putting up her trumpet, thus sparing Captain Hale from having to reply.

Both Fanny and the Admiral answered at once, "He hasn't said anything yet. Angus was speaking."

"What did he say about Angus?"

"He said nothing, my dear," Fanny shouted.

Angus snapped into his sister's trumpet, "Deuce take me, woman, give a fellow a chance to get a word in before you start bellowing at him."

"The bellows?" Harriet said. "No, no, I'm afraid it cannot be repaired. Fanny shall have to buy a new one. Will you be a dear, Fanny, and purchase a new bellows?"

"I shall do so, of course, my dear, but not while we have a guest, though I do not know how I shall get my errands done if I sit here chattering all day, for I am to meet Mrs. George Austen at the Long Rooms to see how they may be fitted for an assembly, and then I am expected at Castle Square with her ladyship's books from the circulating library. The Admiral has made me take my solemn oath not to forget to stop at the tobacconist's, and I have promised myself a card of black lace."

Angus rolled his eyes. "Fanny, if you must go on a deuced errand, then do so, but please do not go on about it so."

Captain Hale heard this exchange with amusement.

The Admiral appeared to regard it as vastly jolly, and turning to his guest, invited him to sit. "As you see, we are delighted to welcome you. I shall send for Emma. She will wish to meet you."

"In point of fact, Admiral, I have already had the pleasure of meeting your granddaughter."

"A treasure she is. And uncommonly good-natured."

"Yes, but the dear flutterbelle has no husband," Angus added, "and she is already twenty-two."

"What did he say?"

"He said Emma has no husband," obliged the Admiral thunderously.

Harriet nodded. "Yes, Emma ought to have a husband,

but only if he will make her happy. I should not like to see her marry a fool."

"Perhaps the captain will marry her," Angus said.

"What did you say?"

"Deuce take me, Harriet, I said perhaps the captain will marry her!"

"Oh, the captain has come to marry her. Well, he is not an ill-looking fellow, but I should not like Emma to marry him unless she wishes to."

The Admiral chuckled. "No, no, sister, the captain is not here to marry Emma. He is here to—I say, why are you here?"

Captain Hale looked from one cherubic ruddy old face to another. Despite their noise and their endless misapprehensions, they were endearing. Perhaps it was the expression of innocence in their eyes. Perhaps it was their hopeful smiles. Whatever it was, they greatly resembled a quartet of guileless children. He felt he could thoroughly comprehend Miss Drenville's touchiness in regard to them.

"I am here," he said, "to further the delightful acquaintance begun at the Dolphin, and to have a word with Miss Drenville, if she is about."

"Come, Harriet, we shall go and find Emma," said Fanny.

"And I shall go with you," Angus said. "A pair of silly nodcocks want looking after."

"What did you say?"

As he bustled Harriet from the room, Angus explained at top voice what mission they were bent on.

The door closed, leaving the Admiral and the captain in unaccustomed silence.

"Well, sir," the Admiral said warmly, "I am very glad to see you again. I am indeed, for you are a sensible fellow. You put me in mind of the purser of *HMS* under my command. Upon opening a cask of mutton, a dozen cuts were discovered to be putrid. The men would have eaten them regardless, but the purser had them surveyed. Even when they were found to be unfit for consumption, the men would have eaten them, and so the purser asked if I would order the casks heaved overboard. As I thought him completely in the right, the sea swallowed the stinking casks and the sailors lived to tell the tale."

"Thank you, Admiral. I do not believe I have ever before reminded anybody of their rotten mutton."

Oblivious to this irony, the Admiral continued, "The men wished to eat the meat so that they might be supplied an extra portion of wine. The ship's surgeon granted all sick men an extra large proportion to promote recovery. You see how it was—the men wished to poison their stomachs so as to be forced to drink more wine!" He laughed rosily at these charming shipboard antics. "Now why did I think to recall the putrid mutton? Ah, yes, the purser was a sensible fellow, like yourself."

"Regarding Miss Drenville," the captain said, turning the conversation. "I am afraid I offended her last evening."

"Oh, I doubt you did. She is the best-natured girl who ever lived. If she can endure my troublesome ways and Old Angus's and our sisters', she is not likely to be easily offended."

Captain Hale regarded the Admiral closely. Apparently he was aware that his conduct and that of his family was odd, and he was aware of Emma's forebearance. The captain could not help but be moved by this acknowledgment.

"Dear Emma," said the Admiral with a sigh. "How shall we get on without her when she sets off for London?"

"When is that, sir, if I may make so bold as to inquire?"

"Tomorrow."

The captain took a moment to think before replying, "A curious coincidence. I mean to set off for London myself tomorrow."

"Do you, indeed?"

"Perhaps I shall encounter your granddaughter on the road."

The Admiral's eyes brightened. "What a boon that would be. I should like her to be looked after by a brother sailor. It would please me beyond anything. She has never been to

Town, you see, and there is only my grandnephew to see to her comfort and safety, and as he has never been to sea and grows seasick on the ferry to Netley Abbey, I doubt he will be able to manage at all."

"I shall look after her. Have no fear."

"Oh, but I would not impose on you for the world!"

"It is no imposition, I assure you."

"Then allow me to write down her itinerary for you, on the chance that it might suit your convenience to adopt a similar route."

"It shall suit my convenience very well, believe me."

"They go by the Portsmouth Road."

"A most admirable highway."

"And they overnight at the Maidenhair Tree."

"A most excellent hostelry. How delightful that your plan should suit mine so well."

The Admiral clapped him on the shoulder. "You are a calm in a gale wind, sir, for I tell you, I have not had an easy moment since she signed on to sail out of home port. Now I may rest easy again."

The captain was touched to see real tears in the old sailor's eyes. It was clear that he treasured his granddaughter, and for this sentiment, Captain Hale honored him; it was one with which he could sympathize.

Itinerary in hand, he soon took leave of the Admiral and the others, whose efforts to locate Emma had sadly failed. Meditating on his next move, he went into the hall. Hearing a creak at the door, he came to a halt. A mass of golden curls appeared at the opening, as though their owner meant to peek inside. In another moment, to his immense pleasure, he saw Emma, endeavoring to steal into the house unnoticed. She froze at the sight of him. By the look of her, she was half frozen anyway. The chill spring air had turned her cheeks pink. Her arms hugged her shivering form. She strove to keep her teeth from chattering. It would have been the work of a moment to stride to her, enfold her, and maker her a gift of all the warmth he possessed.

CHAPTER SIX

Trapped

Dear Grandpapa,

I have asked Mr. Finnerty to send this by the next post so that you may know that George and I are safely arrived as far as the Maidenhair Tree. You will be pleased to hear that our journey thus far has proved as comfortable and uneventful as one could wish. We met with one unlooked for piece of good fortune along the road—the landlady has imparted to me the secret of her Norfolk pudding, which is that she prepares the dough with ground almonds instead of flour and then mixes it with egg white and orange flower water. Dear Grandpapa, commend me to my aunts and uncle. Assure them that I am well and shall write again from Chitting House.

I am your ever affectionate,

Emma

"Miss Drenville," Captain Hale said in a voice meant to soothe any alarms she might feel.

"G-Good afternoon, Captain."

"You are chilled."

"I am perfectly f-fine."

"I congratulate you on your miraculous restoration to good health."

"You do?"

With his eyes, he indicated her foot, which had been bandaged the previous night within an inch of its life.

"Oh, yes. The Drenvilles are famous for healing qu-qu-quickly."

Watching her tremble with cold, he had all he could do to keep from wrapping her in his arms.

"Captain Hale?"

"At your service."

"I am aware you have come to a-apologize but I wish you would not. It is unnecessary, and I do not think I could b-bear it."

His intention to ease his conscience was now effectively thwarted. Much as he would have liked to, he could not ignore this simple, affecting plea. And because he fully expected to meet with the young lady again soon, he forebore to press her while she stood before him, a mass of goosebumps. Formally, he said, "In that case, I shall not keep you, Miss Drenville You will catch your death if you do not get near a fire."

"Yes. G-good day, Captain Hale."

"You mean 'good-bye,' I think."

The blush which flooded her face seemed likely to provide all the heat that had been wanting heretofore. "Of course," she said, "I meant good-bye."

He watched as she hurried away.

The Maidenhair Tree boasted a white front, six peaks on its roof and eight stout chimneys of red brick. The original wing, with a single peak and chimney, had been built in 1278 to house Hospitallers returning from the Crusades. Two centuries later, it had acquired another two wings, with a suitable complement of peaks and chimneys, so that it might be converted to a vicarage. Subsequent generations had constructed additions in the original style, including a stable for post horses when the vicarage became a lodging and posting house for travelers. It was well kept and commodious and boasted an excellent kitchen for such an establishment. A sign hung from a horizontal iron pole over the door and swung creakily in the breeze. It depicted a maidenhair tree with its feathery branches bare of leaves, much the way the actual maidenhair trees surrounding the courtyard entrance appeared to Captain Hale as he rode up.

April had not advanced far enough to do more than tinge the dainty trees with a hint of yellow buds.

It took him all of half a second to ascertain that the Admiral's carriage had not yet arrived. A discreet inquiry that morning had informed him that Miss Drenville and her companions had set out before him. But they had had the disadvantage of traveling by conveyance instead of horseback. Their arrival might not be expected for another hour, perhaps two if they had broken a wheel, or one of the four horses had come up lame, or they had landed in a ditch. They would enter the Maidenhair Tree weary from several hours of jouncing under a drizzly, foggy sky. Perhaps Miss Drenville's strength and patience would be worn so thin that she might be induced to listen to his apology, if for no other reason than to be rid of him. Yes, he had every reason to hope that she might receive him this time.

Having turned his mount over to the ostler, he proceeded inside the main room, where the host, Mr. Finnerty, adjusted his coattails and greeted him effusively. The captain was led to the public room, a darkly paneled hall neatly appointed with plates and tankards.

Captain Hale asked, "Which of the private parlors did Admiral Drenville bespeak for his granddaughter?"

Mr. Finnerty bustled to a table to consult a large book. As he leafed through the pages, he shook his had. "I see no Admiral Drenville listed here," he said, "nor any granddaughter Drenville neither."

The captain frowned. "Is the name Drenville listed at all?"

"I regret to say, sir, it is not."

Captain Hale rubbed his chin. Either the Admiral had forgotten to send ahead for accommodations at the Maidenhair Tree or he had sent ahead to another inn altogether. Perhaps the Admiral had got the entire itinerary wrong. It might be that his coachman had taken the Southampton Road instead of the Portsmouth Road. As the two ran parallel for much of the seventy odd miles to London, the old sailor might have confused them. Captain Hale sighed. His

plan to take Emma by surprise might have fallen victim to
the famous Drenville eccentricity.

On the other hand, the travelers might arrive at the Maidenhair Tree at any moment only to find that no chambers
and no private parlor were to be had. To prevent such an
eventuality, the captain said to the landlord, "Miss
Drenville and her maid and her cousin Mr. George
Drenville will require two chambers in which to refresh
themselves. The Admiral will be most grateful if you can
arrange it." On that, he handed Mr. Finnerty several shining
coins which clinked prettily in the landlord's open palm.

The host lost no time in inscribing the name Drenville in
his book.

"They will also require a private parlor for their supper.
You have one at liberty, I trust."

"I should say I do!" came the reply. "We have four of
them standing empty at the ready."

"Excellent. I shall bespeak all four of them."

The host regarded his guest with curiosity. "All four?"

"Yes."

"But there is only yourself, sir."

"A most astute observation, Mr. Finnerty."

"And the young lady, her maid, and Mr. Drenville."

"Your skill with sums is admirable."

"Were you requiring a separate parlor for each member
of your party, sir?"

"No. I merely wish to have all your parlors available to
me."

"I see. Would it be impertinent of me to ask why, sir?"

"Yes, it would, but I shall tell you nonetheless." He
leaned forward and with an affectation of making a confidence, whispered, "I have a notion that I might wish to
marry into an eccentric family. In anticipation of that event,
I am practicing how to be odd."

The host blinked. Politely, he replied, "Well, then, sir, I
should say you were fair on the road and will not want very
much more practice before you have got the knack of it."

Smiling, the captain nodded his thanks. "And now, if you

will lead me to the best of my four parlors, I believe I should like to order up some supper."

"Will you wish to order up some for your companions as well, sir?"

"Absolutely. As long as I am paying for parlors which will not be used, I may as well pay for dinners which may not be eaten."

Mudge, the coachman, assisted George inside the inn, while Emma held fast to Mary, her lady's maid. Both the young gentleman and the servant looked green and wobbled as they went.

"I am about to be sick as a horse," George complained.

"Oh, I don't think so, sir," Mudge replied, as he steered him around a pair of curious hounds. "You have nothing left inside you to be sick about. I believe you quite emptied everything between Uppark and Haslemere. You will do well from here out."

Mr. Finnerty's hearty greeting faded on his lips as he beheld the two invalids newly arrived. Emma approached and said softly, "We are the Drenville party. I believe you were expecting us."

"Yes, indeed!" said the host. "Permit me to show you to your chambers. If the coachman there will assist the gentleman along the stairs and you, miss, will see to the girl, I shall show you the way." So saying, he smoothed his coattails and led the parade along a series of narrow staircases and passageways.

George was installed in a room overlooking the courtyard, where he immediately prostrated himself on the bed and implored the gods to stop the room from pitching. As Emma closed the door on him, she heard him snoring. *Excellent,* she thought, *sleep will be the best medicine.* Mary was induced to rest herself in the other chamber and avail herself of hartshorn.

Having seen to the others, all Emma could think of was the starved condition of her stomach, which had subsisted all day on dried apples tucked into her pocket by Aunt

Fanny. If she had been home, she might have stolen into
the kitchen, had a pleasant chat with Cook, and warmed a
pigeon pie. The protocol of an inn, however, presented a
difficulty. She tiptoed down the stairs and asked the host
whether she might have a bite to eat.

"I should say so, miss. Your supper has already been ordered," he replied.

"I have never known Grandpapa to be so beforehand in
supplying everything that might be wanted," she observed
in some surprise. "Customarily, he forgets half of what he
has promised and dismisses the remainder as unnecessary."

"Yes, miss. If you will follow me, please."

When he threw open the heavy oak doors and bowed,
she passed into a paneled parlor warmed by a blazing fire.
A table stood in the center, inviting her. The cloth had been
laid, and bread, cheese, hot negus, and other dishes had
been set out. Everything was exactly as she could have
wished, except for one thing. A gentleman stood by the
fire, his hands clasped behind his back, and when he turned
round and smiled at her, he revealed himself to be Captain
Nicholas Hale.

Despite her sudden pallor, her voice was steady. "Mr.
Finnerty, there has been a mistake."

The captain interjected, "I asked our host to show you to
this parlor, Miss Drenville. I saw you arrive just now with
your party and wished you to be well provided for. As all
the other parlors are bespoken, I have the honor to offer
you mine."

"Oh, but there must be another parlor. My grandfather
arranged for our accommodation."

"Mr. Finnerty, did you receive word from Admiral
Drenville to provide for his family?"

The landlord picked up a coattail in each hand. "You
know, sir, that I did not. You yourself arranged for the
chambers, as I am certain you recall."

Emma experienced a sinking sensation in her middle. It
pained her to be beholden to a gentleman she was obliged
to avoid, and this gentleman in particular. "Are you quite

certain there is not a small private parlor that has been overlooked? We should not object to being tucked away in a corner somewhere, so long as it was private."

The captain was quick to say, "Indeed all the parlors are taken. Is that not so, Mr. Finnerty?"

"Aye, 'tis so, as the gentleman knows full well."

Emma, who had not yet removed her cloak, pulled it tightly round her shoulders as though a sudden draught had invaded the room. Venturing one glance at Captain Hale, she said, "You are kind to offer your parlor, but I cannot impose on you." On that, she moved toward the door but was stopped by the sudden appearance of the captain's face as he blocked her exit. She had been wholly unaware of his swift movements. Now she was aware of nothing but his smile.

"If my presence makes you uneasy, Miss Drenville, I shall absent myself so that you may have your supper in privacy. As you see, I have already ordered it up."

Once again, Emma scanned the table. She saw that it contained Leesh of trout, a fat duckling in peas, roasted beef, and other dishes which appealed to her as an aficionado of the culinary arts—and a devilishly hungry one at that.

Although she was sorely tempted, she hesitated. To dine alone with Captain Hale struck her as highly improper, not to say excruciatingly awkward.

She put up a hand as a prelude to declining. Before a word was out of her mouth, however, the captain added, as though he had read her thoughts, "As soon as they are able, your companions shall join us, so that nothing shall appear exceptionable. And we shall say nothing to them of the Admiral's omission in this matter. It will not do any harm to allow them to think he arranged for the parlor and all your comforts and that you have kindly taken pity on me and invited me to share your parlor."

This speech was so obliging as to nearly persuade Emma to sit at the table and take up knife and spoon. Still she debated. Captain Hale was wearing his uniform and was, consequently, in devastating looks. She did not think she could maintain anything like tranquility in his company.

To add to her indecisiveness, the captain added enticingly, "Perhaps Mr. Finnerty will bring you a drink of Constantia to warm you."

The host, who had grown somewhat restless with his guests' indecision and was flapping his coattails, now offered his kitchen's pièce de résistance. "Perhaps Miss will be so good as to taste a bit of Mrs. Finnerty's Norfolk pudding," he said. "It is very much out of the common way, I assure you."

Her attention caught, Emma replied, "Oh, Norfolk pudding! How very interesting. I believe I shall have a taste."

Mr. Finnerty smiled and bowed himself out.

Not looking at her companion, Emma seated herself at the table, aware that he regarded her steadily. He must think her daft, she thought, to be persuaded by an offer of pudding where logic and kindness had failed. She shivered and pulled her cloak about her once more.

"I daresay, you are curious," she said, "as to this sudden change of heart." Though her cloak was now stretched as tautly as she could contrive, she felt compelled to tug on it all the more.

"Not at all. You are excessively fond of Norfolk pudding, I collect."

"I have never tasted a truly well-made Norfolk pudding and I should like to. I am something of a collector of receipts, you see."

As he drew near the table, she calculated the narrowing distance between them. Luckily, he took a chair far from hers.

"If you like the pudding," he said, "perhaps Mrs. Finnerty may be prevailed upon to share the receipt."

"That is what I had hoped."

He lounged in his chair, fixing her with an intent look that caused her to wonder if he meant to mortify her with an apology, but he only said, "You will think me insensible, Miss Drenville. I have always given little thought to what I eat or how it is prepared."

She looked down at her hands. "That is what comes of being a sailor," she said, a little breathlessly. "You have been obliged to make do with such fare as will not spoil during long months at sea. But on shore, that state of affairs need not obtain. The Admiral has always liked to dine well at home. Even when he thought it wrong to feast in war time and would have nothing but parish soup, he liked it tasty with turnips, carrots, beef, and herbs."

His chin rested on his hand as he gazed at her. She had the distinct impression that his profound interest had little to do with parish soup. She spoke quickly now, her voice rising a trifle, "When we lived at Lyme, Cook indulged my curiosity in the kitchen. She permitted me to assist her."

"Did she?" he said softly.

"Oh, yes, and we had our own poultry yard and dairy and killed our own pigs, too."

"Did you?" he marveled, causing her to blush.

All at once he seemed to recollect where he was. Taking a plate, he began to fill it with whatever came to hand—walnuts, gherkins, capers, cheese, jelly, tart. Emma watched as he spooned out ruddy slices of duckling and a gleaming fillet of trout. She wet her lips. When he set the plate before her, she looked at him.

"Please continue," he said amiably. "You had just alluded to a pig slaughter, I believe. I find the subject fascinating."

She stood and said with fire, "You may well laugh at me, sir, as you were pleased to laugh at my family, for my conversation is quite ridiculous, I own. I shall, therefore, spare you any more of it." She pushed her chair away, preparing to leave. The consternation in his expression had not escaped her, but it did little to ease the pain of knowing that she was absurd.

"I do not laugh at you," he stated.

She ignored this declaration, principally because it was spoken with a sincerity which jolted her. Hurrying to the door, she pulled it open and went out. To her mortification, she could not move. The hem of her cloak was caught in the hinge. Tussling with it, she tried to pull herself free. The hem would not come.

Her anguish was now augmented by the approach of Captain Hale, who, if he had had any notion of her feelings, she thought, would have spared her the humiliation of his help.

As he did not divine her thoughts, he came close to assess the difficulty. For an instant, it seemed to her that he was on the point of smiling. That was more than she could endure, and so she closed her eyes. Then, scolding herself for cowardice, she opened them again.

Together, in solemn silence, they contemplated her predicament. At the same time, they knelt so as to work the cloth loose with their fingers. In the process, their foreheads bumped. Both winced, put their hands to their brows, and, at the same instant, apologized. She stopped midway, exhaling in dismay. He also stopped, unable to repress his smile.

Emma set her teeth and resolved not to permit so much as a glimmer of a tear to escape.

"It is a trifling accident," he assured her. "I shall have you free in an instant." Patiently he began to work at the cloth. As he did so, Emma became aware that barely an inch separated her lips from his cheek. When he sat back to consider his progress, he turned to look at her and their noses touched.

She recoiled, as though she had burned herself on a hot stove, and nearly fell back. When he reached out a hand to steady her, she shook him off and stood, unassisted. He stood as well.

"There is no need for you to take up your time tussling with my foolish cloak," she said. "I shall simply untie it and leave it here for Mr. Finnerty to deal with as best he may. If all else fails, he is welcome to rip it to pieces, for it is a perverse thing and I have lost patience with it." It astounded her to hear how much her voice trembled. Nevertheless, she was determined to depart the parlor with at least a shred of dignity.

Frantic now, she fumbled with the tie of her cloak. She saw the captain's eyes lower to her fingers, then lift to her face, then lower again. His attention was so fixed that she grew pale and pink by turns, and then she grew positively crimson when it became apparent that the knot refused to be undone. Far from loosening it and freeing herself, she had tightened it and made a muddle yet again. Only one thing could be worse, she thought—to look up and see him smiling, especially if he smiled kindly, or indulgently, or sweetly.

"May I have the honor of assisting you?" he inquired. She could not be certain whether she heard a smile in his tone, but his expression was as grave as a tombstone.

Before she could refuse, he reached toward her neck and seized the knot. His sailor's fingers worked rapidly and expertly. If there was one human creature who could be counted on to liberate her from this pickle, it was Captain Hale, she told herself. He was, after all, a man whose profession brought him daily in touch with knots. Yet he did not accomplish the work as soon as might have been expected. His fingers moved rapidly enough but to no effect. As a result, the room grew suffocating. Everywhere Emma looked she saw him. When she raised her eyes, she gazed on dark hair done neatly in plain style. When she looked straight ahead, she saw eyes the color of a newly plowed field. When she looked down, she saw his hands moving just above her bosom, which rose and fell so quickly that she wondered if for the first time in her life she was going to faint. Unfortunately, she remained fully conscious, and fully aware of the nearness of the man she was so anxious to escape.

"There!" he said triumphantly. "You are free to run away now, Miss Drenville."

The cloak fell away into his hand. She stood revealed in a traveling dress of hunter's green, and though every inch of her neck and arms was covered, she felt completely exposed.

"However," he added significantly, "I wish you would stay."

"I must go," she said, but stayed rooted to the spot, as though he held her back.

Stepping away, he made a gentle bow, as if to give her the opening she had sought.

Emma felt like a quivering brown rabbit she had once seen. Twelve years old at the time, she had gone out with Angus, who took malevolent pleasure in releasing farmers' traps and nets. They had come upon a young hare that was agitated at finding himself caught. He squirmed violently but to no avail. With Angus's help, she freed the poor thing and set it down on the grass, prepared to see it scamper to freedom. But the fool did not know what to do at this unexpected turn of events. It looked about, blinking, and cocked its head, as though waiting for permission to depart. Angus had obliged by thundering, "Get along you jinglebrains or I shall have you in a ragout!" This threat, or the noise which accompanied it, penetrated the rabbit's brain and at last he went away at a healthy bound.

Like the rabbit, Emma stood transfixed, as if not trusting that she would in truth be permitted to go. Surely, she thought, another catastrophe would befall to keep her in the captain's thrall yet a while longer.

CHAPTER SEVEN

Skirmishes

My Dear Mother,

I have arrived at Fladong's and will stop in Portman Square in hopes of finding you at home. Convey, if you will, my compliments to my father.

I am your most faithful son,

Nikky

Just as Emma had dreaded, a catastrophe did befall. Captain Hale raised her hand to his lips, then, with a silken motion, covered it with his free palm. Holding her fingers between his large wind-tanned hands, he said, "While you are in Town, Miss Drenville, I shall have the honor of calling on you." Thereupon, he uncovered her hand, once more planted a kiss on it, and let it go.

Turning his back, he walked to the fireplace. He leaned a hand on the great stone mantelpost. When it appeared that he considered her already gone, she was able at last to run to safety.

Captain Hale was known in sailing circles for keeping careful logs. It was this propensity which enabled him to set the swiftest and most prudent courses. Thus, he sat down to make a mental log of his late exchange with Miss Drenville.

First, he saw, his original impression of her had been accurate—she was as unaffected a young woman as he had ever met with. She was a surprise, a rarity in a world that he had been accustomed to finding pretentious and puffed up. Her confusion had been undisguised, and he was obliged to confess, he had found it so charming that he had deliberately, and quite wickedly, compounded it.

Second, she had struggled to suppress tears or any outward show of distress, and he admired the pride and strength that struggle revealed.

Third, although she had appeared to regard her cloak as nothing short of demonic, he had blessed it for providing him the opportunity to stand close to her, study her expression, and inhale her scent, all under the pretext of rendering assistance. Her closeness had had a powerful effect on him. He intended to experience it again, so that he might put a name to it.

Fourth, there was a slight hesitation, a hint of awkwardness in her every gesture that struck him as adorable. It was as if she had discovered the means of making gracelessness graceful. The result was that he had been scarcely able to suppress an impulse to smile at her, though he sensed that his smile irked her. No doubt she thought he meant to ridicule her, as he had ridiculed her family. She assumed that because he smiled he did not take her seriously. But she could not have been more wrong. Unfortunately, he had failed to persuade her that he intended no slight.

Even worse, he had been so bewitched that he had forgotten to apologize. That had been his purpose in meeting her at the Maidenhair Tree. Now it appeared he would have to postpone any expression of regret until he saw her in London.

Worst of all, she regarded him with a high degree of antipathy. While he had found her proximity entrancing, she had found his insupportable. She had not *left* his company; she had *fled* it. The more gently he had spoken, the more determined she had been to bolt.

He could well understand her experiencing distress in the company of a man who had impugned her family's honor. What he could not understand was her aversion to *him* personally. He recalled the manner in which she had flinched at his attempt to steady her. It implied that he repelled her, and the implication smarted. In the past half hour, he had not only failed to make amends to the young lady, but he had put her off entirely.

Such a circumstance was unprecedented in his thirty years. He was, after all, the fourth son of an earl, and although all his older brothers were alive and gave no promise of removing themselves any time soon from the path to the title, he was a scion of the noble and ancient Stonewood line and that had always counted for something with young ladies in the past. Moreover, he had made a first-rate reputation in the Red Fleet. Their braided lordships had looked upon his battle wounds and bravery with favor, especially Admiral Nelson, whose notice had brought him advancement. His subsequent capture of prizes, as well as a voyage he had made to China carrying bullion for the East India Company, had enriched his coffers substantially, so much so that his wealth surpassed his father's, and his mother and brothers applied to him for loans instead of to the pater. Because of these attributes, as well as his personal attractiveness, he was one of the most sought after blades of the Town and, consequently, was accustomed to being pursued. Never, until his meeting with Miss Drenville, had a young lady taken him in dislike. Never had one shown a desire to shun his company. Though he found Emma's oddities perfectly enchanting, this was one instance in which he would gladly have seen her behave like other women.

These musings came to an end at the entrance of George, who made straightway for the table and helped himself to victuals. He raised a drumstick and pointed it in the captain's direction, saying, "Emma tells me you have invited us to your parlor. Most kind of you."

Captain Hale could not but wonder how much of their late rencontre Miss Drenville had confided to her cousin.

"She says you would have let it be known that the Admiral bespoke the rooms for us, but she could not permit such generosity as yours to go unrecognized. Besides, we all

know what the Admiral is, don't we? It does not surprise
me that he neglected to provide for us, not in the least."

"How is Miss Drenville? Will she join us?"

"She is tending to Mary. The poor creature has no stomach for travel. Females have weak constitutions, I fear.
Even Emma, who as a rule has the constitution of a dray
horse, claims to have lost her appetite."

Captain Hale suspected that Miss Drenville's uncharac-
teristic infirmity had more to do with her aversion to him
that any reluctance to eat. He therefore rang for Mr.
Finnerty, and when the host appeared at the door, he whispered, "Would you be so good as to bring Miss Drenville
her supper upstairs."

Frowning, Mr. Finnerty said, "Is the young lady ill?
Shall I send Mrs. Finnerty up to her?'

"I believe Miss Drenville would prefer that you sent Mrs.
Finnerty's receipt for Norfolk pudding."

The landlord blinked. "Do you mean to send a sick
woman a receipt in place of a nurse, sir?"

"Yes, but do not regard it, Mr. Finnerty. It is more of my
oddness. I must keep in practice, you know, for I intend to
be a great proficient one day."

Shaking his head, Mr. Finnerty went to do as he was bid.

Captain Hale was now at liberty to converse with Miss
Drenville's cousin. Previously, he had paid little attention
to him. Their meeting at the Dolphin had not given him any
remarkable impression, and the young man had been out
when he had called at Cracklethorne. But now it occurred
to him that the fellow might be a valuable source of information regarding Miss Emma and her stay in Town. Thus,
he experienced a sudden surge of interest in Mr. Drenville.
Seating himself beside him, he smiled cordially. "I have
spoken to our excellent host, Mr. Finnerty," he said. "He
has agreed to provide you with post horses. Everything is
being seen to, I assure you."

George stopped chewing. "Blast, I hadn't thought of the
horses. Truth to tell, I was too green around the gills to

think of anything. Now I am better, I can think only of my supper."

Politely, the captain refilled his companion's wineglass and observed in silence while he ate greedily. When it appeared his appetite was subsiding and he would be able to hear conversation over the sound of his chewing, Captain Hale said, "How fortunate that we should be traveling to Town at the same time."

"Yes, indeed." George cracked a walnut and popped the meat into his mouth.

"Do you and your cousin go frequently to Town?"

"Not frequently enough. That is to say, we have never been at all, for my granduncle detests it, but Emma and I mean to like it prodigiously."

"Perhaps you would like to visit the races?"

George stopped chewing to exclaim, "I should like it above anything!"

"Excellent. I shall take you to Pimlico. Miss Drenville shall accompany us as well, if she likes. And the wax museum. Do you fancy seeing the lifelike figures of every dead king, queen, and prince of Europe?"

"Gad, nothing would give me greater pleasure. You are very kind."

"It is my pleasure. Miss Drenville may accompany us there as well. And perhaps you would have no objection to attending a soiree at the home of my parents. You may have heard of the Earl of Stonewood. My mother's evenings are 'all the crack,' as they say."

Overwhelmed at this attention, George could scarcely find words to accept.

"Naturally Miss Drenville shall receive an invitation as well."

"This is prodigious kindness, Captain. I told Emma London would be the making of us. If she had listened to me, we should have gone up to Town ages ago."

"Miss Drenville is not partial to London, I collect."

"Emma is the best-natured creature in the world, but she has been remarkably obstinate in this instance. She has never before been willing to leave the Admiral."

"What do you suppose changed her mind?"

Inclining his head confidentially, George said in a low voice, "We were already set to go, but I believe Emma would have begged off if not for the assembly at the Dolphin."

Captain Hale pressed his fingertips together.

"She has confided little to me, but judging by what she has said, I believe she wishes to escape from a party or parties who shall remain nameless but whom, suffice it to say, she has lately found offensive."

Sitting back in his chair, Captain Hale damned the offending party, whom he knew to be himself. But though he had done wrong to insult the Drenvilles, and though Miss Drenville despised him as a result, he felt he deserved a chance to redeem himself. After all, he was not such a bad fellow, as Lieutenant Bentworthy and shiploads of men and women could attest. Moreover, he had made a fool of himself in the eyes of Mr. Finnerty for Emma's sake. That entitled him to some latitude, he thought.

Rapt in contemplation, he did not observe that George wiped his mouth and hands with a serviette, stood and walked to the door, exclaiming his gratitude many times over and looking forward to seeing him in Town. By the time Captain Hale came to himself, George was out the door, ready to set off again on the last lap of his journey. He had let the fellow go without finding out the information he required. If he did not move quickly, they would all be off and he might never see Miss Drenville again.

At that moment, George poked his head in the door, laughing and saying, "Do you know, it occurs to me, Captain, that if we are to go to the races together, you will wish to know where to find us."

"I daresay I shall."

"And if you are to send us an invitation to your mother's soiree, you shall want our direction."

"It would be a most pleasant thing to know your direction."

Laughing again, George said, "And to think I nearly quitted the inn without telling you!"

The captain joined in the laughter. Pausing briefly, he prompted, "And where do you stay, Mr. Drenville?"

"At the house of Lord and Lady Chitting."

The captain smiled. Now he was more than satisfied. Had he had been asked to select the single place in the universe in which he would most wish to call upon Emma, he would have chosen Chitting House.

In the midst of writing a note to her grandfather, Emma heard a scratching at the door. She answered "Come," to see Mr. Finnerty enter bearing a covered tray. Mary, who had fallen asleep in her chair, was not awakened by the entrance of the host. In a whisper, so as not to wake the maid, Emma thanked him. "How kind of George to think of me," she said, wiping her pen and setting it down.

"It was the captain who sent it, miss."

"Oh." Uneasy though she was at accepting this attention from Captain Hale, her stomach was even more uneasy at being empty. Therefore, when Mr. Finnerty placed the tray upon a table, she drew near and uncovered it. Among the tempting delights was a dish of steaming Norfolk pudding.

"Oh," she repeated, this time in a tone of admiration. Lifting the dish, she dipped in a spoon and brought it to her lips. She tasted it, then availed herself of another sample, and another. "It is awfully good," she said.

Mr. Finnerty preened. He and the missus were justly proud of their Norfolk pudding.

"What is the secret of it, I wonder."

The landlord took a paper from the pocket of his waistcoat. "The missus has writ out the receipt for you, miss."

Delighted, she took the paper, opened it, and read avidly. "Mr. Finnerty, please do thank her for me."

"That I shall. The gentleman said you would like it. I thought it odd at the time, but it appears he was on the mark."

"Mr. Drenville, you mean?"

"No, miss, the captain."

This was too much for Emma. Plunking down the dish and spoon, she paced back and forth, oblivious to the stares of Mr. Finnerty. "How dare Captain Hale presume to send me up my supper on a tray!" she fumed. "My puddings and receipts are my affair and none of his. He obtrudes himself by ordering chambers and parlors and post horses in my grandfather's name. I vow, he is the most officious, high-handed, hateful man I have ever had the ill fortune to meet." She wrung her hands and would have gone on in this vein but for the accident of glancing at Mr. Finnerty's astonished expression.

It came over her then that she had made a cake of herself. The poor soul was appalled, and she owed him an explanation. Immediately she collected herself. With an assumption of calm, she said, "I beg your pardon. You are not at fault, Mr. Finnerty, and certainly do not merit such a wigging. And, in fact, I did not mean to scold you but Captain Hale, whose attentions, though well-meaning and everything that is kind and generous, are anathema to me." As the illogic of this last sentence penetrated, she added, "I daresay, you think me very odd."

"No odder, miss, than some others I've met this day."

"I shall write to the Admiral of your kindness to us all."

"I shall come for the letter, miss, when I come for the tray."

"I do thank you." On that, she gave him a smile, and the good man estimated that it was worth having an inn full of queer fish to get a smile like that, for it glowed with a warmth that gave a fellow the feeling he had everything he could wish for in this benighted world, and then some.

When he was gone, Emma addressed her supper and her letter, but it was a considerable time before she finished. Her thoughts drifted continually to Captain Hale, and she did not know what she dreaded more, coming face-to-face with him on leaving the inn or meeting him in Town. Either way, she was in for a good deal of uneasiness. Up to now, her attempts to avoid him had warded off an apology, but they had not done anything to allay the mortification she experienced in his presence. She needed a new strategy with which to brave the next encounter. But what that strategy might be, she was at a loss to say.

Although he strolled into the courtyard to see the carriage off, Captain Hale did not engage the Drenvilles in conversation. Instead he contented himself with a wave to George and a bow to Emma. George hung out the window of the carriage to return the greeting with a shout and an energetic wave. Emma, who had permitted her poke to hide nearly all of her face, nodded politely in answer to his farewell, then receded into the darkness of the conveyance. The captain would have preferred to see her demonstrate a modicum of her cousin's enthusiasm, but he was a patient fellow. Any man who could gaze contentedly at ocean waves for eight months at a stretch, he told himself, was nothing if not patient. Miss Drenville would come round. He would see to it that she did.

Minutes later, he set off on horseback, passing the carriage at a dusty gallop, and well before dark, he arrived at Fladong's Hotel in Oxford Street, which, though it did not boast the elegance of The Clarendon or attract the aristocratic clientele of Saint James's Royal Hotel, was the preferred residence of naval gentlemen during a stay in London. The captain was appalled to note that since his last visit, the common room had been filled with "Nelson" chairs, adorned with carved ropes, etched anchors, molded sea creatures, and other nautical ornamentation. He might have gone to the trouble of seeking another hotel, but the host greeted him cordially, informed him that his favorite rooms were at liberty, and offered to order him up a bath.

To his parents' disgust, Captain Hale neither sailed nor traveled with a valet, but while in Town, he did permit himself to be dressed by Mr. Ponce, a skinny gentleman of prodigious refinement and taste. The host sent for the man, so that the captain found him waiting in his dressing room when he emerged from his ablutions, thoroughly scoured of all taint of the road and the sea. Within the space of an hour, Mr. Ponce had decked him out splendidly in cream-colored pantaloons, boots blacked to a dazzling shine, a stylishly cut coat of slate blue, and white brocade waist-coat, and a cravat ironed and starched sufficiently to chafe the neck of the roughest tar. Thus rendered fit to be seen by his father and mother, the captain set forth in a hack to Portman Square.

The butler greeted him with a single raised eyebrow and the information that his lordship could be found in his dressing room. Riggs then disappeared, leaving the captain to make his way along the corridors and announce himself. He knocked and when he heard "Enter," he went in.

"I am home, Father," he said.

The earl stood before a large looking glass, while his valet assisted him into a sumptuous emerald-colored evening coat. He still affected florid dress and especially favored satin breeches because silk stockings showed off his shapely calves, while pantaloons did the world a disser-vice by hiding them.

Hearing a familiar voice, Lord Stonewood squinted into the glass, endeavoring to ascertain the identity of the visi-tor. He did not turn at the sight of his son but patted his coat lapels and said, "Oh, it is you, Nicholas. I had not ex-pected to see you so soon."

"It is eight months since I left London."

"Is it indeed? I had no idea it was so long."

He watched his father continue with his toilette, thinking what he ought to say next. It vexed him to find that al-though he had maintained a warmhearted acquaintance with the likes of Admiral Nelson and had commanded men of murderous strength and violent temper, he had little to say to the pater. The pater had even less to say to him. "You are engaged this evening," he said at last.

"Yes, to Mrs. Leigh. She is recently widowed, and taking pity on her, I have invited her to accompany me to Drury Lane. It is only an Italian opera, but it will serve."

The captain inquired no further. His father's avocation—

consoling recent widows—was well known. The only surprise was Mrs. Leigh's age. She was eighteen, by his reckoning. It seemed that as the pater grew older, the widows grew younger.

"Is my mother well?" he asked.

"I believe she is. I have not seen her these three days. When one rattles around in such a house as this, one may go for decades without setting eyes on another human creature. But had she not been well, I am certain I should have heard." He slapped his dresser's hand when the man attempted to smooth his cravat. The valet bowed himself away and the earl, stepping close to the glass, performed the smoothing himself.

"Is my mother at home this evening?"

"My dear boy, I have no idea."

"I shall go and see."

"As you wish."

At the door, the captain said, "I hope the opera is pleasant, Father."

His lordship had discovered a lack of symmetry in the folds of his cravat and was too engrossed in correcting it to reply.

Captain Hale walked along the well-lit, elegant gallery to another part of the house where his mother's chamber was located. He knocked and listened.

"Who?" he heard.

"It is Nikky."

"Don't be ridiculous. Nikky's at sea."

"Not any longer. I am home and here to present you my compliments in person."

The door opened. His mother stood before him in gorgeous dishabille, one cheek rouged, the other white, one ear red with garnets, the other primed and waiting, one arm gloved in white, the other bare.

"Nikky, what are you doing here?"

"I sent you a note. Did you not receive it?"

"You never sent me any note, you naughty boy, for I certainly never received one."

"I wrote my father from Southampton. Did he not tell you?"

"Well, if he did, I forgot. I have so many engagements that I cannot remember anything."

When she went back inside the room, he followed her. His eyes fell on her dressing table, where his note from Fladong's lay, unopened. Picking it up, he handed it to her. "Here it is," he said.

She waved it away, saying, "There is not much use in my reading it now, is there?" and sat down at her dressing table. Her maid resumed the work of bejeweling her ears and rouging her cheeks.

"Oh, Nikky, I wish you were not here," his mother pouted. "That is to say, there is nothing I should like better than to visit with you, but I am engaged. How unlucky I am."

"Where are you off to?"

"A card party."

"Naturally."

"Have you brought me a gift, Nikky?"

"Naturally."

She waved off the maid and turned to him with a coquettish smile. "Well give it here. What are you waiting for?"

He handed her a small box, which she tore open. Thoroughly perplexed, she removed a tiny beaded pouch. "What is it?" she asked.

"I found it in the Orient. It is a sort of miniature reticule, for your keepsakes."

"It is a strange-looking thing."

"The colors are exotic, are they not? Have you ever seen such a rich purple? And that pink. It is quite extraordinary, I think."

"I look horrid in pink."

"Look inside."

Opening the drawstring, she put two fingers in the pouch and drew out several notes. She unfolded them and when she saw how much money her son had given her, she glowed with pleasure. "You are a pet, Nikky. I declare, I wish your brothers were as generous. I shall make good use of this tonight."

"You will play high, and it will be all my fault." He smiled.

She tucked the notes in her bosom and tossed the pouch on the dressing table. Returning to her toilette, she said, "Nikky, you must dine with us Thursday. Your brothers will be here."

"I am not to see you for a week?"

"Unhappily, I am engaged until then, my dear. Now run along and I shall see you Thursday. Mind you, be punctual."

After kissing his mother's cheek, Captain Hale made his way to the hall, where he was met by Riggs, who, standing stiff as a stick, handed him his greatcoat and his hat. He then opened the door.

The captain paused on his way out. "I was sorry to learn of your wife's passing, Riggs," he said. "I did not hear of it until I was given my letters at Gibraltar. I hope you received my expression of condolence."

His granite expression unchanged, the butler replied, "Yes, sir."

After a silence, Captain Hale said, "It is our family's loss as well as yours. I knew her from childhood. She was a remarkable woman. I shall miss her."

"Thank you, sir."

Again, a pause ensued. Riggs broke it by saying, "I trust you found everything at the house as usual, sir."

The captain smiled ironically, "Yes, Riggs, I have. Everything is just as usual. Not a thing has changed."

CHAPTER EIGHT

Precious Madelaine

Dear Grandpapa,

We have been made wonderfully welcome by Lord and Lady Chitting and their sons, of whom there are four, and very fine-looking young men they are. Upon arrival, I found his lordship suffered the same indisposition of which Lady Landsdowne had informed me earlier, and so I went to the kitchen and set about preparing him a baked apple. I also heated his berberry wine and added a sprig of borage for its excellent healing properties. Cook is pleased to have my company in the kitchen, she says. I believe I shall spend considerable time at her stove, for I do not fancy going about London. Indeed the mere prospect exhausts me. I shall be content to remain in Green Street and scribble out my receipts, which Cook is so good as to say will prove *un vrai benefice*. You have surmised by this that she is French, but be assured, Grandpapa, she does not approve of the tyrant Bonaparte and commends you for your vigilance against him. Please extend my warmest greetings to Angus, Fanny, and Harriet.

I am your devoted,

Emma

Until the carriage crossed the Thames, Emma had no reason to quarrel with Uncle Angus's estimation of London, to wit, that it was the only place in the world where one might bite off a piece of the air and chew on it till he choked. To do Angus justice, the air of the Town, as seen from the carriage window, was thick with smoke, fog, noise, traffic, and crowds. What he had failed to mention, indeed what all her family had failed to mention, was that the London air was also thick with exhilaration. It filled the carriage with a vibrating hum.

Emma glanced at George to see whether he had caught the electric sensation. He had. Their eyes met. They exchanged a smile. "This is wonderfully lively," Emma said, her pulse pounding in rhythm with the city's.

George took her hands. "I am so pleased you like it. I thought you would but I feared you might feel obliged to dislike it on account of the Admiral's disliking it so."

It had not occurred to Emma that she might do more than endure her months in Town. Heretofore, she had looked forward to her visit with unalloyed resignation. Now, feeling the excitement of the city, and seeing the hawkers, the shops, the fashionable equipages, and, the fields of St. James's Park, Green Park, and Hyde Park, it struck her that London might afford her not merely refuge but adventure.

"George," she said, alive with anticipation, "you were right. London is splendid."

He endeavored to smile modestly, then broke into a grin. "And the best thing it is that there are no Drenvilles about, excepting ourselves!"

From the point at which the Portsmouth Road ended at Hyde Park Corner, it was scarcely a moment to Green Street.

"Look, George," she whispered as the carriage drew up in front of an elegant white townhouse, "we shall be close to the park. And I had visions of being indoors the entire time, avoiding what Fanny calls the 'hothouse of vice'!"

He laughed. "I expect we shall have many more such notions and prejudices exploded before we are done. Oh, it shall be capital!"

The door of the carriage opened. A footman helped Emma onto the steps and from thence to the street, which was lined with neat white houses with columned door fronts topped by fanned windows and minuscule gardens surrounded by black iron fences. She had scarcely a moment to take in this simple elegance when she felt herself

embraced. Though it was surprising, the hug was neither
violent nor unwelcome. The arms that held her were cordial
with gentle affection. The words murmured had to do with
being so very glad and being beside oneself with joy. At
last, she was pushed to arm's length and looked over from
top to bottom by an attractive mature lady whose face was
dominated by large blue eyes, two pronounced dimples,
and a smile glowing with sunshine. This beautiful, moth-
erly creature, Emma surmised, was Lady Chitting.

"So delighted, so delighted," she rhapsodized as she led
Emma inside the house. There was no time to ascertain
George's whereabouts, for her ladyship would have another
embrace in the hall after Emma's cloak was removed.

"I have always deemed my sister a most excellent
woman," Lady Chitting crooned. "She has outdone herself
this day by sending you to me."

Emma wondered at this elation. Lady Chitting's sister,
Lady Landsdowne, had never betrayed so much feeling in
all the months of their acquaintance as Lady Chitting had
displayed in the last two minutes. It must be the custom in
Town, Emma concluded, to go quite wild at the arrival of
visitors.

The sound of a thundering herd caused everybody in the
hall to look up. Down the wide carved staircase came four
young men, tagging one another, shouting at the leader to
wait, plucking at each other's coats, and, finally, tumbling
into the hall like a litter of frisky puppies.

Lady Chitting sighed as they landed at her feet. "These,"
she said in a tone of apology, "are my sons."

With frightening energy, they leaped to their feet,
brushed one another off, patted each other's hair and lapels,
and bowed to Emma. Like their mother, they sported saucer
blue eyes, dimples the depth of the quarter moon, and
smiles overflowing with openness and trust. According to
her ladyship's information, they ranged in age from fifteen
to twenty. Emma was at a loss to say which were the
younger and which the older, for they looked exactly alike.
While George shook their hands heartily, Emma bit her lip.

Knowing how cowhanded she was, she felt doomed to address one or the other by the wrong name.

There was no time to be mortified in advance, however, for her ladyship's sons—Nigel, Cecil, Cyril, and Frank— were introduced in form. The four of them blushed several shades of purple as they took her hand by turns and shuffled their feet. It seemed they were incapable of either standing still or looking her in the eye. They remained in a state of mortal shyness until one punched the other in the shoulder and a friendly brawl began, which sent them flying at each other with gusto. At their mother's pleading, they paused long enough to express their pleasure at meeting Miss Drenville and to invite Mr. Drenville to join their high jinks. Mr. Drenville was honored to accept the invitation. After that, the five young men disappeared along the gallery and only occasionally could be glimpsed as one or the other was propelled out of a doorway or slid down the polished floor sprawled on all fours.

"I am a fortunate woman," said Lady Chitting, rolling her eyes to the ceiling, "to have such healthy children. They never tire of sporting with each other at every hour of the day and night."

"It was most agreeable of them to welcome George."

"They are the most agreeable creatures alive. One could not wish for better-natured boys. My only regret is that his lordship and I never had our precious Madelaine." She tucked Emma's hand in her arm and led her along a cheerful, windowed gallery. As they walked, she confided, "I informed his lordship when I agreed to marry him that I should provide him with a son and heir but that afterward, we should have only girls. He agreed entirely."

"Why did you wish for girls?"

"Well, for one thing, we were both so fortunate as to have sisters, and we were both so fortunate as to like our sisters and to get on with them delightfully, and so we wished our children to have and to be sisters wherever possible. You have no sisters, I collect."

"No, only my cousin George."

"Pity."

"He is like a brother to me."

"You poor child. Well, I did as promised. A year after we married, I presented my lord with Nigel. The second child ought to have been Madelaine but it turned out to be Cecil, which was excessively vexing. His lordship took his oath that our precious Madelaine should be third, but who should come along in her place? Cyril! You may conjecture, I think, how dismayed we were. Nevertheless, we resolved that we should have our precious Madelaine at last. But when she presented herself, she was not Madelaine at all. She was Frank! His lordship and I were at sixes and sevens. Though the boys were as dear as a parent could wish for, they set up such a howl in the house that we thought we should go distracted. There was no keeping nurses, governesses, or tutors; they shunned us as though we had the plague. No fewer than sixteen schools sent them down. Their reputation as hellions spread as far as Scotland. Nobody in the kingdom would come within an inch of us."

"Gracious, what did you do?"

"What could we do? His lordship contracted a malady which confined him to his library, where he has been ever since Frank turned two, while I resolved that my precious Madelaine should come to me at last. And thanks to my dear sister, here you are!"

They entered a modern bedchamber fitted out in white and pale yellow. Although it looked out on a stable courtyard in back of the house, traffic along Green Street could be heard as a steady, soothing purr. Emma glanced at the dressing table laden with dainty trinkets, powder puffs, and scent bottles. Sleepy landscapes and portraits of rosy-cheeked girls adorned the walls. Late afternoon light streamed in from the high window. Emma sighed at the cozy luxury of the room and thought that any creature who slept there could not fail to be blissfully happy.

"This is your bedchamber," said her ladyship. Her dimples winked as she spoke. "I hope you will like it."

Emma stared. "But it is so fine. I made sure it was your bedchamber, Lady Chitting."

"Mine is just here." She opened the door to an adjoining room, giving Emma a glimpse of a gorgeously appointed bed draped with crimson velvet.

Touched by this unexpected generosity, Emma sank into a chair. "I must make a confession," she said hoarsely. "I cannot accept your goodness without telling you everything."

An expression of alarm crossed her ladyship's face. She took Emma's cheeks in her hands and said, "What is it, child?" Then she sat on the bed, prepared to hear the worst.

Emma could not meet Lady Chitting's eyes. "As I wrote you, I am accounted awkward. I very much fear that I shall make a faux pas."

Lady Chitting laughed. "But of course you shall make a faux pas! We all make them. That is what makes life in Town tolerable. We should all be a collection of sticks otherwise."

Incredulous, Emma stared. "I do not think you quite understand, your ladyship. I am afraid I shall mortify you and Lord Chitting. Although I should like to please you, I may end up making you ashamed of me."

Shaking her head, Lady Chitting sighed. "My dear girl, you have met my sons. You have heard my story. How could you possibly mortify me more than I have already been mortified? How could I blush for you more than I have for those angelic monkeys who shall carry on the name of Chitting?"

"I am overcome," Emma said. "I do not know what to say."

"Say that I might dress your hair."

"I beg your pardon?"

"One reason why I wished to have girls is that boys cannot sit still long enough for a mother to dress their hair, to curl it and braid it and set bows and baubles in it. Girls, in contradistinction, adore to have their hair dressed, or so I have heard."

"George likes to have his hair dressed, but I have never had it done, except when I or my maid have taken the trouble."

"Alas, that is because your poor mother passed from this vale of tears when you were but an infant. My sister has told me all about it, and my heart goes out to you, child. I believe in my heart that your mother would have dressed your hair if she had lived."

"My aunts never evinced any interest in dressing my hair."

"Then they are ninnyhammers and I have no opinion of them, for your golden curls, my dear, are quite irresistible. I can scarcely keep from plunging my fingers into them this instant."

Emma took a breath hoping that with it she would absorb Lady Chitting's kindness and all the other surprises of the day. "I should be honored if you would dress my hair," she said at last.

Her ladyship clapped her hands. "Oh, we shall deal famously together, you and I. Now you must tell me what it is you wish to do first. Shall we go and have you fitted for new gowns? Shall you like to see the entertainments at Green Park? Shall you like to drive my perch phaeton? Whatever it is, it shall be yours."

"You have been so kind already."

"Dear girl, if you wish to be equally kind you will indulge my impulse to dress you up and show you the Town. Now tell me, what is it you would like?"

"Well, I should like to visit the kitchen."

Lady Chitting's jaw dropped.

Emma was quick to explain, "You have been so good. Perhaps I might repay you in some small manner by preparing his lordship one of the dishes I customarily make for my grandfather when he is feeling down-pin. I am accounted quite skilled in the preparation of restoratives."

"Gracious, child, I can deny you nothing, not even a visit to the kitchen, but I do not know whether I can take you there, for I have scarcely been there myself and do not rec- ollect where it might be found."

Emma smiled. "I have never," she said, "had difficulty locating a kitchen. If your ladyship will follow me, we shall come upon it in a trice."

Lady Chitting took Emma's hand. They shared a giggle and together made their way belowstairs.

Half an hour later, her ladyship put an ear to the library door, then knocked. A growlish voice answered, "Get away!"

"It is only I, my sweet," she said, opening the door wide and walking inside. "I have brought you our precious Madelaine. She is an angel. You will like her prodi- giously."

Emma followed Lady Chitting inside. She carried a tray meant for Lord Chitting, which she set down on a table next to his high-backed chair. After she was presented to him in form, she curtseyed and said, "I have made you a baked apple and also a drink of hot wine, my lord. I hope you will like them."

He regarded her with suspicion under a bushy brow. His head was covered by a cap, and he wore the dressing gown and demeanor of an invalid.

"It is true, my sweet," said his wife soothingly. "She has made them with her own hands and though Madame De- Pois was very much put out at first having a stranger in her kitchen, she has come round to liking it, and so you must oblige us by eating and drinking these excellent delights. We should not wish to offend our precious Madelaine on her first night in this house."

Furtively, he looked about the room. "What of the boys?" he asked in a low tone. "Do they know she is here? Has she seen them? Have they frightened her off yet?"

"Do not fret about the boys, my sweet. They have under- taken to entertain Miss Drenville's cousin. The five of them were last seen scrambling into a carriage, off to some gaming hell, I expect. I doubt you will see them this night, my sweet."

His lordship exhaled with relief.

The countess kissed his creased forehead and spread a serviette over his knee. When she handed him the dish of baked apple, he leveled a cautious glance at Emma and ate a spoonful. After several additional bites, he conceded, "It is tasty."

"Will you have some of this excellent wine, my sweet?" encouraged the countess.

His eyes shifted from one female to the other. Then he drank. The wine must have had a calming effect, for he sighed and said to Emma, "You appear to be a quiet enough young person. You may sit down, if you like."

Emma did as she was bid.

"My dear," he whispered to his wife, "I suppose I shall have a bit more of that wine. You are certain the boys have gone out and will not be back?"

While she poured a bit of the berberry brew, Lady Chitting said, "Why yes, my sweet, I am quite certain. I am very much afraid our precious Madelaine will not see them at all this evening."

"She will bear up," he assured her ladyship. Taking her hand, he induced her to sit beside him.

Emma was charmed to see that the two resembled a pair of lovebirds, holding hands and calling each other endearing names. Having no memory of her own parents, and having grown up in a household of bachelors, widowers, and spinsters, she had little notion of how married people comported themselves at home. It pleased her to see that they were quite as civilized as unmarried people.

She sat across from them and smiled. They smiled back. Indeed, smile was all they did, for nobody said a word. It seemed they were content just to gaze upon her in blessed silence with expressions of inordinate pleasure. Though it was gratifying to be beamed upon, Emma found herself a little discomfited. Those smiles reminded her stingingly of her family's. Thoughts of her family reminded her sting-

ingly of her reason for leaving them. Thoughts of leaving
them reminded her stingingly of Captain Hale. She sighed.
All mental paths led eventually to the same destination.

"How peaceful we are," observed his lordship.

"I wonder if I might ask a question," Emma said.

In unison, they nodded and smiled, encouraging her to
ask to her heart's content. "As long as you do it quietly,
Madelaine," his lordship said.

"I recently formed an acquaintance who spoke of coming
to London, and I wondered whether we might happen to
meet. In point of fact, I scarcely know him, but I am curious as to whether there is any likelihood of our coming
upon one another by chance."

The earl and countess looked at one another to consider
this.

"London is an immense city," said his lordship. "It is
devilishly crowded as well. One might easily get lost in
such a crush of strangers. In my estimation, Madelaine, it is
most unlikely that you will meet your acquaintance."

Emma found much comfort in this answer.

"Yes, my sweet," said Lady Chitting to her lord, "but
one must acknowledge that polite Society is a small circle.
One is always meeting the same few faces wherever one
goes."

This extinguished Emma's comfort.

"Quite right, my sweet," Lord Chitting said. "I had forgot that one is always meeting one's acquaintance in the
theaters and drawing rooms and ballrooms of the Town."
He turned to Emma to explain his lapse of memory. "I
never go anywhere that is likely to be noisy, and as every
place is noisy, I never go anywhere."

By this time, Emma did not know what to think.

"On the other hand, my sweet," the countess put in,
"whenever I expect to meet somebody, I never do. It is only
those I do not wish to meet who turn up."

That was precisely what Emma had feared.

His lordship added, "I venture to say that the way to
meet an acquaintance would be to tell him where you in-

tend to stay so that he might pay a call. Did you supply him with your direction, Madelaine?"

"No I did not," Emma said, taking heart. Her smile broadened. "He has not the least idea where to find me."

"Ah, a pity. In that case, it is quite possible you might not set eyes on him the entire Season."

Emma endeavored to mask her joy.

"You are entirely correct, my sweet," said Lady Chitting. "However, it is possible that she will find him at the very first party she attends."

Once more, Emma was cast down.

"Indeed," continued her ladyship, "I suspect strongly that she *will* meet with her acquaintance, for I mean to take her to every gala, musicale, play, assembly, and card party the Town affords. She shall be all the rage. I shall see to it. And best of all, before we go, she has promised to permit me to dress her hair."

While his lordship congratulated his wife on having found their precious Madelaine at last, and such a mild spoken one at that, Emma considered her position. There was no guarantee that she could avoid an encounter with Captain Hale in London. If Lady Chitting had her way, she would meet him every day. Therefore, she must find the means of confining herself in Green Street. On no account must she leave the house, even if it meant foregoing the opportunity to explore the beautiful parks and animated streets she had viewed on her ride through the city. She must find an excuse to keep indoors for the next three months. Moreover, she must find the fortitude to withstand Lord and Lady Chitting's invitations. Their arguments, she felt certain, she could endure; their affectionate kindness, however—that presented a difficulty which might well prove too much for her.

Business in the City prevented Captain Hale from seeking out Miss Drenville immediately. Once he was at liberty, however, he frequented those places to which Lady Chitting was most likely to escort her guests. He attended a play at the Haymarket, an exhibition in Spring Gardens, and a concert featuring a soprano and Mr. Clementi at the pianoforte, but all he got for his trouble was a stronger dose of *Richard III* than he felt anybody deserved, a look at the *Panoramic View of St. Petersburg,* which set him back a shilling, and a nap interrupted by shrieking in a foreign tongue.

Wherever he went, he met an abundance of young ladies who were in raptures to learn that he had returned from his recent voyage. As they listened to his seafaring adventures, they regarded him with worshipful eyes and fanned their luscious bosoms. These attractions were not lost on him. They reminded him that ladies who sought his company instead of avoiding it were excessively charming. He took himself to task for having expended so much thought and effort upon Miss Drenville.

Nevertheless, he could not get her out of his mind. Thoughts of her obtruded at the most inconvenient moments, such as when he was whispering in a shapely ear or nibbling a perfumed neck. Miss Drenville, he concluded at the end of three days, was interfering with his pursuit of pleasure. His only recourse was to make his apology to her forthwith, and if that did not do the trick of winning a smile from her, he would put her from his mind altogether. Why pine after what was out of reach, he reasoned, when there was so much satisfaction to be had close at hand?

At Astley's, he came upon Nigel, Cecil, Cyril, and Frank, along with their new boon companion, George Drenville. The young men greeted him with their customary energy, tripping over each other's feet in order to be first to shake his hand and clap him soundly on the back, but the one thing he wished them to do—produce Miss Drenville—they could not. She was at home in Green Street, they reported mournfully. They had been unable to tempt her out-of-doors since her arrival, not even with the promise of a pantomime at Sadler's Wells and their own jolly company.

"What is the matter?" he inquired.

Nigel, Cecil, Cyril, and Frank stopped thumping each other's shoulders long enough to ponder this question and shrug in helpless ignorance. They then resumed their boisterous conversation.

The captain turned to George. "Is your cousin ill, do you think?"

With ill-disguised exasperation, George confessed, "I do not know what keeps her indoors. She seemed to like London, or what little she saw of it on our arrival. She told me so. I believed she wished more than anything to see the sights. I cannot imagine what prevents her."

Captain Hale was equally puzzled.

"I hope we may still visit the races," George said, "but I fear we shall not have the pleasure of Emma's company. I wish I knew what the matter was. I declare, I am almost out of patience with her."

One thing was clear to the captain. If he was to meet Miss Drenville, it would not be by chance. He would have to take the bull by the horns. He would have to pay her a call in Green Street. And so to Green Street he made his way.

CHAPTER NINE

A Cookery Book

Open Apple Tart

Prepare a small quantity of fine short crust and add a generous dust of cinnamon and a spoonful of sugar. Roll out thinly and line a well-buttered pie plate. Stew windfall apples with 4 cloves and brown sugar till solid and clear as amber. Spread a very thin layer of pork scratchings on the pastry, cover with the apple amber and put four pretty wide, straight bars of pastry, which you may nail down with 4 cloves used in stewing the fruit. Bake in a hot oven. This excellent tart may be served with whipped cream spiced with rum. For the scratchings, use small scraps of crisp fat, scratched up from the bottom of a pan in which a pig has been roasted. Render down flead for lard so that it will make a base under the apple pulp.

Emma found herself more and more in the company of Madame DePois and more and more at a loss as to how to explain her odd behavior to her hosts. The Chitting boys had overcome their diffidence enough to slip notes under her door containing invitations to an outing of one sort or another. She refused these kindnesses as gently as she could. Nigel whispered at dinner one evening that if she wished, he would endeavor to elude his brothers so that they might go to Piccadilly alone. Emma would have loved to see the famous street, but she declined. Cecil and Cyril offered to dress her up as a boy and take her to a cockfight. This invitation she also felt obliged to refuse. Frank had no adventures to suggest; however, one morning in the breakfast parlor, he did offer to marry her.

"You are only fifteen!" she said.

"Yes, but of the four Chittings, I am the tallest."

"You are no taller than your brothers."

"Well, then, I am the jolliest."

"They are wonderfully jolly, too."

"Well, then, I am the loudest."

Emma could not dispute this fact. Therefore, she made what excuse she could and went as fast as she could to the kitchen, not so much to indulge her fancy for interesting cuisine as to hide. Nobody ever followed her there.

George accosted her one afternoon in the hall as he was preparing to go out. He exhorted her to accompany him to The Mall, where a parade and a review were promised as well as an appearance by the Prince himself.

Emma's look of longing at this suggestion was apparent. Nevertheless, she declined.

"Come now, Emma, you would like to see it. You know you would. Why will you not come?"

Sorrowfully, she shook her head. "I am very sorry indeed, but I cannot."

He patted her hand. "Tell me why."

She evaded his eyes. "I cannot."

"I hope you are not pining for the Drenvilles. For my part, I am vastly relieved to be at a great distance from them."

Coloring, she remained silent.

From his pocket, George took the ring she had given him, saying softly, "Did you not make me a present of this, and does it not signify that we may rely on each other completely?"

"Yes, I did, and yes, it does."

"Then tell me, cousin, what keeps you indoors?"

Fighting back tears, she said, "I must go to the kitchen," and before he could protest, she was gone.

As difficult as it was for Emma to disappoint George and the boys, it was even more heartbreaking to know that she was the cause of Lady Chitting's unhappiness. The countess had had such hopes for her precious Madelaine, hopes of taking her about the Town and showing her off. Now they were being utterly dashed because the silly chit would not step foot from the house. In an effort to make it up to her, Emma knocked on her chamber door and asked, "My lady, would you like to dress my hair?"

This suggestion brightened her ladyship's face for three entire hours, during which time she washed, brushed, curled, crimped, ironed, ribboned, and decked the golden curls it had been her ambition to get her hands into. But at the end of that time, when Emma's hair was a ravishing sweep of Grecian locks, her ladyship experienced a letdown. "What shall we do now?" she asked plaintively, and when Emma heard her mention Bond Street and Saville Row, she inched toward the door, and said, "I must go to the kitchen." Without looking back, she ran belowstairs, racked with remorse at having left her kind hostess so dejected, but not so racked that she could bring herself to change her mind. She threw herself into preparing skate and tomatoes with a garnish of green fried parsley, but even that exquisite dish could not shake her of the conviction that she had let everybody down.

Everybody except Lord Chitting, that is. He was the single member of the household who did not find Emma's conduct deplorable. It seemed to him that her reluctance to go out was a mark of uncommon good sense. He congratulated her upon it and informed his wife that she did very wrong in encouraging their precious Madelaine to venture forth where she would certainly encounter nothing but folly and noise sufficient to deafen a post. "My sweet," he added, "you must tell the boys I forbid them to plague Madelaine to accompany them on their outings."

"You may tell them yourself," grumbled her ladyship.

"I cannot speak to them, for they shall answer me, you see, and then I shall have a vile headache."

It was so painful to Emma to be the cause of unhappiness that she began to contemplate returning to Southampton. She did not wish to return. Her feelings were still at war in regard to her family. The shame she felt at their absurdity had not abated. The shame she felt at her own disloyalty was as fresh as a new stab wound. At the same time, she could not continue indefinitely to be unresponsive and ungrateful to Lady Chitting and the boys. She could not keep fobbing off George and distressing him by her continual refusals. The choices before her were, in her view, misery on the one hand and woe on the other, and she knew she would have to choose one or the other soon.

She was debating this choice when she opened the door to the saloon and to her dismay found that she had been putting herself and everybody else to a good deal of bother for nothing. Captain Hale was sitting on a sofa beside Lady Chitting and submitting with very good grace to her coos, kisses, and squeezes.

The sight of him froze Emma. Her first thought was that he looked splendid in a smoky green coat and fawn pantaloons, the next that his visit would most assuredly be followed by others. Indeed, it appeared he might camp there if he liked. One did not have to be a fellow of the Royal Society to deduce that Captain Hale was a favorite with her ladyship and an intimate of the household.

When Captain Hale looked up and saw Emma, his resolution to forget her was forgotten. She stood with an air of uncertainty which made him wish to go to her at once and take her hand. However, as Lady Chitting was in the act of pinching his cheek, he did not stir.

Seeing the direction of his eyes, her ladyship looked round. She rose and greeted Emma preparatory to making an introduction.

Captain Hale also rose. He said with a smile, "Miss Drenville and I are already acquainted."

"Oh, I am disappointed. I had hoped to be the means of bringing you together."

He noted that Emma blushed at this felicitous choice of words.

"Have you been acquainted long?" the countess inquired.

"Long enough to know that Miss Drenville and I share a similar taste in crockery and a propensity to admire sailing ships in the moonlight." He hoped this reference would remind her of the kiss they had exchanged on the dock, a kiss which had lingered on the fringes of his memory ever since. From the flutter of alarm in her eyes, he guessed she recollected the incident vividly.

"Well, you shall not induce Miss Drenville to admire sailing ships or anything else in Town, I fear," said Lady Chitting sorrowfully. "Miss Drenville has conceived a horror of London."

Surprised, Captain Hale studied Emma. "Is that so?" Emma looked at the carpet.

Her ladyship mourned, "Yes, it is so. She will not so much as peek outside. I have failed to tempt her from the house."

"Perhaps *I* may tempt her."

Emma regarded him with anguish and cried, "No!"

He found himself singularly goaded by this vehemence. Had he offered such a hint to any of the other young ladies of the Town, they would have danced for joy. Devil take her! he thought.

"It is no use, Nikky," her ladyship lamented. "Miss Drenville is quite devoted to the kitchen. She spends every waking hour between the bake oven and the cook stove. I cannot imagine what she does there all day but whatever it is, it is vastly more interesting than anything London appears to offer."

To contain his vexation, he moved to a table and fingered a clock encrusted with seashells. Irritably, he set it down again, saying, "Perhaps she is collecting receipts for pudding. Miss Drenville infinitely prefers puddings to people."

"Is that what you are about, my dear," asked the countess, "collecting receipts?"

Emma swallowed. "Yes."

Captain Hale regarded her with narrow eyes and shot, "And once you have collected every pudding receipt in Britain, what do you intend to do then, Miss Drenville? I dare not hope that one may tempt you from home at long last."

Lady Chitting echoed the captain's question. "I, too, am curious, my dear. What do you mean to do with a collection of receipts?"

It seemed to Captain Hale that Emma's eyes clouded with the same look she had worn at the Maidenhair Tree, when she had caught her cloak in the door. So unsettled did she seem that he regretted having quizzed her. He would have saved her from having to answer but she prevented him by saying in what struck him as almost a gasp, "I am writing a cookery book!"

Lady Chitting beamed and dimpled. "So that is why you have hid yourself belowstairs, dear precious Madelaine!" she cried. "Oh, and I was so afraid the boys had put you off and that you disliked us all and wished to have naught to do with us."

Emma said wretchedly, "Please do not think such a thing. It is entirely untrue. I like you all prodigiously."

Her ladyship drew Emma down beside her, caught her in an embrace and the two women shared a sniffle.

Captain Hale smiled. So Miss Drenville was writing a cookery book. There was no end to the surprises she handed him. If there was one thing he liked it was surprises.

Holding Emma a little away, her ladyship said, "I am overcome to think that you are so ambitious as to write a cookery book. Gracious me, my lord will be all admiration. But why must it be such a secret?"

Emma glanced at Captain Hale. He saw that caught look again in her eyes and wished to know what it meant. Writing a cookery book was nothing to be ashamed of, in his estimation. He admired her enterprise in undertaking such a task.

At that moment, George put his head in at the door to announce in a pained whisper, "Lady Chitting, there has been an accident. Will you come?"

"Merciful heaven!" Lady Chitting cried "It is one of the boys!"

"I am afraid it is Frank. He has broke his arm."

"Oh, dear. How did he do it this time?"

"He went to retrieve his cap and fell."

"Where was his cap?"

"On the chandelier."

Her ladyship sighed. "Say no more, Mr. Drenville. I cannot bear to hear it. Has the surgeon been sent for?"

"Nigel went after him."

"And his lordship? Has he heard any of this?"

"Cecil and Cyril went to the library to inform him."

Lady Chitting leaped to her feet. "They must be stopped!" She ran from the parlor, followed hastily by George.

Alone, Emma and Captain Hale exchanged a glance. He could not mask his intensity, but he guessed his expression would put her out of countenance, as it had in the past.

She shivered. "I think I must go to the kitchen."

Unable to resist, he came closer. "To write your cookery book?"

From the stricken expression on her face, he might as well have plunged a dagger into her throat. She moved her lips, but no words came forth.

Attempting to put her at ease, he smiled softly, saying, "I should like to read your cookery book. I expect it would prove quite interesting, especially as I am entirely ignorant on the subject of cookery, except of course as one who daily ingests examples of the art."

She did not return his smile. For an instant, she closed her eyes. Somehow, he suspected, he had contrived to mortify her by his words. It seemed she might well collapse on the spot.

Stepping close, he asked, "What is the matter?"

She blurted out, "There is no cookery book! It is only a pretext. I have confined myself to this house and its kitchen for one reason only—to avoid meeting you!" In despair, she shook her head.

He whipped around so that he would not see her face. With icy fury, he said, "Say no more, Miss Drenville. You have now made it quite plain that my presence is disgusting to you, so that any doubts I may have cherished in that regard are effectively answered. If you will kindly sit down, I shall make my apology and then be gone. If you will not kindly sit down under your own power, I shall make you sit down. Either way, you will hear me out so that I may be done with the deuced apology and leave you once and for all."

He glanced at her briefly. She sank into a chair, stunned.

While she stared at him one moment and lowered her eyes the next, he paced and talked. "Miss Drenville, I am aware that during our delightful stroll on the dock, I made allusions to your family, before I knew they were your family, which made it appear that I laughed at them and thought them ridiculous. I freely confess that my words were careless, hurtful, and unjust. I wish you to know, however, that the next day, when I called at Cracklethorne, I had the opportunity to further my acquaintance with the Admiral and his brother and sisters. At that time, I came to regret even more the words which I had spoken, for I respect your family and fully understand your tenderness where they are concerned. There is nothing for me to do but apologize. Having done that, I bid you adieu."

He paused so that she might reply. Meanwhile, he inspected the rosewood frame of a chairback. Hearing not a sound from her, he turned sharply and made for the door.

When he reached it, he found Emma there. Her cheeks were pink with heat. "Will you stay a moment?" she asked. It was clearly an effort for her to speak.

He doubted whether he ought to remain another moment with a female whose dislike was so evident. But a plea was written openly and unaffectedly in her eyes, and though he cursed himself for a fool, he stayed. Abruptly, he moved to the window to look out at the carriages and pedestrians filling the street, seeing none of them. He became aware all at once that she had drawn near his back.

"Captain," she said, "I cannot permit you to leave thinking that you have caused offense. It is not true."

Skeptical, he faced her. It hit him that she was a remarkable woman, with a full, soft figure and hair that was so gorgeously thick and curly that he could imagine burying his face in it. In spite of himself, he took a step toward her.

"It was not, it has never been, your words which induced me to avoid meeting you. It was the conduct of my own family."

He endeavored to absorb the significance of this statement, hoping he might find in it something more flattering to his attractions as a man than he had found in their conversations of late.

She appeared determined to make him understand. "What I mean to say is that I do not blame you. You merely spoke the truth, and in doing so, you made me conscious of what I have blinded myself to in the past, namely, that it is not for nothing the Drenvilles are laughed at and called 'the Dreadfuls.'"

"You will think me obtuse, Miss Drenville, but if my words did not offend you and you do not blame me, then why have you conceived such an aversion to me and my company?"

She stepped back, her eyes wide with amazement. "Aversion? What gave you the notion I had an aversion to your company?"

"Merely that you flee my presence on every occasion."

Pressing her hand to her lips, she glanced away. He had the impression that her eyes gleamed with tears. At last, she contrived to get out the sentence, "I assure you, sir, I do not have an aversion to your company."

An idea gripped him. He said, "I begin to suspect that your unwillingness to hear my apology was stronger than I imagined. I had thought, you see, that your protest was made out of politeness. I was not aware till now how deeply distressing the prospect was. It may be that I ought to apologize for apologizing."

The look she gave him contained depths of meaning, like a whirlpool in the sea. After a strained pause, she said,

"Yes, that is why I was obliged to avoid meeting you. I wished to avoid hearing your apology."

"So you do not hate me, after all."

She inhaled. "No, I do not hate you. I have never hated you. Indeed, I have never hated anyone so little. I can scarcely express to you how much I do not hate you."

The warmth of her tone, along with the earnestness of her face and the clumsiness of her words, greatly pleased him. He rubbed his palms together. "Then fetch your bonnet and spencer, Miss Drenville. We are going out."

Because she did not move but only blinked at him, he explained, "You have heard my apology. It is no longer necessary for you to fear my company. The calamity you dreaded has come to pass, and both of us remain alive to tell the tale. Now you are at liberty to do as you like, and, as you confess you do not hate me. I conclude it is time I showed you the Serpentine."

"Why, you are right! I need no longer fear your apology."

As she gazed at him, an expression of joy flushed her face. She looked at the room as though she had noticed for the first time that it was magnificent. "I am no longer a prisoner in this house!" she cried.

"Exactly so. And you owe it all to me."

In answer, she smiled at him. It was, in his estimation, as though a rain-soaked month had been obliterated by a burst of sunshine.

"I suppose there is nothing to prevent my going out now," she said with pleasure.

"I suppose not," he agreed, "unless it be the want of a bonnet."

"A bonnet! I shall just go and fetch it."

While she went in search of her things, he congratulated himself on having won his point. Now, he vowed, he must turn it to account.

As Emma issued from the house on the arm of Captain Hale, she experienced a rush of anticipation. Until this instant, she had not realized how very confining confinement had been. A lack of fresh air, stimulation, freedom to wander about as she was used to doing, and, most of all, a lack of forthrightness and truthfulness on her part, had worked together to oppress her spirits. Thanks to the captain's apology, however, that situation had been reversed. Stepping out into the fresh spring air, which had lost its chilly edge in the five days since her arrival in Town, she breathed in deeply and promised herself that she would make up for all the time that had been lost.

The captain's curricle awaited him at the bottom of the steps. It was a spanking equipage, pulled by two dappled grays. As the day was fine, the top had been rolled down. A servant held the horses, and taking the reins, the captain invited him to avail himself of refreshment in Lady Chitting's kitchen. "I have Miss Drenville's word on it that the kitchen at Chitting House is well worth visiting," he told the man.

She smiled at this allusion, meeting his eyes without flinching. What a luxury it was to be able to look the gentleman in the eye. What a luxury it was to be able to feel him by her side in a curricle instead of running from him.

They drove a short distance along the lane which bordered the park, then turned inside on a muddy path. "This," said the captain, "is Rotten Row. Every visitor is obliged to see it. Here one may view the grand parade of London. Every class and degree of citizen may be found in the vicinity, whether on foot, horseback, or wheels."

Emma thought the avenue most attractive. It was spacious, lined with elms which showed promise of bursting into leaf in another week. Here and there she caught sight of beds of crocus and daffodils. The ladies and gentlemen who strolled, rode, and drove were sumptuously trimmed out in dress Emma had seen only in fashion plates. She felt somewhat dowdy in her coatee, seeing that most of the ladies sported a barouche coat with a girdle at the waist which accentuated the round bosom. When Lady Chitting

took her to Bond Street, she vowed, she would purchase a
barouche coat.

She was thinking that she had never seen so many beautiful women and handsome men collected in one place
when the captain turned the subject.

"It occurs to me," he said, "that though you proposed it
merely as a pretext, you really ought to write a cookery
book."

Her thoughts had been so far from kitchens that she
looked at him and laughed.

"It makes perfect sense, you know, given that you collect
receipts and are familiar with dairies and pig farms and the
like. Indeed, if you include a chapter on brewing beer, I
myself shall purchase a copy of your book. Sailors, as you
no doubt know, are prodigiously fond of beer."

Emma said, "I am well versed in the making of beer. I
also know something of laundering, teething balms, and the
keeping of cats. Do you require that I include these price-
less gems of wisdom in the book as well?"

"Your gems of wisdom shall absolutely be included, and
you shall entitle your book *The Englishwoman's Book of
Cookery and Sundry Household Matters*."

Serious now, she folded her hands in her lap. "You are
quizzing me. I daresay the notion is ridiculous."

Suddenly, he pulled the horses to a stop in the middle of
the Row, blocking the way and causing the drivers and rid-
ers traveling in both directions to shout at him in protest.
Ignoring them, he leaned close to Emma, startling her, and
said, "What must I do to persuade you that I am not laughing at you, that I am completely and deadly serious?"

She felt a dryness in her throat that prevented her from
answering.

"Say you believe I am serious," he insisted. "We shall
not move from this spot until you say it."

The noise from the traffic about them had grown shrill.
Numerous insults were hurled their way. Emma's eyes
shifted to one side, then the other. An incensed driver
flicked his whip in their direction, causing her to jump. An-

other offered to separate Captain Hale from his manhood if he did not bestir himself on the spot.

"Well?" said Captain Hale to Emma, paying no attention to the hullaballoo he had stirred.

A rider banged his crop insistently against the curricle wheels. "Get along!" he snapped. "Are you bosky?" causing Emma to wonder at such rudeness.

"I am waiting," the captain said to Emma, whom he regarded steadily, as though they were the only two people on Rotten Row at that instant. "Say you believe me."

She closed her eyes. "I believe you. May we please drive on?"

"I do not think you mean it. You are merely humoring me."

"I do mean it. At least, I shall endeavor to mean it."

"Will you write me a page of your book and show it to me?"

"What?"

"Damn your eyes!" cried a driver who had been forced to interrupt his gallop. The tangle of traffic, Emma noted, had grown alarmingly large.

"Yes," she declared breathlessly, "I shall write you a page."

"I shall look forward to reading it," said the captain. Making a click with his tongue, he urged his grays forward.

To Emma's relief, the traffic dispersed without mishap. Though a few parting verbal shots were fired, they were not accompanied by any physical punctuation. It was astonishing, Emma thought, that Captain Hale would go to such lengths to convince her of his sincerity. Astonishing, and deeply gratifying.

In a brief time, they arrived at the edge of a curved ornamental lake, which the captain informed her was called the Serpentine. He pulled the horses to a stop out of the path so that they might admire the fine view.

"It is an engineered water," he told her. "It was formerly a collection of small ponds and marshes. John Bridgeman, the royal gardener, oversaw the design. In some aspects, his accomplishment much resembles the writing of a cookery book, which, like the Serpentine, is a gathering of disparate items in a graceful and organized fashion."

Emma laughed. "You are nothing, Captain Hale, if not persistent. But I have already promised to show you a page from my book. What more do you wish from me?"

Leaning towards her, he brushed away a wisp of hat feather that the breeze had caused to tickle her cheek. The sensation of his finger on her skin made her forget to breathe. He said, "You are about to learn, Miss Drenville, that I wish a great deal more from you."

CHAPTER TEN

A Perfect Family

Winter Salad

The Rev. Sidney Smith has devised an ideal salad which may be served with cold roast chicken and ham. If you will select the most hardy lettuces and greens, you may then add the pounded yellow of boiled eggs and two boiled potatoes passed through a kitchen sieve. A sprinkling of onion is added here. The temptation to omit the onion must be resisted if the salad is to succeed. To prepare the sauce, mix together a single spoon of mordant mustard and a double quantity of salt, four spoons of oil of Lucca and two of fine vinegar. Toss the salad, then season with a soupçon of anchovy. You will find that winter salad is consistent not only with sensible eating, but with aristocratic dining as well.

Emma burst in the door to the parlor where Lord and Lady Chitting sat reading together from *The Morning Advertiser*. "We have been invited to dine at Lady Stonewood's!" she announced. It pleased her to speak the words aloud, for she could scarcely believe that Captain Hale had been so gracious as to make the invitation.

Earlier, as she had gazed with him at the Serpentine, she had been unable to imagine what would follow his pronouncement that he wished more from her. To her relief—and pleasure—he had wished for her presence at a dinner to be given by his parents.

"My precious Madelaine," his lordship said gently, "you know I never go out."

"You need not put yourself to any trouble, my lord. George and the boys will be delighted to escort us," Emma assured him.

"Oh, I doubt the boys are invited," said Lady Chitting. "They are never invited anywhere."

"I am so sorry," Emma said, her ecstasy now abated. "George and I shall not go either, in that case."

"Poof!" said her ladyship. "I have no intention of staying away on the boys' account. The three of us shall go to dinner at Stonewood House. It will be a perfect opportunity to introduce you and your cousin to Society. The pink of the ton are certain to be there."

This prospect daunted Emma somewhat. She had imagined a family party, such as she enjoyed at Cracklethorne. It had not occurred to her that the occasion would be formal, that there would be a number of guests who would be curious to see a visitor new to the Town, and that she must be watchful of her skirts and her awkward feet.

On the other hand, she had enjoyed an hour's outing with Captain Hale without mishap. Her hem had not caught in any doors, she had not knocked heads with him, and no knots had plagued her with their refusal to be untied. The only event which had served to discomfit her had had to do with his very evident admiration, which was discomfiting in a thoroughly pleasant way. To sit next to Captain Hale in elegant surroundings and meet his family—that was too delicious a prospect to allow other thoughts to obtrude. It was more than delicious. It was an honor, and she was sensible that he would not have told her to expect an invitation from his mother if he had not liked her a great deal.

These charming reflections came to an end as Emma realized that Lady Chitting was talking to her.

"In a year or two," her ladyship was saying, "Nigel will be invited everywhere, for he will have come into his fortune and will be thought an excellent catch. Going into Society without his brothers to incite him to mischief will civilize him, I daresay."

"Poor lad," said the boy's father. "He will be required to go out every night of the week. I hope he does not have an attack of the megrims as a result."

"As for the other boys," continued Lady Chitting, "their

time will come. For the present, I do not take offense at their being excluded. Gracious, I should never be invited anywhere if I did!"

"What shall I wear?" Emma asked.

Her ladyship beamed, so that her dimples danced. "Aha! You shall be forced to permit me to take you shopping! You shall have no excuses now. Instead of spending your days in the kitchen, you shall spend them with the modiste."

Demurely, Emma replied, "I shall do whatever you say, your ladyship."

My lord and lady exchanged a glance. They had never heard such complaisance from a young person in their lives.

"And you shall dress my hair," Emma added.

Clapping her hands together, Lady Chitting vowed that she was the most fortunate creature on Earth.

"And now," said Emma, "I shall go and prepare a cup of twig tea for his lordship," and before Lady Chitting could stop her, she was gone to the kitchen.

After delivering the tea, along with a warm seed cake, she retired to her bedchamber, where she wrote out instructions for preparing open apple tart, which was one of the Admiral's favorite desserts. It recalled fond memories of dinners she had eaten surrounded by the loving smiles and contented gastronomic sounds of her family. For the first time since her arrival in Town, she began to miss her grandfather and the others. The homesickness, though it was slight, gave her hope that she might soon return to Southampton restored to her former self.

So satisfying was the writing of her first receipt that she essayed another, Reverend Sydney Smith's famous winter salad, the directions for which he had imparted to her in person upon his return from one of his visits to France. It seemed to her that the style of this receipt was much livelier than the first. Her writing was less stiff, less reserved. The tone of it struck her as cordial, agreeable. That was the sort of cookery book she wished to write—one that en-

gaged the reader in conversation and gave the impression
that knowledge was being shared rather than dictated.

During the next half hour, she made fair copies of the
pages. She then folded and sealed them and, thanks to Lady
Chitting's information, was able to send them by way of a
servant to Captain Hale at Fladong's.

Having kept her promise to him, she sat back, thinking
that when they sat side by side at dinner, he would tell her
what he thought of her cookery book's beginnings, and she
would have all she could do to fix her mind on the subject.
It would be a struggle to conduct a lighthearted conversation with a man whose nearness electrified her. The
prospect excited rather than daunted, so that she was impelled to pull out all her dresses from the wardrobe and
hold them up to her nose as she stood before the glass. It
was crucial to appear before the captain's family in the first
stare of fashion. Above all, she must not wear a color
which sapped her complexion.

She had just decided that she looked pallid in Aurora,
Egyptian brown, pea green, and every other color the fashion plates advertised, when she heard a scratching at the
door. The maidservant handed her a note from George.
Throwing her dresses on the bed, Emma went to meet him
in the sitting room.

"Is it true? Are we to go to Lord and Lady Stonewood's
Thursday?" he asked.

She smiled, delighted to see that he was in a high state of
excitement. "It is true. Are you pleased?"

He gestured wide. "To tell truth, Emma, I am anxious. I
do not know whether I shall behave as I ought."

"You! Why you always behave as you ought."

"That is kind of you, cousin. I used to think so, before I
came to Town. I vow, the gentlemen here are so elegant
that I am quite awestruck."

Emma laughed. "You are not awed by Nigel, Cecil,
Cyril, and Frank, I hope?"

Smiling, he shook his head. "They are good-natured lads
and I am prodigiously grateful to them for taking me about.

But everywhere I go, I see men of fashion, the sort we shall meet at Stonewood House. Their elegance is quite beyond my reach. The best I can hope for is that I shall not make a cake of myself."

"Captain Hale likes us well enough to invite us. That is all that matters."

He sighed. "Perhaps you are right. Perhaps his liking us well enough to offer the invitation is a sign that we are presentable and shall not be entirely cut dead."

She took his hand and patted it. "Perhaps we may assist each other Thursday. I shall whisper in your ear if I see you on the brink of a misstep, and you shall give me a quiet hint in a similar circumstance."

"It might serve," he said, relenting. "And I suppose I may take solace in the knowledge that there are no other Drenvilles beside ourselves to make us laughingstocks."

"You are feeling sanguine now. I am glad."

He regarded her with curiosity. "I say, Emma, you are amazingly insouciant. I should think you would feel some apprehension. After all, we are Drenvilles. There is no occasion on which blood is so likely to show itself as one in which we shall have the cream of Society inspecting us and pronouncing us acceptable or unacceptable."

Her high spirits would not be repressed. She had devoted too much time already to fretting over her family's reputation and her own tendency toward gracelessness. The upshot was that she had permitted misunderstandings to come between herself and Captain Hale. That was a mistake she would not make again. Hugging her arms tightly, she said, "I will not permit my happiness to be destroyed by apprehension. Besides, what have I to fret about? I shall not be dancing, shall I? Therefore, nothing can go amiss."

The dressmaker fell into a fit of indignation when Lady Chitting informed her that she had twenty-four hours in which to fashion a gown for the young lady. Madame Milledeux was one of the leading modistes of Bond Street. Fully three-fourths of her clientele were titled ladies. Not only were all of them appallingly rich, but there was not a mushroom in the pack. Lady Chitting's request appeared to her, therefore, as an affront.

Her ladyship's soothing persuasions, however, soon convinced her otherwise. It would be a feather in Madame Milledeux's cap, so to speak, to have one of her gowns dine at Stonewood House. Moreover, it would be an additional advantage to have it worn by Miss Drenville, whose figure would do the dressmaker's skill credit, which was far too rarely the case. As these blandishments were accompanied by a handsome payment, Madame was at last brought to consent. Immediately, she threw her shop into a frenzy of activity, calling upon her assistants to strip Emma of her walking suit while her ladyship selected a fabric.

Emma was lifted onto a tiny platform, and once she had been divested of her outer clothing, was given to understand that her underthings would not do at all. Her stays were made in such a way as to force the bosom up, which was now esteemed a highly unnatural fashion. The undergarment was replaced with one that was lightly boned. Roughly one-quarter the size of the old one, it covered only a quarter of her bosom. Unfortunately, it still pinched the ribcage, so that Emma was obliged to plead for room to breathe.

Her shift was dismissed with a clucking of the tongue and a shake of the head. The seamstress removed the inferior garment and tossed it away. When it came to the wearing of gowns, Madame Milledeux declared, she favored only the sheerest of drawers, shifts, and petticoats. Linens mussed the lines of a dress, which ought to cling. If a lady was wreathed in underclothes, she would appear lumpy. Emma cried out that she could not possibly appear in Society virtually shiftless but was assured that was not to be the case. Madame Milledeux caused an invisible petticoat to be brought in. When Emma had contrived after a time to squeeze into it, it was pronounced perfect. However, when it was discovered that the young lady was unable to walk in it, another solution was sought. It was found, after two hours, in the form of pantalettes, silk stockings, and the filmiest of chemises.

Lady Chitting showed Emma samples of Georgette silk and grenadine in Spanish fly, which was "all the kick" in greens now, she said, and would have Emma looking "in prime twig." As everything looked splendid to Emma, she was amazed to see how her ladyship discarded one pattern after another, pronouncing it either "monstrously" gaudy or "monstrously" old-fashioned. In the end, her ladyship selected a simple dress in the Greek style. The fabric consisted of delicate white Indian muslin which did not "put on airs" and which would make Emma look "complete to a shade." Emma had unwavering confidence in her ladyship's taste in dresses but wondered at the phrases which issued from her mouth, phrases which were unfamiliar to her and which, she concluded after some hours of being fitted, squeezed, pinned, and adjusted, invaded her ladyship's vocabulary only in the seamstress's shop, where she was consumed with fashion rather than sense.

The following day, Thursday, Emma returned with her ladyship to Bond Street to receive her final fitting. She was certain that a fleet of little elves had spent the entire night stitching her gown, for it was magnificent. Madame Milledeux held it up with justifiable pride and Emma could scarcely wait to be helped into it, but when she was, and she saw herself in the glass, she despaired. So filmy and light was the dress that she was certain she would freeze, and so she said. Her ladyship and the dressmaker assured her that her white silk gloves would keep her arms warm. Emma protested that gloves did not answer the difficulty of her bosom, which was scarcely covered, and her neck, which was entirely bare, and the scant material about her legs which permitted her pantalettes to show. Her advisors waved their hands, dismissing her concerns. "You will require a fan to cool you, dear Madelaine," said her ladyship. "London rooms are kept unbearably hot precisely so that ladies may wear so little!"

* * *

While Emma was being tended to, George was taken in hand by Nigel, Cecil, Cyril, and the injured Frank, whose broken arm did not prevent him from punching his brothers and inviting their friendly blows in return. The boys graciously put at George's disposal every stitch of clothing they owned. But unlike Emma, George had gone out of the house since his arrival in Town. Indeed, he had ventured forth every day in search of fine things, especially clothing. He had discovered that though the Chitting boys were irrepressible tusslers and whoopers, they were possessed of exquisite good taste. With their assistance, and the final approval of an alarmingly dignified tailor, George had outfitted himself nicely.

On the evening of the fateful dinner, his vanity was greatly flattered by Lord Chitting's taking an eleventh hour interest in his success. His lordship sent his own valet to him to assist him in dressing. And so George, despite his self-doubts and mistrust of the Drenville blood, appeared in the hall dressed to the nines.

Emma was still doubting the wisdom of wearing practically nothing when she emerged from her bedchamber, her hair dressed by Lady Chitting with a fillet of white satin and pearls twining through her gold curls. In answer to the complaints about her bare neck, her ladyship had given her a gold chain with a tiny pearl pendant. To her disquiet in regard to her bosom and legs, Lady Chitting had replied, "I daresay, the gentlemen will think you look well enough and the ladies will wish you to the other end of the Earth, which is all one can desire," and as she would not budge from this position, Emma had been forced to resign herself to the prospect of catching her death the instant she emerged from her bedchamber. As she walked to the hall, she endeavored to glide but when she tripped on the toe of her slipper, she thought better of it. She had all she could do to keep from reaching a hand into her stays and loosening them, let alone trying to glide.

In the hall, she was met by her ladyship and George, as well as by the boys and his lordship, come to see them off.

Glancing from one face to the other, she became aware that something was amiss. Either she had made an unforgivable error in her dress, manners, and taste, or they had eaten a curry which stuck in the throat and caused the eyes to bulge. They appeared stupefied as they looked at her. Quelling the pang which gripped her, she mustered the courage to say, "I am very sorry, your ladyship. I did my possible to appear 'in prime twig,' as you say. I shall change my dress, if you like."

"Do not change a thing!" cried her ladyship, a plea which was echoed strenuously by the others.

Lord Chitting was the first to collect himself. "You are quite magnificent, Madelaine," he said, and though he wore his customary dressing gown and cap, he seemed quite regal as he put her hand to his lips.

George, determined to take his cue from his elegant host, also kissed her hand. "Ah, Emma," he said, "I know now that it was not a mistake to urge you to come to London. At last someone has done you justice!"

She blushed at this attention, thinking that she had never heard so much praise in her life.

Nigel stepped forward to bow and compliment her, Cecil and Cyril to grin shyly and hope she might have a jolly evening, and Frank to stare at her bosom and whisper that he meant to marry her as soon as he was grown up.

Emma gleaned from these responses that far from disapproving, the others thought she looked very well. That assurance pleased her, for if Captain Hale also approved, then she would have nothing left to wish for.

Stonewood House had been designed in the neoclassical style by Robert Adam for the third Earl of Stonewood. The architect's talent for fitting grand rooms into a narrow space was brilliantly exemplified at Number 20 Portman Square, for not only had he contrived to construct a domed main saloon fronted with a facade in the shape of a triumphal arch, but he had made it so large that Lady

Stonewood never invited fewer than one hundred and twenty to one of her evenings.

Confronted by this stately chamber and the crush which filled it, Emma gave over all thoughts of an intimate family dinner with Captain Hale and his relations. Among the elegant ladies and gentlemen who swarmed round her, she could not even find Captain Hale. He had been whisked away by an admiring lady the instant he had presented Emma to his mother and father. She had scarcely got a look at him, nor he of her. There had been no time to ascertain whether he admired her costume as much as George and the boys had done. She was obliged to defer her plan to discuss with him her initial book pages.

George had been swallowed up in the crush as well, and though Lady Chitting remained at her side, she soon expressed perfect willingness to turn her over to the charge of Lord Stonewood, who intimidated her into silence with his impeccable dress, his grace of movement, and his polite inanities uttered in silky tones.

With Emma on his arm, Lord Stonewood located his wife by a divan and informed her that in honor of Nicholas's return from an arduous voyage, the boy ought to perform the duties of host and take the Marchioness of Poulet down to dinner. Meanwhile, it would be his own pleasure to escort Miss Drenville. The countess eyed Emma sharply, shrugged, and went to inform her son of the honor just bestowed upon him. Emma, who had hoped to sit next to Captain Hale at dinner, did her best to smile at his lordship's gallantry but could not help wishing he had not put himself to the trouble.

When the doors were thrown open, Emma was glad of the gentleman's arm to steady herself, for the lavishly laden table seemed to stretch for miles. Candles and confections gleamed in the center under dazzling chandeliers. The wineglasses struck her as magnificent. Never had she seen such large ones. Since the tax on glass and the subsequent shortage, her grandfather had drunk his wine from pewter goblets and crockery cups. The few wineglasses they possessed at Cracklethorne were tiny. Aunt Fanny kept them in a special locked case to be brought out on rare occasions, such as a toast to the defeat of Bonaparte.

The sparkling tableware was equally impressive. It was silver, Emma guessed, not Sheffield plate. Among the glasses and the silver stood tureens, ashets, and cover dishes in a fine flowered blue-and-white china. The cover was the softest linen, and the table stood on a single mahogany platform ornamented with clawed feet in gilt.

Emma was overcome by the grandeur of the scene. Nothing in it, not the lowest-born liveried footmen, not the humblest finger bowl, not the simplest candle, bespoke anything but riches, splendor, elegance, and style. There was only one thing in the vast hall which did not seem to fit, she felt, and that was Emma Drenville. She began to regret that Captain Hale had arranged for her to be invited to dinner.

She found herself on Lord Stonewood's right hand near the center of the table. When she heard the gentleman who sat on her other hand addressed as Stonewood, she deduced that he was the captain's brother and the future earl. The gentleman across from her, it later developed, was also a brother. It seemed she was abundantly provided with Hales on all sides. Unfortunately, none of them was the Hale she preferred.

He, it developed, sat in the host's chair at the bottom of the table next to a ferociously rouged lady who must have been the Marchioness of Poulet, but he might as well have been seated in Southampton as far as Emma was concerned. She could not hear him or speak to him. All she could do was observe as he attended to the comfort of his dinner companions. Just then, he looked her way. There was a quality in his smile that convinced her he had not looked her way by accident. That was sufficient to cheer her a little.

George's situation was superior to her own, Emma thought. He was seated on the right hand of Lady Stonewood at the top of the table and was engaged with her in animated conversation. Her ladyship struck Emma as a

most remarkable woman. She was so youthful and pretty,
so charmingly fetched out in ribbons and bracelets, so de-
mure in unadorned white, so full of liveliness and grace
that she might have been Captain Hale's sister instead of
his mother. Added to these attractions was the countess's
warm cordiality to George. It gratified Emma to see him
welcomed and made happy. Her ladyship's attentions were
everything that must gratify her cousin, for she spoke to
him without pause, all the while tapping his cheek with her
fan from time to time before spreading it wide to cool her
bosom.

That technique of fanning the bosom intrigued Emma.
Though she tried not to stare, she could not help it. Her ladyship opened her black lace fan with a snap that seemed to
speak. Then she waved it in the most curious manner, for,
though it was done with vigor and speed, it could not possibly have had much of a cooling effect. It was held so low
that it really fanned the waist instead of the bosom. Emma
was puzzled by this practice until it occurred to her that her
ladyship deliberately only appeared to fan her bosom. It
was a sensible antidote to the thinness of evening dress,
Emma concluded, and the perfect means to keep from
catching cold.

Glancing about her, she saw the others engrossed in conversation and serving out dishes, and so she spread wide
her painted fan and fluttered it, just above her waist. The
result pleased her. She had something to occupy her hands,
she appeared to be part of the goings-on, she looked as if
she actually belonged in that magnificent company, and
none of the breezes she stirred up chilled her bosom. It
soon became apparent, however, that her fanning had a singular disadvantage. It fixed the eyes of her male companions on that part of her anatomy which appeared to suffer
an excess of warmth. Their stares put her violently to the
blush.

Emma could not understand what she had done wrong.
As far as she could tell, she had imitated the countess's
movements exactly. Nevertheless, she ceased fanning at

once and directed her attention to the dishes. To her relief, the eyes of the gentlemen soon found objects less mortifying to gaze upon.

She wished she could see what dishes had been set near Captain Hale so that she might ascertain what his favorites were, but she was too far away. The dishes near her consisted of salmon with shrimp sauce, sweetbreads, and chicken fricassee, Florentine rabbit and beef olives, tongue with red currant sauce, and roast turkey. There appeared to be countless removes for every dish. Emma could not imagine the hours of labor which had gone into the preparation of such beautiful and—once she had sampled them— delicious creations. Immediately she conceived a great curiosity to see the kitchen and speak with the cook, but a glimpse at Lord Stonewood's imposing countenance convinced her that it would be unwise to suggest it. Besides, Lady Chitting would not like it, and George would be horrified. She therefore kept mum and endeavored to look as though she understood the conversation which swirled about her.

It was not long before she was required to contribute to that conversation. The earl leaned toward her to inquire, "We are speaking of service à la Russe, Miss Drenville. What is your opinion?"

He looked at her, waiting expectantly. The two brothers, who greatly resembled Captain Hale but were not as handsome, also regarded her with encouraging expressions. The ladies nearby stopped their chattering to permit her to speak. All, it seemed, hung on her answer.

Emma had grown up in a household which, for all the faults of its inmates, have never taught her deception. Indeed, her relations were as open, honest, and outspoken as a family could be, which was one reason why they had been anointed with the epithet *dreadful*. Consequently, it was impossible for Emma to pretend to know what was meant by service à la Russe, and she was incapable of inventing an answer ambiguous enough to persuade her listeners that she was au courant. She answered, "If you will be so good as to tell me what service *à la Russe* is, I shall see whether I have a opinion."

The others put up their glasses to inspect her, as though she were an odd specimen, all except his lordship, who put his finger to her chin and said, "Good heavens, an honest woman, and at my table! It is unprecedented. No wonder Nicholas put the bee in his mother's bonnet to invite you. You are a tonic."

From the smiles which followed this pronouncement, Emma concluded that her answer had not absolutely disgraced her.

"Service *à la Russe*," said the earl smoothly, "is the custom of Europeans. Servants pass each dish to the guests so that they may help themselves."

"Oh, I see. Thank you very much."

"What is your opinion?" he prompted.

Taking their cue from their host, the others patiently awaited her reply. It appeared to Emma that there was nothing to intimidate in their air. Indeed, they smiled as amiably as one could wish.

Emboldened, she said, "I should like to be invited to a dinner with service *à la Russe*, to see whether I liked it. No doubt it has its advantages, as long as the servants do not spill the dishes on the guests."

When his lordship laughed, they all laughed, which alarmed Emma until she saw that they did not laugh at her. Their laughter implied that she had made a delightful sally.

His lordship smiled warmly and said, "In that case, Miss Drenville, I shall instruct her ladyship to employ service *à la Russe* as soon as possible, as a sort of experiment, and you, of course, shall be invited so that you may render your opinion with full knowledge of the facts."

She looked at her hands in her lap. "I daresay, you all think me vastly ignorant, which is no less than the truth."

None of them knew how to respond to such directness.

His lordship, however, said, "Your candor must disarm all criticism. Besides, it is a sign of wisdom to be aware of one's own ignorance. In London, we have a vast supply of rattles who claim to know everything. We have far too little wisdom."

Smiling at him, she said, "My lord, you are the most polite gentleman I have ever met, for no matter what I say or how awkwardly I say it, you contrive to turn it to my advantage."

He gazed at her appreciatively and patted her hand.

Emma felt that all the stories Angus and the Admiral had told of London—of its high and mighty ton, its sneering gentlemen and snubbing ladies, its shallowness, pretension, and sham—had been the result of some deplorable misunderstanding. Her reception could not have been more gratifying, not in her wildest dreams. True, she had not sat next to Captain Hale, but his father and brothers had treated her with the consideration one might accord a princess. They had admired her, encouraged her, drawn her out, and complimented her. They had been kinder than she felt she deserved, especially the Earl of Stonewood.

She did not attribute any of this complaisance to her own attractions. It all rose from their good manners, she felt. Her conduct was exactly what it always had been and therefore necessarily spotted with missteps. Theirs, on the other hand, was perfect.

Again she glanced at Lady Stonewood, who had managed this entire feast, the likes of which Emma had seen only in imagination. Her ladyship seemed a veritable queen out of a fairy tale. Like her husband and sons, she was perfect. As a family, the Hales were as far from the Drenvilles as it was possible to get. She envied the captain. Surely he must know how fortunate he was to have relations it was not necessary to blush for.

All at once, she paled as an old and hideous fear overcame her. What if she permitted herself to fall in love with Captain Hale? What if he should then conceive a disgust for her family or, what was worse, for her? She was half in love with him already. Indeed, she was on the brink of being in a hopeless case. It would break her heart to lose him on account of the Drenville reputation. Even more, she dreaded repulsing him by her own awkwardness.

These reflections were nothing new, but they were so painful that Emma did not hear the conversation. She neglected to return Captain Hale's smile from the bottom of the table. She was unaware that an exquisite whipped syllabub garnished with fresh violets had been set before her. And it escaped her completely that Lord Stonewood looked at her with meaning and squeezed her knee.

CHAPTER ELEVEN

What Was Brewed in the Kitchen

Lavender

The scented part of the lavender is the flower and is a great favorite. The spike, which consists of the leaves and stems, gives off a pungent odor best rubbed on the inside of oak chests to ward off flies and moths. Flowers should be collected in muslin bags and used in linen chests. They should never be left loose near woollens, for they will produce tiny holes. To clear the air of a sick room, burn a handful of lavender stems before an open window, allowing the breeze to blow the smoke throughout the chamber. Lavender water may be mixed by combining a pint of spirit of wine with half an ounce of oil of lavender, thirty drops of nutmeg oil, another thirty of essence of Bergamot, and a bit of essence of ambergris. The mixture is especially . . .

From the moment he saw his father attach himself to Emma's side, Captain Hale recognized it had been a mistake to invite her to Stonewood House. He ought to have known how it would be. His mother's note ought to have forewarned him.

He had written to her requesting that she send an invitation to Lady Chitting and the Drenvilles. She had replied by saying that she would be only too happy to oblige but would he mind very much franking the expenses for the dinner as she was frightfully out of pocket and knew not where else to turn. His father would not oblige her, his mother complained; Mrs. Leigh had thrown him over for a young dandy and there was no reasoning with the man.

The captain had sent the money, and his mother had sent the invitation, which, he told himself, was all that mattered. Now he would be able to convey to Emma something of his regard for her. If the attention appeared very particular and gave rise to speculation that he had conceived a *tendre* for the young lady, he did not care, as long as Emma knew that he wished her to be pleased.

But he ought to have cared. He ought to have known that the pater, in the absence of Mrs. Leigh, would see Emma's appealing face and delightful form and would affix himself to her like a leech. He ought to have known that his plan of sitting next to her and carving out lamb roast for her would be thwarted by the superior craft and experience of his father. He ought to have known that he would be obliged to sit practically at the opposite end of the Earth from her, reduced to watching while his father and brothers ogled her and pretended to be fascinated by her every syllable.

As disagreeable as all this was, however, it was nothing to the sight of Emma wielding her fan in the manner of an egregious flirt. It stunned him to see her drawing attention to her bosom in such a manner. Even without the allurement of the waving fan her breasts were captivating. The obvious ploy to win the attention of his father and brothers was infuriating. It put him in mind of his mother, who employed the selfsame stratagem to attract prospective lovers.

More important, it signaled to him the end of Emma's innocence. No longer was she the unaffected young lady he had met in Southampton. An hour in Society had rendered her indistinguishable from every other female he knew—vain, silly, vapid, and sly. And if Miss Drenville had been spoiled by the influence of the ton, he had nobody but himself to blame. He had set her down in the midst of folly and conceit and had foolishly expected her to come through unscathed. Naive and unprotected, she had succumbed. It was the most natural thing in the world. If he had been a rational fellow, if he had not been half demented with infatuation, he would have seen that; he would have had no difficulty quelling his impulse to leap onto the table and hurl the dishes at every male who had the temerity to leer at her.

He calmed considerably when he saw her give up fanning herself and join the conversation. She held her head in an attitude of interest, and he could not help but envying his father and brothers. They did not deserve such rapt attention, in his estimation. They were capable of only the most empty, frivolous thought. He devoutly wished Emma would throw politeness to the winds and give out with a great yawn.

When he saw his father put a finger to her chin, he ground his teeth. When he saw him pat her hand, he muttered an oath. But when he saw him reach under the table, he started so violently that Lady Chitting, who sat nearby, asked him if he was choking on a fish bone. He watched, waiting for Emma to jump up in indignation. When she did not move, he pushed away his plate. He could not eat while jealousy ate at him.

After what seemed a century, the ladies withdrew and the gentlemen were left to their port and cigars. He rose so that he might speak to the pater but was intercepted by his eldest brother, who said, "Nikky, old fellow, lend me a hundred, will you? There's a good fellow."

He laughed. "You might at least ask me how I do after eight months at sea."

"Yes, of course. How forgetful I am. I should have asked at once had I not been in such a frightful state. I am being dunned wherever I go. I thought you might have a bit of the ready. I should pay you back, of course."

"Stonewood," Captain Hale said, "I should as soon sit before my fire, burning pound notes the live long day, as give you money and expect to be repaid."

His brother squinted. "Are you saying you do not intend to lend me the blunt, or that it will not be necessary to repay you?"

Captain Hale eyed him ironically. "I must go and pay my compliments to the pater," he said and left without further ceremony.

At his approach, his father rose and inhaled luxuriously on his cigar. "Your Miss Drenville is quite delectable," he remarked.

It grated to hear Emma spoken of in such a manner but the captain said nothing, knowing that his father was incapable of alluding to a female in any other terms. But though he was silent on that head, he got right to the point. "I ought to have sat next to her at dinner," he said. "It was unkind to seat her entirely with strangers. It was not well done of you, Father."

"I made certain she was well entertained."

"You made certain that *you* were well entertained."

His lordship raised an eyebrow at this challenge from his son. "What is your interest in the girl, Nicholas? You do not mean to be serious about her, I hope."

"Why should I not be serious?"

The pater sipped elegantly at a brandy. "Have you any idea who she is? Admiral Drenville's granddaughter."

"What is that to say to anything?"

"Only that you may do as you like with her as long as you do not ally yourself to her family. They are not merely parvenus. They are called 'the Dreadfuls,' and with good reason."

"Thank you for the sage advice."

"I do not advise. That is too mild a word, my boy."

The captain smiled. "In short, you mean to threaten me, is that it? Do you mean to disinherit me if I disobey, Father?" For the first time in his life, he saw his father look ruffled.

His lordship cleared his throat. "*Threaten* is such a disagreeable word," he said.

"I am glad you think so, for I am well aware there is nothing left for me to inherit."

"Let us not quarrel, Nicholas. It is vulgar."

"I shall refrain from vulgarity if you will refrain from slighting Miss Drenville and her family."

"As you wish. It is a matter of complete indifference to me."

"And you will refrain from attaching yourself to her when we join the ladies."

"I merely wished to be civil, my boy."

"And you will refrain from squeezing her hand or touching her, with or without her permission."

Caught, his lordship flared, "You speak as though you meant to call out your own father!"

"I mean to remind you that you are my father and not my rival."

"All those months at sea have not done a great deal to improve your manners."

"Perhaps my manners are so execrable that you will disdain to borrow any additional funds from me."

Lord Stonewood paused with his cigar in the air. Uncharacteristically at a loss, he replied with a weak smile.

Captain Hale nodded. "I can see that my manners will never be as execrable as that."

When the gentlemen joined the ladies, Captain Hale found Emma seated with his mother on a sofa. He drew near to observe them more closely. On his way, he was intercepted, first by a persistent young lady who flirted with him mercilessly, and then by his youngest brother, who had come in late, very much the worse for drink, and had only just met Miss Drenville. He offered to take the chit off old Nikky's hands when he tired of her, in exchange for a few hundred crowns.

Attaining the sofa at last, Captain Hale lingered behind it and overlistened the conversation.

"May I ask a question?" Emma said.

"You may ask anything you like," said his mother. Her voice was thick with charm.

"I shall ask, but you must tell me if I do wrong in asking. I should not like to offend. But I cannot help asking. And yet I am certain I ought not to ask. Oh dear, I am making a muddle and I have not begun to ask the question."

This was the Emma Captain Hale knew and liked. He

smiled to think that perhaps dinner at Stonewood House had not ruined her altogether.

Her ladyship laughed. "If I do not like your question, my dear, I shall evade it quite prettily, have no fear."

"Thank you. My question is this—how do you contrive to fan yourself so gracefully without causing the gentlemen to stare at your bosom?"

Her ladyship choked on her coffee. "I beg pardon?"

"I watched as you waved your fan, my lady, and I was so full of admiration for your grace and style that I endeavored to imitate you, but when I did, I soon found the gentlemen's eyes fixed upon my bosom until I quite blushed. And so I thought I should ask you what I had done wrong."

Captain Hale smiled. So Emma's escapade with the fan had been conducted with perfectly guileless intentions. He had misjudged her. He had been jealous and leaped to absurd conclusions. It amused him to see how her innocence unsettled his mother, who regarded the girl as though she had suddenly sprouted two heads.

"I shall show you how I did it," Emma said, and promptly fanned herself just above the waist. A dozen or so gentlemen nearby turned to observe. Like them, Captain Hale found himself gripped by the sight of the two creamy orbs which rose and fell above a glow of motion.

"There, you see!" Emma declared.

Her ladyship scowled and replied, "You are a strange creature. Wherever did Nikky find you?"

"In Southampton."

"That explains it."

The tone of sarcasm was not lost on Emma. "I have offended you," she said. "I am very sorry."

"Don't be ridiculous. It is always flattering to be imitated. But it is manifestly clear that you have your own unique style. You ought not to copy others."

"You are very kind," Emma replied uncertainly.

By this time, Captain Hale had heard enough to assure him that he could not let another moment pass without speaking to Emma. He therefore came round the sofa and showed himself to the ladies, bowing before them and asking his mother whether he might steal her companion for a moment.

"You may have her as long as you like," his mother replied sweetly.

He handed Emma up and led her to a corner of the drawing room where he hoped they would not be interrupted. Unfortunately, he was not in luck. He saw his middle brother bearing down on him from across the room. In another moment, he would be beseiged with more pleas for funds. To forestall such an eventuality, Captain Hale took Emma's hand and pulled her through the door, saying, "Come, I shall show you the gallery," and before she could protest, off they went.

Emma realized too late that she was steering a course directly into the maelstrom. She had intended to keep her distance from the captain, determined not to like him any better than she did already; yet here she was accompanying him along the spacious white pillared gallery, gazing at pictures of his ancestors, searching their solemn faces for a hint of his fine features, knowing all the while that if she found such a hint, it would merely serve to torment her, just as his nearness tormented her now.

Her thoughts leaped to their late drive in Rotten Row. It had been wrong of her, disastrously wrong, to let down her guard with him. She had deceived herself into thinking that his apology had freed her to resume their former friendly terms. But in fact, nothing had changed. Her family was still what it had ever been. She was still what she had ever been. And he was what he had ever been—the son of an ancient, noble, refined, worldly, worthy family. Only one thing had changed. He was more out of reach than before.

"That ugly devil," he said, "is my namesake, Nicholas Hale." He directed her attention to a uniformed gentleman with white hair and large hands. "He was a younger son and therefore never acquired a title. He did, however, have the distinction of being the first sailor in the family."

She studied the wind-tanned face. It was the only one in the entire row that did not appear on the point of biting one's head off. The face drew her with its strong jaw and penetrating eyes, which seemed equally capable of gazing far out to sea and seeing through the heart of a woman. Emma became aware that her heart was pounding in her ears.

"Do you like him?" Captain Hale inquired.

Emma could not deny it. "Yes."

"I suspect you are partial to sailors."

She sighed at her weakness. "Yes."

"I am going to kiss you."

She blinked at him, backing away until she came flat up against the wall. "I expect it would be better if you did not," she said when she could breathe.

"You do not wish me to kiss you?"

"Yes. No. I beg your pardon?"

Instead of repeating the question, he came near, too near. Emma fidgeted and assessed the routes of escape. To her right was the dark end of the gallery with no one and nothing to run to. To her left was the domed saloon with a multitude of ladies and gentlemen among whom she might safely hide. Unfortunately, Captain Hale's sturdy form blocked escape on the left. She did not think she could run round him without his grasping her arm or somehow stopping her. And the instant he touched her, she would be done for. She would melt like butter in a saucepan.

The debate was made moot by Captain Hale, who tipped up her chin and looked intently into her eyes. She lowered her eyes. She was now as stiff as a pole, with chin high and eyes low, an awkward position if ever there was one. Any desire he had felt to kiss her must not be effectively stifled, she thought.

"Look at me," he said.

She kept her eyes averted.

"Very well. Do not look at me. I shall look at you."

At that, she stole a glance at him and saw that he was

about to kiss her. She turned her head. His lips landed on her earring.

"Oh, dear," she rasped, "I am so sorry. It did not cut you, did it?"

He rubbed his lips. "Just a graze. Nothing to send for the ship's doctor about." On that, he again brought his lips close to hers. Before they touched, however, she ducked under his arm and would have fled down the gallery except that he caught her in his arms.

"My dearest Emma," he said, "stop squirming."

He held her firmly by the cheeks and kissed her. After a time, she felt his hands leave her face and drift down along her shoulders and sides. He pressed close, murmuring a sound that told her how much he desired her, and it was too much for her. Without a thought for anything else, she threw her arms around his neck and answered his kiss in equal measure.

She had known that he would affect her. What she had not known was that he would bring her to abandon. All the reason and logic which had cautioned her to avoid him was now just so much seaweed tossed by waves onto the shore. Her head, toes, fingertips, mouth, belly, earlobes, teeth, thighs were a jumble of sensation. She clung to him urgently, let her lips seek his eyes and ears and brow as well as his mouth. Her hands reached to his hair, his cheeks, and his chest as though she could not convince herself of his reality unless she burned his imprint into her palms.

Slowly he released her and swallowed. Clearly her response had surprised him as much as it had her. She rested against the wall. Both breathed unsteadily. They looked at each other without speaking.

He required a length of time to collect himself. Putting a hand on his breast, he smiled, though there was more aching in his expression than gaiety. "Emma," he said. The word made her shudder. It woke her.

Sense returned then. Ashamed that she had permitted the situation to go this far, she vowed to be strong in future, before it was too late. She was in love with him and must do everything in her power to keep from being hopelessly in love.

Pushing away from the wall, she said, "I do not ever wish to see you again, Captain Hale." On that, she walked toward the saloon. She moved confidently because a new determination had seized her. This time, she knew, she would not give in.

On the following day, Emma did not endeavor to avoid Captain Hale. She knew he would come eventually. He would come because he would accurately read into her kisses an invitation that belied her express wish not to see him. He would come because he was a gentleman of steadiness and feeling and would not have asked his mother to invite her, nor kissed her, if she had not meant a great deal to him. He would come because he would not be able to stay away. And so she steeled herself to face him.

When he did come, she vowed, she would *not* behave as she had done in the past—inventing excuses to run from his presence. She would stand her ground and explain herself as truthfully and as urgently as she could. Try as she had, she had never been able to make him understand the obstacles which stood immovably in their path, namely, her family and his. The explanation would cause her untold mortification, for she would be obliged to reveal sentiments which she would have given anything to have kept hidden; nevertheless, she would not hang back.

Having thus made up her mind, she did not decline invitations to go out. If they were to meet in the world at large, so be it, she thought. Consequently, she accepted Nigel's arm on a stroll through Kensington Gardens. She sat between Cecil and Cyril at a tea garden. She permitted Frank to take her to the Tower, and when he proposed marriage to her near the spot where the executioner had divided Ann Boleyn from her head, she asked him what he would do if she said *yes*.

"I should consider myself and my heart engaged," he answered promptly.

"You are too young to be engaged."

"I am not too young to fall in love."

"Do not fall in love until you are forty or fifty, dear Frank. It is not the joyous ecstasy the poets make it out to be."

"Oh, what a bore."

"Exactly so."

"Still, if my heart must be broken, I should just as soon you were the one to break it."

"We shall not discuss your broken heart until your broken arm has had an opportunity to mend."

"Very well, and after it is mended, we shall become engaged."

Emma also accompanied Lady Chitting on morning visits to the myriad fine ladies she had met at Stonewood House. She drank tea in their sumptuous parlors, said what was required, and received compliments on her appearance, all the while thinking what was in store for her when Captain Hale came to call. Although she dreaded the moment, she acknowledged its inevitability, and like the aforesaid Ann Boleyn, though she was not precisely eager to meet her fate, she was reconciled to it.

Days passed and she did not see him. He left his card on two occasions when she was out, and on a visit to Lady Stonewood she learned that she had just missed him. Instead of Captain Hale, her cousin George was there. It seemed her ladyship had kindly taken the young man under her wing. Since the momentous Thursday at dinner, he had been invited to visit the countess every day, and to escort her to a fashionable gaming house every night. Emma saw that George had permitted his head to be turned a little by these attentions. He gazed at Lady Stonewood with a perfectly daft expression. But she did not blame him. The Hales were an attractive family, an irresistibly attractive family. It was difficult not to admire them. Was she not in a similar case? Was she not in as pitiful a state as poor George, wholly under the spell of a Hale who was utterly unattainable?

Whenever she could, Emma kept on with her cookery book. She had warmed to the writing, not only because Captain Hale had encouraged her to persevere, but also because she liked it for its own sake. She found herself deliciously absorbed when she began to separate the book into chapters: meats, poultry, breads, puddings, soups, and the like. Thinking out receipts and choosing words took her away for a time from the cares of the present. And going belowstairs to test out the receipts was a welcome respite from thoughts of the man she could not chase from her thoughts. It was wrong for a female to think of nothing but gentlemen, she told herself. A woman ought to have something to engross her, something important, interesting, difficult, and exciting. Something that did not depend on one's family. Something that could not be spoiled by one's propensity to make a muddle of things. Something that had nothing to do with love. Thank Heaven she had her cookery book.

She was in the kitchen, engaged in mixing lavender water and recording her notes in a little book, when a soft noise interrupted her. Madame DePois had gone to the market. The scullery maid had gone off to find a hand to flirt with in the stable. Housekeeper and butler had set themselves the task of polishing the silver in the dining parlor. Alone, she felt the unaccustomed emptiness of the kitchen and started at each imagined footfall.

"You are writing your cookery book. I am glad," said a voice behind her.

So, she thought, *he has come at last.* Setting down the ladle, she wiped her hands on her pinafore and turned to face him.

"I have not had an opportunity before to tell you how delighted I was to read the pages you sent me."

She inhaled for courage. "I have been expecting you," she said.

Something in her gravity evidently shook him, for he evaded her eyes. "A kitchen is a vastly interesting place," he observed lightly. "I have never been in a kitchen before. You must give me a tour."

"It was not necessary for you to come belowstairs, Captain. I would not have been denied to you had you come to Lady Chitting's saloon."

Fixing her with a look, he said, "I had no way of knowing that, did I?"

She shook her head. "No, you did not. Judging from my past behavior, you might well have assumed I meant to avoid you at all costs. However, I meant no such thing."

"Excellent. Then you will give me a tour of the kitchen. I have a prodigious curiosity to see a place which so fascinates you."

There was not a great deal of room for walking, as the center of the kitchen was dominated by a large pine worktable containing the bowl of lavender water surrounded by the cook's equipment. She led him round the table, pausing whenever he paused to test the scales, examine the mortar and pestle, scrutinize the utensils, and toss an egg into the air and catch it again. They stopped at the oven and plate warmer so that he might peek inside the doors and hold up the irons for review. At the open range, he inspected the drip pan, cauldron, and kettle. His determined interest made her wonder whether he was as anxious about this meeting as she was and wished to forestall their talk until he had calculated exactly what to say.

At last, they came to the batterie de cuisine. The captain pursed his lips as he scrutinized the copper pots, pans, and molds. Turning to her, he said, "I see that a kitchen is like a ship. Everything has its place. Nothing is there that does not have its use. All must be kept scrubbed and polished and shipshape. From this time forward, whenever I am homesick for *The Ambuscade*, I shall visit a kitchen."

His smile sent a pang through her. She guessed that his words reflected none of his real thoughts and feelings.

"Now that you have come, Captain Hale," she said, "we must speak candidly."

"Indeed we must, and I must begin. By apologizing."

"Oh, dear, another apology."

"Well, the last one was prodigiously successful. I never quarrel with success."

In spite of herself, she smiled. "At the risk of repeating myself, you have nothing to apologize for."

Her response appeared to interest him. "I should have thought, Miss Drenville, that I might be expected to apologize for my excessively warm behavior Thursday last."

Puzzled, she shook her head. "Truthfully, I neither expected nor wished for an apology."

"You did not take exception to my conduct?"

"I was not offended."

"Young ladies are always offended when a gentleman kisses them, especially when he does so in a manner which indicates his inclination to continue doing so for the rest of all eternity."

"Are they? Well, I am not in a way to know what young ladies do. I am odd, Captain, in case that fact has escaped you. That is what we must speak of now."

"You may be rare, perhaps, but I would not say odd."

"You would not say so, because you are polite and a gentleman and everything that is good."

He laughed. "Well, if you think that I am such a paragon, then perhaps you are a bit odd after all, but not disagreeably so, I assure you."

"I am more than odd. I am utterly graceless. My hems catch in doors. My ties become knotted. My earrings scrape gentlemen's lips. Your mother noticed my awkwardness. I should not be surprised if your father did as well. It is a wonder I did not disgrace you at Stonewood House."

His face seemed to swell with emotion. "Is that what you think, Emma?" He moved round the table to come close.

Quickly, she moved away. Her head banged against a pot hanging from the batterie de cuisine. Humiliated, she said, "It is what I know, and what you ought to know. I have tried to make you see it, but my words have been inadequate, perhaps because I wished them to be. Now, however, I wish your eyes to be fully open. I wish you to see that I am a Dreadful. My family are forever mortifying everyone within earshot, and I am no different."

He grasped her hand, gripping it in both of his. "Yes, your family are out of the common way. Yes, they are capable of behaving in a manner which leaves them open to ridicule. But they are kind and earnest and affectionate. You are exactly like them in that regard. The only difference is that I do not think I should like kissing Harriet or Angus as much as I like kissing you."

Exasperated, she pulled her hand away and cried, "How can I make you see that this is not a matter to be dismissed with quizzing and lovemaking? You say that you think well of my family and have the highest esteem for me, but the day will come when you shall retract it all."

He picked up a wooden spoon from the table and pointed it at her. "Not possible."

"If you will not think of your own interest, think of what your family will say."

His eyes burning, he demanded, "What have they to do with anything?"

"Only that they will not like your intimacy with a Dreadful. Only that they will soon learn that I am not their sort, if they have not learned it already."

"Their opinion weighs not at all with me."

"It must weigh with you!"

"Why?"

"Because one owes a duty to one's family. Because one cannot escape what one is. And because the day will come when I shall disgrace your family as well as you. It is inevitable, if we continue like this."

Wearing a wry smile, he tapped the spoon against his palm. "It is far more likely," he said, "that my family will disgrace you."

She erupted. "How can you talk so? They were as kind to me as any family I have ever known outside my own and Lady Chitting's. Your mother sat with me a full ten minutes. Your father pointedly included me in the conversation and refrained from laughing when I made a cake of myself.

He even patted my hand. Your brothers were as courteous and attentive as I could have wished. I will not hear you abuse them!"

"Emma, your impression of my family is based on one night's observation. You must know them better before you judge."

"I know them well enough to know that they are perfect, and instead of disparaging them, you ought to go on your knees before them every day and thank them for it!"

To her amazement, he looked pained. He half turned from her so as to hide his emotion. She saw him in profile, struggling, thinking, debating, suppressing the instinct to do more with his fist than merely open and close it.

Fearing to disturb his thoughts, she remained still, though after what seemed a very long time, she wished to go to him and lay a soothing hand on his arm.

He did not look at her but said simply, "Come with me."

"What?"

Taking her unceremoniously by the hand, he pulled her up the stairs and along the corridors, opening and closing the doors until he had found the parlor which contained Lord and Lady Chitting.

CHAPTER TWELVE

George in Disfavor

Dear Admiral Drenville,

I had the good fortune to meet Miss Drenville on the road to London, as we had planned. Since that time, I have met with her frequently and have come to regard her with esteem and affection, and that is what prompts me to write to you. May I have your permission, and that of your excellent brother and sisters, to pay my addresses to Miss Drenville?

I am your most obedient servant,

Nicholas Hale

Seeing Lord and Lady Chitting in front of the fire, holding hands and congratulating one another on having sent the boys to Surrey for the entire day, Captain Hale pulled Emma inside and said, "You must tell Miss Drenville what you know of the Stonewoods."

Lady Chitting looked from one to the other, bewildered.

"This looks to be a noisy conversation," Lord Chitting said with a grimace. "Perhaps I ought to retire."

The captain blocked his path. "I beg you will stay, my lord," he said with more passion than politeness. "Miss Drenville wishes for the truth to be told, and as you know a good deal of it, I ask that you enlighten her."

His lordship rubbed his eyes, sighed, and sank into a chair, lamenting, "It seems that even when one's own children take themselves off and leave one to a bit of peace and quiet, someone else's children will come to plague you."

Because the high state of emotion in the room was contagious, Lady Chitting said to her husband something she had never said in twenty-three years of connubial bliss, namely, "Be still, Godfrey!"

When he raised his brows at her, she explained apologetically. "Our dear Nicholas and our precious Madelaine require our help."

"Quite so," he said, resigned to having his serenity exploded.

With clucking noises, she persuaded Captain Hale to let go of Emma's hand. He went to the mantel and glared so fiercely at it that it would have been difficult to say which blazed more heatedly—him or the fire. At the same time, she brought Emma to a settee and when they had both made themselves comfortable, she said, "Nikky, dear boy, I shall be happy to tell Miss Drenville of the Stonewoods, but you must calm yourself first. It is very hard to have to relate a history when your listeners are in a pet."

"I am calm," he said through his teeth.

All this time, Emma had been trying to quell a persistent pounding in her forehead. It was clear that during her late conversation with Captain Hale she had gone too far, said too much. The difficulty was that she could not imagine what she had said to set him off. How could he be infuriated by hearing his family praised? She would have given the moon and stars to hear hers praised in such terms.

After clearing her throat, Lady Chitting began, "The Stonewoods are an old and noble family, whose title was created by one of the Charleses, I believe, not the one beheaded by that frightful fellow Cromwell but the other one. I believe the first earl had chased some poor savages off an island somewhere and had claimed the land and its coconuts for England, for which the nation proved not ungrateful."

"Your ladyship," Captain Hale interrupted impatiently, "we may read all that in the history books. Tell Miss Drenville, if you will, what the Stonewoods are like now."

Lady Chitting shrugged. "What do you mean, Nikky? They are a family, like any family. They have four sons, just as we have four sons. What more can there to be say?"

He smiled cruelly. "A great deal more. You see, Miss Drenville thinks they are perfect."

"Gad," said his lordship, "my poor Madelaine! You will be disillusioned, my dear, for they are not perfect, any more than the Chittings are perfect."

Emma looked from him to Lady Chitting, trying not to let her glance wander to Captain Hale, who had put a hand on the mantelpost and drummed his fingers on it.

"Well," said Lady Chitting, attempting to put a bright face on things, "the Stonewoods do have their little faults. They would be very odd if they did not."

Captain Hale could contain himself no longer. Coming before Emma, he said, "Yes, indeed, they have their little faults. The pater is a rake with a penchant for young widows. My mother is an inveterate gamester. My brothers are idle scapegraces. And the lot of them have only one quality of note—a talent for running up debt."

Emma was appalled. She had never heard of so much corruption gathered together in one house.

Captain Hale said, "I have shocked you. I am sorry, but you had to know."

Her ladyship sighed and wagged her head. "My poor Nikky," she said.

Emma's heart went out to Captain Hale. How it must wound him to know such things of his family. In comparison to the Stonewoods, the Dreadfuls seemed rather bland.

Lady Chitting rose. "The faults you have laid to them are neither here nor there, Nikky," she said in a gentle tone. "Their great fault is that they do not know how to value you. They do not treat you as you deserve or speak to you with consideration unless it is to borrow money. That is the true defect of the Stonewoods."

"It is lamentably so," said his lordship, shaking his head. "I never once saw your father shake your hand. Jove, I have even shaken Frank's hand, when his arm was not broken. I have shaken Cecil and Cyril's hands, too. Just yesterday, I shook Nigel's hand, though I cannot recall why. It is a father's duty to shake his son's hand from time to time."

"You are right, my sweet," said Lady Chitting. Turning to the captain again, she said softly, "And while Lord Chitting has never seen your father shake your hand, I have never seen your mother kiss your cheek, not even when you were a lad." On that, she stood on tiptoe and planted a kiss on his cheek. Then she confounded him by throwing her arms about him and weeping on his coat.

Emma's eyes stung with tears as she observed this scene. She could not imagine anybody living in a family and not being petted and coddled and caressed as she had been. She could not imagine anybody neglecting to pet and coddle and caress Captain Hale, if given the opportunity. London had certainly opened her eyes to a great many strange truths. The question was what was she to make of them?

She saw the captain look at her over Lady Chitting's shoulder. He smiled. Emma understood now why he submitted to her ladyship's effusions of affection where most gentlemen would have squirmed for dear life. She returned his smile.

When Lady Chitting released him, she wiped her eyes with her linen and said, "La, I have not wept so much since I read *Clarissa*. The poor girl died of a broken heart after that frightful fellow ravished her. It is a wonderful thing to have girls, but one must always be on the watch over them, I fear, or they shall end like poor Clarissa, alone, ravished, with nothing to wear but rags."

"My sweet, you take a rather dismal view," Lord Chitting remonstrated. "I think our precious Madelaine will do well enough." With his eyes, he directed her attention to Captain Hale, who regarded Emma seriously.

As she observed the two young people, Lady Chitting's saucer eyes grew larger. Then her dimples played as she exchanged a significant look with her husband. "I believe," she said, clearing her throat, "that Lord Chitting and I have business elsewhere. Do we not, my sweet?"

His lordship pushed himself from his chair and adjusted his invalid's cap. "Yes, my sweet. Here, let me take your hand, and if you have any kisses to spare from Nikky, you may lavish them on me."

When they had left the parlor, Emma stood and approached the captain. "You have proved," she said, "that your family is not perfect. I wish I knew what to make of it all."

"Nobody's family is perfect, Emma, and what we are to make of it is this: we must resolve that our families shall not be an obstacle to our happiness."

Lowering her eyes, she nodded. "Perhaps you are right. They ought not to be an obstacle. But having said that, I must confess, I am bewildered. I have vowed, you see, that we should part forever. I have no idea what we ought to do now."

"That is simple. We must dance at a ball."

She looked at him, horrified. "Dance?"

"Yes, dance."

"Oh, Nicholas, must we dance?"

"Naturally, we must dance. As I am too much of a gentleman to allow my violent passion for you to overtake me, except now and then of course, there is nothing left for us to do but dance. It is the only means by which I may court you and touch you and hold you and make love to you that is sanctioned by civilized Society."

In despair, she sank onto the settee. "I cannot dance," she said.

"You are not afraid of what my family will say, I hope."

"No. It is worse than that. You see, I am a loppet."

He sat next to her. "I do not believe it."

"Do you recollect when we met at the Dolphin, and my foot was bound? Well, it was a hoax."

"Your foot was not really injured?"

"No, I pretended it was, so as to please George. He would have been mortified to see me dance, and so will you be, if you are ever so unfortunate."

"I am glad your foot was bound. It gave me the opportunity to carry you down the steps."

She sighed. "I am glad you are glad, Nicholas, but that does not answer the difficulty."

"Very well. I shall ask Lady Chitting to hunt up a dancing master who will exorcise all the loppetry out of you."

She smiled thinly.

"I should like a little more rapture from you, if you please. Unless, of course, you do not wish me to hold your hand and twirl you about, or bow to you and point my toe at yours, or admire you from close range and permit you to admire me. If the prospect is repugnant to you then naturally we shall say no more of dancing. The word shall not pass my lips. I shall not utter . . ."

He stopped, principally because she had put her forefinger to his lips. With a smile, she apprised him of her willingness to submit to dancing lessons. He kissed her finger, then lightly bit it, then covered it with his mouth.

The following morning, Captain Hale visited his club, which, because it was a tedious place, would permit him to think undisturbed. His brothers owed debts to so many of the members of Boodle's that it was highly unlikely they would show their faces there, and his father rarely frequented locations inhabited exclusively by men. He sat down in an enormous creaking chair, raised a copy of the *Times* in front of his face, and proceeded to log his progress.

He had succeeded in winning Miss Drenville's trust for the moment, but she was skittish as a colt. Where her family were concerned, she was still so sensitive that she was vulnerable to another attack of scruples, followed by a declaration that they were doomed to "disgrace" him. Even more vulnerable was she to the fear of making an unforgivable faux pas and thus disgracing him herself. Her awkwardness, which roused his tenderest sensations and made him wish to hold her and kiss her, merely made her ashamed. It would not be an easy task to persuade her that he loved the very attributes she loathed in herself. He must be careful to do and say the right thing, lest he send her fleeing from him again.

Hence, he could not propose marriage to her quite yet. She required time to learn confidence in him, to see that he was not likely to be driven off by missteps and falls and the sniggerings of others, time to learn that she was so far superior to any woman he had ever met that it was ludicrous to doubt herself. And he would give her time—three weeks, in fact. He did not think he could hold out much longer than that.

It was clear she was meant to be his wife—she knew and liked the sailor's life, she never got seasick, she was intelligent, good hearted, principled, able to busy herself with the kitchen and a cookery book in his absence, and she loved him to distraction, to name just a few of her most sterling qualities. Therefore, he saw no point in waiting any longer than he absolutely had to before making her his own. In any case, he did not think he could keep himself in check longer than three weeks. He could not think of her without wanting to look at her, and he could not look at her without wanting to have her.

Satisfied with his decision to wait three weeks before making her an offer, he turned to the second order of business—he must write to her family. Calling for pen and paper, he set down a few words and found a servant to seal up the note and get it sent off by the next post. That done, he considered what to do next.

He had thought to delight Emma by mentioning a ball. Instead he had terrified her. It had taken a great deal of gentle teasing and encouragement to soothe her alarms. No doubt, as soon as he had gone from Chitting House, they had returned. Some means must be found, he felt, to allay her fears and make her look forward to the ball he had promised. Rising from his chair, he set forth to do just that.

If she were any happier, Emma felt, she would levitate, and if in the past she had dreaded what others might say of her, she must certainly dread it now, when all of London

might see her floating above their heads, bussing the ruddy
cheeks of the cherubim on the painted ceiling, tinkling the
crystals of the chandelier with her toes, and declaring to all
the world by her daft expression that she was in love. Luckily, she lived in a household where exuberant spirits were
not unknown. Indeed, compared with Nigel, Cecil, Cyril,
and Frank, she was a model of tepidness. Still, Lord and
Lady Chitting were themselves an affectionate couple and
recognized her condition for what it was. They indulged her
with smiles, drank her salutary concoctions, ate her heav-
enly confections, and kept to themselves their curiosity regarding the date of her nuptials. Their knowing
forebearance assured Emma that she was a fortunate creature indeed.

When Nigel got wind that there might possibly be a
match between Miss Drenville and Captain Hale, he presented her with a posy and took her for a boat ride up the
Thames. Cecil and Cyril bought her a book of Italian love
sonnets and allowed her to test her latest dishes on them.
As she was amassing cabbage receipts at the time, the poor
lads were pathetically bilious for a week. They did not
complain, however, but contented themselves with knock-
ing each other about. As to Frank, he drew Emma aside one
evening following supper and vowed to be stoical in the
face of her defection, despite his broken heart.

"Naturally, I wish you felicitations," he concluded in a
martyred tone.

"I am glad you do. And I wish you well, Frank. I hope
you shall fall in love and be in raptures."

"You gave me to understand that love was not as raptur-
ous as it is made out to be."

"Gracious, did I say that?"

"Yes, and now you have gone and changed your mind.
What is a fellow to believe, I ask you?"

"Believe this, that you are like a brother to me. I adore
you, and I wish you very happy."

"I wish you happy, too, but if you are not happy, then I
beg you will remember that I love you and wish to marry

you and will plant Captain Hale a facer if you like, though he is the best fellow I ever met."

She smiled. "He is a great deal larger than you. It would not be wise, I think, to attempt to hit him."

"It would be utter folly. No doubt he would break my other arm. Nevertheless, I should deem it an honor to be injured on your behalf."

Hearing this, Emma was certain that she was going to levitate. The world was the most hilarious, the most charming place, and she was its most fortunate inhabitant. Everywhere she turned, there was a friend. Everywhere she looked, she saw flowers bursting into bloom and fields and trees growing green. Every time she closed her eyes, she saw the countenance of Captain Hale smiling at her. It was like a dream, except that it would not end when she awoke.

The only one who had heard nothing of Emma's impending engagement was George, who had scarcely stepped foot in Chitting House since the fateful Thursday on which he had been introduced to Lady Stonewood. He met Emma late one morning as he was coming in and she was going out. Immediately, she noticed that he had a desperate look about him. She had thought he was happy. Certainly, she had wanted him to be happy. Even though she was on her way to meet Captain Hale at Piccadilly, she stopped to question her cousin. Nothing gave her as much anxiety as seeing those she loved unhappy.

"Are you unwell, cousin?" she asked. "You look as though you had not slept in a week."

"That is very nearly the case. I have been to card parties and assemblies and Vauxhall and a masquerade. I have lost fifty guineas at *vingt-un* and forgotten to eat. I have raced a curricle, though I had no notion how it was to be done, and I have had my face slapped by two ladies in one night. In short, Emma, I am dished. I shall return to Southampton and embrace my destiny, which is to be a Dreadful, and a lonely, obscure one at that."

"Come, you must go to bed." She led him along the corridor to his chamber, and, defying propriety, she opened the door and gestured to him to go inside. "Once you have rested," she urged, "you will see things in a less tragic light."

He leaned on the doorpost as though he had not an ounce of strength in his body. "It is worse than tragic," he mourned. "It is comical. I am a laughingstock. You will be ashamed of me when you hear what I have done."

"Nonsense. I shall not be ashamed."

"Yes, you will."

"No, I will not."

"Yes, you will."

"Very well, George, tell me what has happened."

He rubbed his brow, then his stubbled chin. "Gad, I must look a fright," he said, and Emma had to acknowledge that for George to be so careless of his appearance, something had to be profoundly wrong.

"As you recollect, Lady Stonewood was so good as to befriend me. In my turn, I regarded her in the light of an angel. I never meant anything but the greatest respect and esteem for the lady."

"I believe you, George."

"Yes, well, Lady Stonewood was so good as to make me an intimate of her household. She admitted me to her boudoir, which will shock you, I know, but is a very common practice in Town and not at all frowned upon, and she confided to me something of her situation, which is quite wretched when one is apprised of the facts. Her ladyship is kept on the most paltry allowance and Lord Stonewood, though he is an excellent creature, neglects her abominably."

Having learned something of the Hales in recent days, Emma did not view the matter precisely as George did. In fact, she began to wonder whether he might have been imposed upon.

To her distress, George said, "Naturally, I have lent her all the money at my disposal, but it is a pittance to what she ought to have. I would write the Admiral for more, but I doubt it would do any good now. It is too late for that."

Pleased that George's plan to write her grandfather had been abandoned, she waited for him to go on.

"At one of the assemblies to which I escorted her ladyship, I was introduced to a Mrs. Leigh, a young widow of passing good features and modest manners. She and I engaged in conversation for several minutes, I forget how long. We talked on the most unexceptionable topics, and it seemed to me that neither of us would go out of the way to speak to the other again. Then, suddenly, I found myself seized by the neck and hauled off to an anteroom in the roughest manner."

"George! I cannot believe you were waylaid by ruffians inside a house! Is no place safe anymore?"

"I was not waylaid by ruffians but by Lord Stonewood. It appears he was jealous of what he took to be my attentions to Mrs. Leigh. I could not persuade him that I had no interest in that quarter. He would have it that I meant to force myself on her and he was determined to blow my head off."

"He challenged you to a duel?"

"Yes, in Green Park. All the best duels take place in Green Park, it seems."

"Oh, George, you cannot fight a duel. I shall not permit it. What if you were to be hurt? What if you were to hurt Captain Hale's father?"

"No need to get in an uproar, Emma. There is not to be a duel. You see, Lady Stonewood heard of the affair. She summoned her husband and me before her and forbade us to shoot at one another at Green Park or any other venue. And if we persisted in making cakes of ourselves, she said, she would give it out that I was a fortune hunter and that Lord Stonewood was a eunuch!"

"Gracious, Lady Stonewood is a formidable creature, is she not?"

"Yes, she is. Naturally we agreed to her terms."

"Then all's well that ends well."

"No, for she will not speak to me. She believes that I was flirting with Mrs. Leigh, just as his lordship says. She accuses me of deserting her for someone young enough to be her daughter. She says I have no notion of friendship and must never darken her doorway."

This caused Emma to smile with pleasure. That he would be forbidden entry to a house full of those who would use him for their own devices could only be for the good, *his* good. She sighed, relieved, and said, "I am sorry you have been treated unjustly, cousin, but perhaps it is for the best."

Weary from too many sleepless nights, he nodded dejectedly. Then, he sprang to attention as a new thought occurred to him. "Emma, you do not think that I was flirting with Mrs. Leigh, do you?"

"Why should I doubt you, dear George?"

"I will confess, I have made an ass of myself, dangling after Lady Stonewood, and I did think Mrs. Leigh was quite pretty and charming, but I have not forgot what I owe to you, Emma."

"What do you owe to me?"

"We have sworn to be loyal to one another in the face of all impediments. We said we should look out for one another and always have the other's best interest in view."

"We said that?"

"We did not say it precisely, but that is what we meant, is it not? Is that not what you meant when you gave me this ring?" He searched in his pockets for the ring but could not produce it. "It must be in another coat," he said. "If I have lost it, I shall fling myself from the Westminster Bridge."

"You shall do no such thing. I shall give you another ring, George. But first, you must go to sleep. One cannot think clearly until one has slept and eaten properly. I shall give orders for Madame DePois to make you a cup of chamomile tea. It will enable you to sleep peacefully. And when I return, I shall prepare a restorative broth which will have you back in the midst of the Chitting boys and ready to laugh again."

"You are very good to me, Emma. I was afraid you might be angry. I was afraid you might think I was not to be relied upon, despite my avowals in the past, and would wish to break with me altogether."

Firmly, Emma pushed him inside the door and went to find a servant so that he might be readied for a good twenty-four hours' nap. Afterward, she located Madame DePois, and together, they created a regimen which would set the blood to flowing again in Mr. Drenville's veins. Emma was sorry to think that in addition to all his other troubles, George fretted that she might be angry. What had she to be angry about, after all? If he had harmed anybody, it had been himself. But he was out of danger now. He was done with the Stonewoods. That was the important thing.

On that thought, she went to the door. She was to go in Lord Chitting's carriage to Piccadilly. Captain Hale was to meet her at Hatchard's, and after making purchases there, they were to take in the shops and the parade of fashionably dressed ladies and gentlemen, endeavoring to appear ordinary instead of what they were—a pair with a lamentable tendency to levitate, to cavort among the clouds, leaping from one star to the other, taking an excessive delight in each other's company.

When the door was opened, Emma passed into the May sunshine. She could not help humming an air as she started down the steps. Midtune, midstep, she stopped. Captain Hale was there under a slender birch. He tipped his hat. From the expression he wore, it was evident that he had been unable to wait for her to get to Piccadilly. He shrugged, as if to say he had been caught in the act of loving her and was ready to make a full confession. As he came up the steps to meet her, Emma felt herself levitate.

CHAPTER THIRTEEN

The Caper-Merchant

Avast Captain Hale!

If all that is wanting is an order from Southampton to set sail on your course, then consider yourself rigged complete from stem to stern. Along with my loyal crew, I wish you fair weather on your voyage. May you end by capturing the prize!

Yours etc.,

Francis Drenville, late of His Majesty's Service

For the next several days, Emma's happiness was complete. With Lady Chitting and the boys as chaperons, she and Captain Hale savored the best entertainment London had to offer, including an evening of Grimaldi at Covent Garden, a tour of Madame Tussaud's, a day at the races, and an excursion to Twickenham to see the garden of the Wicked Wasp. So delighted was she with everything that met her eye that she scarcely noticed George's absence. It did not occur to her that the last time she had seen him, he had been en route to his bed and for all she knew he was there still. Her own contentment, and that of Captain Hale, engrossed her entirely.

This exquisite happiness culminated as happiness generally does—by ending. The end came crashingly, when Lady Chitting announced at dinner that a dancing master had been engaged and that instead of going about the Town, Emma would spend her days learning the minuet, the mazurka, the Boulanger, the reel, and other country dances. If she showed any aptitude at all, her ladyship said, evidently thinking it would be an added inducement, she might prevail upon the dancing master to teach her the cotillion and the quadrille. Hearing that, Emma could not eat a bite, though she and Madame DePois had prepared pork rissoles and apple pie.

Shortly afterward, furniture was removed from the parlor which housed the pianoforte. The rugs were rolled up and stored. Nigel, Cecil, Cyril, and Frank were warned that they must not mortify Miss Drenville by peeking in the door during her lessons. Lord Chitting was provided with beeswax for his ears, while her ladyship offered herself as accompanist on the instrument, should one be wanted. Thus, in a short space, all was in readiness to receive Mr. Grozett, his fiddler, and his less-than-eager pupil.

As they inspected the dancing parlor, Captain Hale reassured Emma, "Your efforts shall not go unrewarded. Very soon after we have danced, I shall present you with a prodigious surprise."

"Yes, and I shall present you with a surprise as well," she said bleakly, "bruised ankles and crushed toes!"

"You must not take such a gloomy view. You will do perfectly well."

Emma doubted it, but she did not say so. It was difficult to quarrel with a man who willfully blinded himself to her faults and persisted in thinking the world of her, especially when he punctuated his soothing speeches with light kisses on her brow.

Mr. Grozett arrived in much state. He was tall, rail-thin, carried a staff of carved ebony, and flowed rather than walked. His voice was deep and melodic, as though a composer of music had formed his sentences. Above all, he was elegant. On another man, a dark green coat, white muslin cravat and cuffs, and shiny black pointed shoes would have constituted clothing. On Mr. Grozett, they were sacred vestments.

Lady Chitting led him to the dancing parlor, whereupon Mr. Grozett stared at her until she became aware of being superfluous. She colored and hastily excused herself on some matter of business. The gentleman then signaled to his fiddler, who struck up a dirgelike tune.

"The minuet!" proclaimed Mr. Grozett and proceeded to glide in stately fashion, his footsteps echoing in the bare room, one arm raised as though he held a partner's hand in his. From time to time, he paused to bow or curtsy—he performed both with equally stunning grace—then proceeded to glide again.

Emma watched from her post at the pianoforte, thinking that if she praised the gentleman sufficiently, he might be content to demonstrate steps the rest of the day and not ask her to dance. But though she gave out with many expressions of admiration, he soon beckoned to her to join him, holding out his hand commandingly. Remembering Captain Hale's soft expression as he had whispered of the "prodigious surprise" in store for her, she inhaled for courage and went to meet her fate.

Just as Emma feared, the first trial displeased Mr. Grozett. "Miss Drenville must not bound," he remonstrated. "Nor must she hop or jump."

Emma was quick to apologize. "I did not mean to bound. It is only that I dance with uncommon energy. Even Lord Landsdowne has noticed."

"Miss Drenville must conserve her energy for the mazurka and the country dances. The minuet is an old and revered dance. All that is required is stateliness and grace."

At the mention of those two qualities, Emma despaired. With a sigh, she looked away and spied Nigel, Cecil, Cyril, and Frank peeking in the door. They waved to her, then ducked out of sight. "I cannot do it," she said.

"Oh, but Miss Drenville *can* do it. I have never had a pupil who could not master the minuet. It is mere walking. I shall demonstrate."

Mr. Grozett stood a moment as though in the middle of a line of dancers, then sidestepped, walked in a circle and bowed. So beautifully did he glide that Emma envied him from her heart. When he turned to repeat the movement, the boys stole inside and proceeded to walk behind him with mincing steps, all the while holding their fingers to their lips. Their pantomime was full of exaggerated daintiness and clowning grimaces. Emma had all she could do to appear to remark nothing out of the way. The fiddler, who had his eyes closed, played his tune, oblivious to the mischief going forward.

"Now Miss Drenville will give me her hand," said the dancing master.

Obediently, she took Mr. Grozett's hand. Out of the corner of her eye, she observed that Cecil took Cyril's hand, while Nigel took Frank's.

"I shall bow and Miss Drenville shall curtsy."

Emma lowered herself as best she could but lost her balance as she attempted to rise.

Cyril and Frank performed flawless curtsies.

Emma practiced her curtsy until her knees were quite sore. Numerous times, Nigel and Cecil traded places with their partners and practiced curtsies as well. All four of the boys were more adept at curtsying than Emma ever hoped to be.

It was not long before they wearied of dancing and tiptoed away as silently as they had come. They gave her a heartening farewell wave and left her to the mercy of her teacher.

While Emma was engaged in the dancing parlor, Captain Hale attended to two matters of business. The first concerned the ball at which he and Emma were to dance in less three weeks' time. It was to be a momentous occasion. Much—his entire future with Emma, in fact—hinged on its success. He therefore hoped it would be given under the auspices of Lady Chitting. But when he approached her, the lady demurred.

"It is not possible, Nikky dear. You see, if I were to give a ball, I should be obliged to invite my children, or at least the elder three. I cannot insist that others invite them, but as their mother, I should be required to. It is unavoidable."

"Well, then, invite them."

"You must be joking!"

"How am I to propose marriage to Miss Drenville if there is not to be a ball?"

"You mean to propose marriage!" Her ladyship clapped her hands together and beamed, her dimples etched deep. "Oh, I told Lord Chitting it would be so. Or rather, he told me. Oh, I could not be happier, dear boy."

He smiled. "I thought you might approve. In any case, I promised myself an evening of unparalleled delight, climaxed by going down on bended knee and doing the pretty to the loveliest, best-natured creature in all the world, and now it is all spoiled."

"It shall not be spoiled. Lady Windolph means to give a cotillion-ball. I shall arrange for all of us to be invited."

"My mother and father as well."

"Oh, dear, your mother and father! I fear they may not approve the engagement. Though Emma has a handsome dowry, her connections will not suit their grand notions."

"Once they come to know her, they shall love her nearly as well as you and I."

Her ladyship beamed, showing her dimples. "Of course they shall. They shall not be able to help themselves."

"A cotillion-ball," he mused. "That will give Emma a splendid case of the fidgets. She has a notion that she cannot dance at all, let alone dance the cotillion."

"Do not give it a thought," said her ladyship. "We shall contrive to arrive late, after the cotillion is over. You shall have her for the country dances, and for anything else your heart desires. Oh, it gives my heart a flutter just to imagine it!"

Leaving Lady Chitting to her flutters, the captain addressed his next order of business, which was to visit his mother, whom he had not seen since the dinner at Stonewood House. He had been reluctant to see any member of his family since that evening, for their incessant petitions for money must, he knew, dissipate his newfound contentment. Still, if he intended to marry Miss Drenville, he owed it to his mother to inform her. He therefore set out for Portman Square. To his surprise, he met George there, anxiously pacing the hall.

Captain Hale handed his hat to the butler, who went off to announce his arrival to her ladyship, and greeted Mr. Drenville warmly. "What a pleasure to see you. We missed you at the races."

"I was obliged to send regrets," said George sorrowfully. "It was necessary to attend Lady Stonewood."

The captain regarded the young man with pity. "Is that how you have spent these past days, my friend, dancing attendance on my mother?"

George nodded wretchedly. "I must do my possible to restore myself in her good graces. You see, I inadvertently offended her, and she was good enough to write to say that she would receive me again, but not until I had proved my steadiness and fealty."

"I see, and to that end, you haunt her hall day and night."

"Do you think she will see me today?"

"I could not possibly say, Mr. Drenville. I do not depend on her seeing me, her own son. She has many engagements."

"I sent her a locket, a garnet in gold filigree. I thought perhaps she might like it well enough to see me today."

"You do not make a habit of sending her gifts, I hope. There are ladies who quarrel with a gentleman solely in order to induce him to send gifts by way of apology. Sending those gifts merely encourages them to quarrel further."

"Oh, dear, I had not thought of that. To tell the truth, I have given her tokens of my esteem from time to time."

"From time to time? You have scarcely been acquainted with her very long."

"That is true, which is why I have sent only a few trinkets. She is fond of trinkets, you know."

"May I presume on our acquaintance so far as to advise you, Mr. Drenville? Lurking about Stonewood House will only bring you to grief. My mother will keep you hanging in suspense as long as you permit her to. You will end by being perfectly miserable. I urge you to go home and eat a hearty dinner. Your cousin will be delighted to cook one for you, I have no doubt."

As though a bolt of lightning had struck, George cried, "Emma!"

"She prepared an excellent turbot last night. If you hurry, I am certain she will warm a bit for you."

"Blast it, I have forgot Emma! She will think I have neglected her abominably. And it is no more than the truth!"

"You have neglected yourself as well. Now run along, my friend, and see to your dinner."

Frantically, George begged, "You will say nothing of my visits here to Emma, I hope. Ladies do not understand this sort of thing as gentlemen do."

Captain Hale smiled. "You mean she might disapprove of your dangling after my mother."

George also smiled, but thinly. "Emma is an odd creature. She has no notion that an acquaintance which might raise gossip in Southampton might be all the crack in London."

"Yes, that is why I admire her."

"Oh! And so do I! I admire her prodigiously! Still, you will keep mum, I hope."

"I shall not breathe a word, on condition that you look after yourself."

With no further word, Mr. Drenville was gone.

On the butler's reappearance, the captain was led to his mother's boudoir, where she was being fitted by a modiste for a new gown of white satin seeded with pearls.

"Nikky, dear, what an inconvenient time for you to come. I am engaged this evening."

He picked up a powder puff from her dressing table and sniffed it. "Mother, why are you tormenting Mr. Drenville? He cannot possibly interest you."

She turned, so that the dressmaker might pin her bosom. "Of course, he interests me. I have determined to make him a splendid match."

"He is half in love with you."

She glowed. "Yes, he is. It was the work of a moment.

All one was required to do was to appear to be in high dudgeon on some pretext or other. He has been entirely devoted ever since. Even so, I shall make him fall in love with
Mrs. Leigh."

"Mrs. Leigh?"

"Yes, your father's squeeze. Your poor pater is already
jealous of Mr. Drenville and half a dozen other fellows on
her account. Now I shall drive him quite frenzied." She
laughed.

"I do not presume to interfere in your relations with the
pater, but I will ask you to spare Mr. Drenville. I like him. I
do not wish to see him come to harm."

"I do not intend to harm him. I shall merely educate him,
and provide him with a pretty and silly bride in the bargain.
He shall be forever in my debt."

"Let him go, Mother."

Pushing the dressmaker aside, she pouted, "Eight months
at sea have made you dull. You never used to spoil one's
fun, you loathsome boy."

"I shall be happy to frank any other manner of fun you
may undertake."

She treated him to a dazzling smile. "In that case, of
course, I shall dismiss him. Generous boy! I shall do anything you say."

"Excellent, then you shall see no more of George
Drenville. Oh, and bye the bye, I intend to ask his cousin to
marry me."

Under her rouge, her cheeks whitened. Her hand fluttered to her throat. "That green girl who came to dinner and
made such an improper fuss over her fan?"

"That is the one."

She rolled her eyes. "Are you aware that she is Admiral
Drenville's granddaughter? Are you aware that he is called
Admiral Dreadful? Are you aware that she is the most ill-
mannered young chit I have had the misfortune to meet in
some time, excepting Mrs. Leigh?"

"You have now said every vile thing you could say on
the subject, and my reply is simply this: you and the pater

will soon receive invitations to Lady Windolph's ball, which you will be so good as to accept. Miss Drenville will be in attendance that evening, and you will kindly bestow upon her every cordial attention in your extensive arsenal."

His expression was so severe that it gave her ladyship pause. When her son wore such a look, it was unwise to argue with him, for he was liable to withdraw his generosity and then she would be in a pretty fix. Therefore, she said, "I understand perfectly, Nikky dear. I should like nothing better than to comply with your wishes. The difficulty is that I shall need a new gown."

"I believe you are being fitted for one, even as we speak."

"Very true, but I shall require another for Lady Windolph's ball."

He shook his head and laughed. "Nothing would give me greater pleasure than to give you a new gown, Mother."

"Oh, you are a darling boy! I am so pleased."

"I thought you might be." On that, he took his leave, congratulating himself on having gotten off so cheaply.

The day came when Mr. Grozett deemed Emma's curtsy "almost acceptable," and they passed on to toe pointing and exchanging places in a circle. These two exercises confounded Emma entirely. It was especially dismaying to find that no matter when Nigel, Cecil, Cyril, and Frank stole into the parlor, they gracefully executed each and every step before stealing off again, whereas she, no matter how many hours she spent with Mr. Grozett, could not dance without bursting out occasionally in a bound.

After a week thus spent, Mr. Grozett shouted at the fiddler to leave off. Sighing he said, "Perhaps Miss Drenville would be more amenable to another approach. Perhaps if she understood the philosophy of the dancer's art, she might not feel herself so resistant to its refinements."

Emma nodded. "I should very much like to know the philosophy." Anything was better than actually dancing, she felt.

With a flourish, Mr. Grozett leaned upon his staff and intoned, "Dancing is nothing more nor less than the oldest and liveliest of the arts. Indeed, it has been the inspiration for the drama, the opera, and the ballet, not to mention the making of sculpture and painting."

At this point in the lecture, the boys silently entered the parlor. When the fiddler's eyebrows rose at their appearance, they gestured with fingers at their lips for him to keep mum. Shrugging, he complied. This complaisance permitted the four young men to form a line behind Mr. Grozett and move their lips and arms in the manner of a self-important orator. Emma could scarcely repress her laughter.

"In every age and clime," the dancing master continued, with the boys mimicking him from behind, "ladies and gentlemen have responded to rhythm with movement. Such movement has been polished over the centuries until it has reached its height of elegance in our present age. Unlike former times, where the dancing was expressive of religious sentiment, the dancing which takes place in our ballrooms is social in nature. It provides companionship, deepens acquaintance, and grants relief from the sameness of everyday life."

By this time, the boys were on the floor, feigning sleep. When Frank let a snore escape, Mr. Grozett jumped and turned to discover him, lying with his brothers in a heap, their eyes closed, their heads pillowed in their hands. Opening their eyes a little, they saw that they had been found out. Instantly they leaped to their feet and complimented Mr. Grozett upon his excellence as a teacher.

"Miss Drenville evidently regards dancing as a jesting matter," the dancing master said, offended.

"No, no," she protested. "It is absolutely serious, terribly serious, frighteningly serious, I assure you."

Mr. Grozett studied her anxious expression a considerable time. "I do believe Miss Drenville is afraid of dancing," he remarked at last.

Closing her eyes, Emma nodded.

"But there is nothing to fear," he declared. Turning to the boys, he asked, "What is there to fear in dancing?"

They looked from one to the other and raised their hands in helpless ignorance.

"I'm damned if I know," said Frank.

"It is not dancing that is at fault," Emma said. "I am the one at fault. I am a loppet."

The dancing master refused to credit it. "I will not have a pupil of mine call herself by such an epithet," he said.

"And neither shall we!" Frank declared. "That is to say, we shall not have Miss Drenville call herself by such a name. If there are loppets skulking about this house, they are we, or rather, we are they. Is that not right, Nigel?"

Nigel agreed with vigor, as did Cecil and Cyril.

"I say," Frank went on, inspired, "suppose the four of us were to assist Mr. Grozett! Suppose we were to dance with Miss Drenville, taking our turns. Miss Drenville could not possibly fear dancing in that case. We are the least terrifying creatures who ever lived. What to you say to that, Mr. Dancing Master?" He concluded his question with a thump on the man's bony shoulder.

Brushing his coat, Mr. Grozett replied, "I am agreeable if Miss Drenville is."

All eyes were turned on her.

"Any port in a storm," she said with a sigh.

From that moment on, she disappointed five dancing partners instead of only one. As the fiddler played, he watched the partners take their turns and shook his head mournfully. Mr. Grozett grew so disheartened that he bargained with Emma, taking his oath she would never have to learn the quadrille if only she would try to go down the line without bouncing. Even the boys grew discouraged. The case seemed hopeless, until Captain Hale paid a chance visit to the dancing parlor.

He had just received a letter from Southampton which had put him in excellent spirits. Consequently, he entered with a sprightly step. He took in the gloomy faces one by one, came to rest at last on the face he loved best, and smiled.

Emma said, "We have done our best, Nicholas, but it is no use. We shall have to give it up."

"Never," he declared with force. "Why, what would Admiral Nelson think if we surrendered our ship without a fight? I shall tell you what he would think—that we deserved to have our faces painted on plates!"

CHAPTER FOURTEEN

My Lady's Brooch

Dear Grandpapa,

You will be pleased to know that I am occupied with writing a cookery book. I mean to include hare pasties, venison cutlets, and all your other favorites. Do assure Uncle Angus, Aunt Harriet, and Aunt Fanny that I shall include pigeon pie, too, in their honor. Madame DePois makes the double crust for her pigeon pie with a Huff Pastry which takes the place of potatoes or bread. It is wonderfully savory and you shall have a taste, as soon as I am able to bake it for you. I must not forget to mention, I am to dance at a ball with Captain Hale.

Your ever devoted,

Emma

The boys welcomed the captain with boisterous halloos and mock punches to each other's abdomens. After a time, he calmed them sufficiently to be heard when he suggested that they take his curricle and horses for a drive. Cheerfully, he waved to them as they raced from the parlor, tumbling over each other's feet.

He then turned to Mr. Grozett and the fiddler. It was no very great task to persuade them that the lesson might be declared finished for the day. They left with a promise of returning on the morrow.

When he was alone with Emma, Captain Hale said, "I have got rid of them solely in order that I myself might teach you to dance."

Her hand went to her heart.

Gravely, he took it. "Come," he said and led her forward as though he were leading her to the top of a line of dancers. "You are stiff, Emma. Do not be uneasy. It is not as though I meant to pull your tooth, you know."

She blurted out, "Why is it necessary that we dance? Why may we not simply go on as we are, seeing the sights of the Town? I should adore to visit Mr. Wedgewood's shop and buy a teapot for Aunt Fanny. I am perishing to visit the museum."

Gravely, he shook his head and considered the hand he held. "You must dance with me. The invitations have been arranged. It is all settled."

She sighed.

He drew close. "I have excellent reasons for insisting upon dancing with you, aside from the obvious ones, which have to do with courtship and lovemaking and all that sort of thing."

"Courtship?"

"Exactly so. Ordinarily, I should not dream of asking you to do the very thing you dislike most. But only by doing so will you see that you are not a loppet. More important, you will see how little it matters whether you are a loppet or not. I wish you to know that you are the woman I love, exactly as you are, and that I do not wish you to be otherwise."

"The woman you love?"

"Exactly so. That is why I cannot have you banishing me from your sight every fortnight or so, under the mistaken notion that you have disgraced me or will disgrace me. Our future depends upon your not banishing me from your sight ever again."

"Our future?" She could not repress a smile.

"Exactly so. However, I shall say no more on the matter, lest I spoil the surprise."

"Oh, by all means, let us not spoil the surprise!" Her smile was full now.

"Will you dance with me, Miss Drenville?"

"One moment please."

"What is the matter now?"

She put her free hand lightly on his chest and kissed him on the lips. Then, just as he reached for her, she pulled away and performed a perfect curtsy. "It shall be my pleasure to dance with you, sir," she said.

He bowed and they danced.

It would be delightful to report that Emma danced gracefully with her captain the remainder of the afternoon. Unfortunately, the words lately spoken by the captain inspired her to bound vigorously. All his patience and persistence were required to keep both of them from losing hope.

After half an hour, he paused, wiped his brow with his linen, and observed, "The difficulty is, you have persuaded yourself that you are a loppet. That is why you dance like one. Your feet are following the instructions given by your intellect."

"What am I to do? I cannot lie and tell myself that I am as graceful as a gazelle."

"And why not?"

"Because I should burst out laughing at such a hum!"

"Then do not think at all."

"If I do not think, I shall lose the count."

"I do not wish you to count. I do not wish you to look at your feet or anticipate the next step. I wish you to forget entirely that you are dancing."

"It is too disagreeable to be forgotten."

"Look at me. Look into my eyes. Think about my eyes. Think about the way my eyes look into your eyes. That is what you must think about."

"Yes, but Nicholas, if I do, I shall grow very warm."

"Exactly so, too warm to bound and hop overmuch."

They danced several turns with only a few mishaps.

Thus encouraged, the captain sent a note by way of the servant inviting Lady Chitting to accompany them on the pianoforte, and before another hour's practice was completed, Emma had learned the minuet.

"One wishes the minuet were danced more often," her ladyship lamented. "I fear it is regarded as the dance of the ancient, the infirm, and the married. Everybody else prefers the livelier dances."

"Oh, dear," said Emma.

Captain Hale was not to be daunted. Taking Emma's hand once more, and holding her eyes with his own, he taught her the reel, and because a modicum of bounding was appropriate to the dance, Emma's efforts met with success.

"The reel is all very well when you are dancing with Nikky," said Lady Chitting, "but what if you should dance with somebody else?"

Emma grew alarmed at the prospect.

Her ladyship said, "I shall persuade Lord Chitting to accompany us to the ball. He shall not refuse to dance with his precious Madelaine."

The captain added, "Mr. George Drenville shall certainly claim his dances. And I shall have all the rest of them."

"You shall have two, you scamp," Lady Chitting corrected, "three at the outside. Anything more would be very particular and kick up a dust."

At that moment, Nigel, Cecil, Cyril, and Frank entered to report that they had run the captain's curricle into a pothole on the Strand, but the horses were unhurt and there was only a little damage to the wheels. Their entrance was deemed auspicious. Each in turn was enlisted as a partner to Emma, thus demonstrating that it was possible for her to dance with a gentleman other than Captain Hale and not make a botch of it.

The following day, when Mr. Grozett returned, Emma was able to show him that she had made great strides. Although gazing into the dancing master's eyes was not at all as pleasant as gazing into the captain's, she found that thinking too little about dancing was preferable to thinking too much. She scarcely stepped on her teacher's toes above half a dozen times, and even the fiddler gave it as his opinion that Mr. Grozett would live to see his reputation enhanced by the young miss.

* * *

While Mr. Grozett drilled Emma in her steps, Madame Milledeux was far from idle. She fabricated for Lady Chitting's young protégé a frock of delicate white Anglo-merino. Its en coulisse was crisscrossed with gold thread under the bosom. That same gold thread embellished the melon sleeve and hem. It also adorned a white ribbon which Lady Chitting wound through Emma's hair. On the night of the ball, her ladyship inspected her minutely.

"My dear Madelaine," she said with sigh, "something is wanting."

Emma thought that, contrary to what her ladyship had declared, nothing was wanting. In fact, everything was perfect. Captain Hale was going to make her an offer of marriage that night; she was certain of it. Therefore, it was her obligation to give over all gloom and savor the joy which had come her way, just as she might savor a ragout she had devised for her cookery book. She must smile at everybody she saw, dance with relish, and accept Captain Hale's proposal with every appearance of not expecting it. In short, she must permit herself to be precisely what she was—the most fortunate creature alive.

"Well," said Lady Chitting, "are you not perishing to know what is still wanting in your costume?"

"Oh, yes," Emma fibbed.

"A jewel, dear girl."

"Very well. I shall wear the locket my grandpapa gave me."

Her ladyship's face fell, causing Emma to say, "Perhaps the locket will not do after all."

"It is a fine locket, Madelaine. It is only that I hoped you would wear something of mine."

Emma's eyes filled with sentimental tears. "I should like it of all things, my lady."

Lady Chitting flew into her dressing chamber and returned an instant later with a brooch. It was of the finest gold, worked in the shape of an oval and studded with diamonds. Emma gasped when she saw it.

"It belonged to my mother. I have had it reset, and I believe it does not look excessively outmoded."

Emma, who had never seen anything so beautiful, said, "I am afraid I shall lose it. Oh, I should never forgive myself if it were to fall off and come to harm."

"Nonsense. I shall fasten it to your bodice just here." She pinned it to Emma's frock and stood back to admire the effect. The brooch rested just at the décolletage and, in her ladyship's opinion, set off the rosiness of Emma's bosom very prettily. If the captain had not already meant to make Emma an offer that night, Lady Chitting mused, the strategically placed brooch would certainly have put the notion in his head.

There were those among the ton who speculated that His Majesty the Prince was the only living Briton who still professed a passion for chinoiserie, which, as all the world knew, had long since passed its peak. They were wrong. Lady Windolph had maintained a taste for things Chinese for the past quarter century, and though her guests might tire of paper lanterns, ceramic dragons, and red wallpaper ladened with lotus leaves and serpents, she persisted in imitating the Pavilion at Brighton, especially in its excesses. Thus, her ladyship's ballroom was festooned with symbols of the Orient, including junks, birds' nests, and even life-sized pagodas. There were three of the latter, placed on the fringes of the parquetry floor so that guests might go inside to contemplate the marvels of Cathay or to bill and coo with a lover, according to their taste.

Emma entered this lavish ballroom between Lord and Lady Chitting, both of whom hoped aloud that their precious Madelaine would not be intimidated by the crush, which was so thick and noisy as to cause his lordship to exclaim. In point of fact, Emma was not the least intimidated. She had observed a little scene in the cloakroom which had given her an entirely sanguine view of the ball. The scene had consisted of nothing more than a mother scolding a beautiful young lady on having twisted her silk shawl into a knot. While the two women restored the shawl to a presentable condition, the young lady received her mother's reproofs with ill-concealed yawns, until saying at last, "How tiresome, Mother, to be always thinking of ways to be anxious."

The words had struck Emma as wise beyond the girl's years. It *was* tiresome to be always anxious. Worse, it was flying in the face of heaven's gifts, of which she had lately known many. Yes, Emma thought, there would be missteps, but the crime was not in making them; it was in stewing over them to the ruination of everything else.

This bit of sage philosophy enabled her to enter the ballroom without trepidation. Indeed, as she was greeted cordially by her acquaintance, Lord and Lady Stonewood among them, she saw that since coming to London, fear of making a faux pas had caused her to focus attention too narrowly on herself, as though all the world had nothing better to do than to laugh at her. Thus, she had missed the magical sensation of being fully present to her surroundings.

Now, however, she was alive to them. She sensed electricity in the air, admiring glances, lilting music, murmurs of conversation, and tinkling laughter. As she took it all in, she discovered it was more delicious than any confection she might include in a cookery book. Even the pagodas, garish and fantastic though they were, were delicious.

Her delight lent her a radiance of which she was completely unaware, so that when Lord Chitting led her down to the dance for the first minuet, he could not help whispering, "I am very glad to have left the peace and quiet of my house to dance with you tonight, Madelaine."

She received this compliment with becoming modesty and concentrated on not counting her steps. Luckily, she was able to occupy herself with searching for the face of Captain Hale, who had not yet arrived as far as she could tell. Anticipating his appearance heightened the deliciousness of the evening.

When Lord Chitting had had his two dances, George

came to claim her. As they joined a square with seven other couples, he exclaimed, "Emma, you are slap up to the mark tonight. I vow, I am not ashamed to lead you down the set."

She gave him an arch look and accused him of arrant flattery.

"You think I am bamming you, do you? Well, I am not. I am entirely sincere. And if you wish to know how I can profess to be sincere and yet spend my time neglecting you and loitering about Stonewood House, I shall answer that I intend to reform my ways. Hereafter, I shall be entirely at your disposal, for you see, Lady Stonewood will have none of me."

A little confused, Emma said, "It was weeks ago that you made a similar announcement. What has happened in the meanwhile?"

"Ah, it is too painful to speak of."

"Do you mean to tell me that since we last spoke Lady Stonewood forgave you and then banished you again?"

Sheepishly, he confessed, "I do."

"Oh, George!" she cried. "I ought to have kept an eye on you."

"No, it is I who ought to have kept an eye on you. After all, we made a pledge to one another. We swore our fealty. It is true I have disregarded that pledge of late, but henceforth, I do not intend to forget what we are to each other and what promises we have exchanged. Tell me you will not forget either."

To her amazement, George slipped. George, the most fastidious creature on earth, the one most determined to be elegant, the one most mortified at the sight of her dancing!

His slip reminded her poignantly that she was not the only human creature who displayed an occasional awkwardness. More important, she was aware that she did not love her cousin the less for stumbling. All at once she comprehended how it was that Captain Hale could love her despite her myriad faults, and she exulted.

Unfortunately, exultation inspired her to bound, and her third bound caused her to miss a step. Anxiously, she scanned the faces of the other couples and found, to her delight, that her blunder had gone unnoticed. Even George did not seem to remark it. Indeed, they all ignored her, being completely consumed, she saw, with their own concerns.

At that moment, she spied Captain Hale by a pillar that had been painted to resemble a stand of bamboo. He was dressed in his uniform. Its dark blue color enhanced his dark hair and fine figure. If Emma had had any doubt before that this was the man she was destined to love and marry, it was now put to rest. He seemed too intent on his thoughts to smile.

"Emma, you have not answered me," George complained.

"Dear me, I am afraid I have forgotten the question."

He sighed. "You choose the oddest times to forget my questions."

Because her eyes met Captain Hale's at that moment, she could do no more than reply, "Yes, George, dear."

"Just say that you forgive me and have no objection to our being exactly as we were before."

"Yes, George, dear."

The dance ended, and, conscious that the captain was still watching her, she performed a curtsy. As she rose, she took satisfaction in knowing that not even Cecil and Frank could have done it better.

At the approach of the captain, George relinquished Emma's hand and bowed himself off. Captain Hale and Emma greeted each other formally, then took their places in the lines which were forming longways. Immediately, they were required to separate as each wove through the lines. But they soon met again, clasped hands, and danced to the bottom of the set. Emma observed that no matter where they stood, whether together or apart, his eyes never left her.

A welling of gratitude suddenly filled her, for she realized how right he had been to insist upon their dancing at a ball. The evening had taught her much that she would never have learned at Mr. Wedgewood's warehouse or the museum—for example, that a misstep was not necessarily a horrific calamity, that the most graceful creature alive could slip from time to time, that a stumble was not tantamount to a fatal flaw in one's character, and that a loppet was still entitled to love and be loved. When their hands joined for the circle, she felt a surge of confidence such as she had not known before.

Because the next dance was more sedate, Captain Hale was able to catch his breath and say, "At last we shall be able to have a little conversation."

Smiling, she said, "Mr. Grozett said nothing to me of conversation. He assured me I would not be obliged to do anything except keep the time and check my unfortunate inclination to bound."

"My dear Miss Drenville, there is no dancing without conversation. It is imperative to demonstrate that one is capable of speech and movement at the same time."

"I see. What is one obliged to say?"

"Well, I ought to inquired whether you are pleased with London. Are you pleased with London, Miss Drenville?"

"Oh, yes."

"You must give me a sly look now."

"Why?"

"That is what young ladies are expected to do. Words convey only a small particle of one's intended meaning. The rest is communicated by dint of expressions. You must learn to cultivate the simper, the snigger, and the sigh."

"I am afraid I shall have to make do with a smile." She smiled at him in such a manner that he seemed to forget the necessity for conversation. As a number of couples had begun to stare at them, she was obliged to say, "What else shall we speak of, Captain Hale?"

"I ought to ask you whether you have heard the latest *on-dit*."

"As I spend all my time indoors, practicing my dance steps, I am obliged to confess that I have heard no gossip."

"Neither have I, but we need not despair of continuing

the conversation, for I have yet to deliver my best smirk. Here it is, and I hope you admire it prodigiously."

She laughed at his affectation of smugness.

"My next duty is to tell you that you are in great beauty tonight. I wished to say something to that effect earlier but in dance conversation, one must not be overhasty. Besides, 'in great beauty' is an overused phrase which scarcely does credit to your appearance tonight."

Regarding him under her eyelashes, she remarked, "Is this flummery, Captain?"

"The only flummery is the pretense that I am enjoying this dance."

"Oh, dear, you are disappointed."

"Yes. I suddenly find that my passion for dancing has been replaced by an ambition to leave the floor with you and enter one of Lady Windolph's pagodas."

She answered his look directly. "I should like that."

He laughed. "Emma, you overturn every notion I have ever held of women. I half expected you to protest that you could not possibly and it would look so particular and so forth and so on."

"Why should I say such a thing? Your wish to visit the pagoda can mean only one thing, that you mean to reveal the surprise you promised me, and I shall tell you plainly, I cannot think of anything I should like better."

Captain Hale lost no time in leading her to the nearest pagoda, which was large enough to accommodate two people, if they were not overlarge. After they entered, he drew the curtain and they looked about them. The walls were papered in brilliant green and embossed with pagodas in silhouette. While there was no furniture, there were several pictures of pagodas in pen and ink. "One has the impression," the captain observed, "that her ladyship is fond of pagodas."

Emma reminded him gently, "We came to speak of the surprise, Nicholas."

He appraised her. "Did you think I had forgotten?"

"No, but I do not know how much longer I can contain my impatience."

"Very well, though I have a notion it will not be much of a surprise." Here, his expression grew serious. "Emma," he said, taking her hand, "the instant I met you, when you caused me to break that infernal plate, I found myself unaccountably drawn. I do not mean merely that I admired your beauty, though I did. I mean that I admired *you,* your candor, your lack of conceit, your strength of character, your excellent understanding, even your scruples, though they have occasionally proved inconvenient. It is no wonder then that I fell in love with you and . . ."

She did not permit him to finish but threw her arms around him and kissed him. To her gratification, his response was immediate. So tightly did he hold her that even if her lips had not been engaged, she would have been unable to utter a word. She understood suddenly what it was to be desired. When at last she was able to catch her breath, she said, "Yes, Nicholas, I shall marry you."

She had taken him by surprise, but it was such an agreeable surprise that he forgot for the moment where they were. When he remembered, it required a manful effort for him to collect himself. Gently, he set her at a distance, though within the confines of the pagoda, that could not be very far. "Emma," he said, aware that the words he was about to speak were among the most difficult he had ever uttered, "it would be best if we conducted ourselves discreetly." He saw her eyes go wide.

She cleared her throat. "You did not mean to ask me to marry you?"

"Of course I did. I was just getting round to it. I merely wished to avoid our being discovered in an awkward situation. As your affianced husband, I have a duty to protect your reputation."

He had the pleasure of seeing her smile. "My affianced husband? Then we are engaged?"

"Yes, we are, but as my bride to be, you must understand one very salient point."

"What is that?"

"Simply that I like your affectionate impulses far better than my deuced discretion."

So saying, he caught her to him and kissed her. Then, with a laugh, he lifted her high. He looked up to see her throw her head back and inhale the glory of sensation. Suddenly, she gazed down at him and bent her head. As their lips touched, he lowered her to a standing position. His mouth traveled eagerly over the skin of her cheeks and neck. As his hands coursed over her, he felt the trembling of her frame. It was both bliss and pain to realize that her urgency equaled his, that she loved him as much as he loved her, and that she wanted nothing from him but his love. She was the one human creature he could depend on to prefer his love to his lucre.

He said her name until he became conscious that once again they had gone too far. Reluctantly, he let her go.

He was disconcerted to find that though he no longer held her, he could not part from her, not because of any lack of discipline on his part but because her brooch had caught on his button. They were firmly attached to one another and no amount of pulling or wriggling succeeded in setting them free.

When she looked up at him, wearing a woeful look, he could not help laughing. "A most agreeable pickle," he observed.

Emma, it was plain, did not quite share his amusement. In some distress, she attempted to unpin the brooch. When that failed, she worked her fingers round it, hoping to loosen it from the button. This maneuver was no more successful than the last.

Patiently, he permitted her to struggle with the bauble, all the while conscious of her fragrant cheek and delectable ear. At last, when it was clear that she had made no progress, he offered his services. "I have lately had some success at untying knots," he said gravely. "It was not long ago that I released a young lady from her cloak, which had rudely imprisoned her. Perhaps I may be of use in this instance as well."

With an attempt at a smile, she dropped her arms to her sides and waited.

He gazed down, contemplating the best manner of attempting such a delicate operation. To put his hands to the brooch was to place Emma in an uncommonly distressing situation. However, as their situation was already very bad, he considered it was worth the risk. Hence, he fixed his attention on the brooch, endeavored not to notice its tantalizing surroundings, and attempted to unpin it. After a struggle, which proved fruitless, he thought he might have more success if he tried to loosen the button. While he was in the throes of this operation, the curtain parted, letting in the light of the ballroom.

Captain Hale looked up to see his father and Mrs. Leigh.

"Beg pardon," said the pater with a slightly raised eyebrow. "We did not know the pagoda was occupied."

Mrs. Leigh, meanwhile, stared openmouthed at the captain's hands. He looked down at them, too, as did Emma.

When the captain looked up again, he saw that his father and Mrs. Leigh had been joined by Lord and Lady Chitting. The latter were so shocked at what they saw that their lips trembled. His lordship gasped the words "precious Madelaine"; tears ran down her ladyship's cheeks.

He felt Emma start violently at the sight of them; he saw that the blood had drained from her cheeks.

"Lady Chitting," he said, more for Emma's comfort than his own, "please allow me to explain this foolish predicament. It is all on account of this ridiculous brooch."

"My mother's brooch!" Lady Chitting exclaimed, appalled.

"Oh, no, it is a beautiful brooch," Emma pleaded. "Please permit Captain Hale to explain."

Lady Chitting bowed her head and sobbed, "I thought that nothing could overset the mother of Nigel, Cecil, Cyril, and Frank, but to find my precious Madelaine in such a, such a *circumstance*! It is too much to bear."

Solicitously, Lord Chitting said, "Come, my sweet. We shall locate a vinaigrette at once." With a woeful glance at Emma, he led his tottering wife from the hall.

"Please, do not go!" Emma cried, and would have run after them if she had not been joined to Captain Hale.

The captain endeavored to calm Emma but she would not be calmed.

"I must speak with them," she cried. "I must set things to rights."

"We shall do exactly that," he told her gently, "as soon as we can undo this brooch." He would have made another attempt to free it, but because Mrs. Leigh, his father, and a fair-sized crowd were watching in what struck him as ghoulish fascination, he was reluctant to touch the offending bauble. As soon as he put his hands to it, their position would appear even worse, if that were possible.

He saw Emma close her eyes, in an effort, he guessed, to avoid seeing the growing number of spectators. Determined to free the brooch, he cast discretion overboard and set to work.

All at once, George Drenville and Lady Stonewood appeared. Her ladyship wore an expression of cynical amusement. George was aghast. "What has happened?" he demanded.

"George, you must go and find Lady Chitting," Emma begged him. "You must entreat her to hear me out."

"I cannot leave you, Emma!"

"Do not concern yourself with me. Captain Hale will undo the brooch and I shall be free in a moment. But Lady Chitting must be made to understand that I never meant to mortify her."

George slapped his hand to his forehead. "Blast it, Emma! There will be a scandal! It shall make the Admiral's oddities seem as less than nothing."

Captain Hale would have soothed George's alarms, but Emma said, "It is no use, Nicholas." She was not weeping. It was as if she was too grieved to weep. "There is nothing to be done. It is too late. I have disgraced you and everybody, exactly as I knew I would. The Drenvilles have won. Everything is lost." On that, she pulled herself from him, tearing the bodice of her frock, revealing a great deal of smooth pink skin and, in the process, freeing herself. She pushed her way through the crush and ran from the ball-room.

Seeing her disappear, Captain Hale felt bereft, as though he had been robbed. A moment ago, Emma had been his and the world had been theirs. Now he was alone, except for the pitiless bystanders. He would have followed her but was prevented by George, who blocked his path, lamenting, "This is entirely my fault. I ought to have kept an eye on her. If I had not abandoned her, she would not have had the leisure to fall into mischief."

Scarcely able to contain his anxiety to be gone, the captain said, "I shall go after her, have no fear. I shall calm her, and I shall prevent any scandal. You have my word on it."

George said gravely, "You are very kind, but it is my place to go after her."

"You take your cousinly duties far too much to heart. Believe me, when I say it shall be my pleasure to go after her."

"My cousinly duties be damned!" George wailed. "I am engaged to Emma. I must protect her and get her out of London at once."

"Engaged to her?"

"Yes, but I wonder if I it would be prudent to marry her, now that she has caused such a stir. She will not be able to show her face in Town again, which means that I shan't ei-ther."

"Mr. Drenville, did you say you are engaged to Emma?"

"Yes, but though I may not be able to marry her, I can at least look out for her welfare."

"You cannot be engaged to her," the captain said in an unnaturally quiet tone. "*I* am engaged to her."

George looked puzzled. "You cannot be engaged to her, *I* am engaged to her."

The crowd overlistened this conversation with avid interest. It was the juiciest tidbit in ages. The granddaughter of
Admiral Dreadful had not only been caught in a compro-
mising situation with a dashing sea captain, but she had engaged herself to two gentlemen at the same time! Who
would have suspected that such an innocent-looking creature could turn out a hussy and a heartbreaker? The faces of
the spectators registered an appropriate measure of shock
and indignation.

Captain Hale paid no attention to the crowd. Sternly, he
said to George, "She accepted my proposal of marriage just
tonight. Indeed, she accepted me even before I had the opportunity to make my offer. Therefore, she cannot be engaged to you."

George's brow wrinkled as he endeavored to piece out
the difficulty. "She gave me this ring to seal our betrothal,"
he said, drawing Emma's gift from his pocket. "Did she
give you a ring as well?"

Captain Hale took the ring and examined it. It was in-
scribed with a graceful *E*. "When did she give you this?" he
asked darkly.

"Before we left Southampton."

Taking George by the cravat so that he gasped, he said,
"Do you mean to tell me that she was engaged to you before you arrived in Town?"

"Oh, yes, well before. As I recollect, it was just before
the assembly at the Dolphin, at which I had the honor of
making your acquaintance."

Captain Hale let George go with a snap.

"You see," George explained as he straightened his cravat, "the Admiral has settled an amount of money on each
of us which we cannot touch until we are married. And so
we agreed it would be best to marry and have our own establishment, far from the Drenvilles."

"Why was it a secret?"

"It was not a secret. We merely did not mention it."

Captain Hale turned away. He did not wish to believe
that Emma had deceived him, that she had been playing a

deep game in order to gain an advantageous establishment, that finding him richer and better-connected than her cousin, she had ended by engaging herself twice. He did not wish to believe it, but then he did not wish to believe that his mother was what she was or that the pater was what he was. Wishes were a very different thing from facts, and the facts were, it seemed, that Emma was no different from anybody else he knew intimately.

A black look clouded his well-formed face. He remembered that this was not the first instance of Emma's deception. She had pretended to have an injured foot at the Dolphin. She had invented a cookery book out of the air. She had endured his father's touch without protest. She had flashed her fan under her bosom, summoning the leers and ogles of every male creature within a hundred yards, and had professed not to know what she was doing. In short, contrary to what he had thought, she was an accomplished prevaricator, and she had succeeded in beguiling him better than any Town-bred miss had ever done.

He was recalled to the present by a touch on his arm. Lady Stonewood had come to him and was smiling. "It was best that you found out now, Nikky, before it was too late. You shall see, one day you will be grateful to have been spared a disastrous marriage to your Miss Dreadful."

Although his mother's words mirrored his own thoughts, the sound of them was revolting. He scanned the crowd with an expression of contempt, wilted their expressions of glee, and strode away. As he exited the hall, he heard the hum of excited gossip rise and swell to a roar.

CHAPTER FIFTEEN

The Rescuers

Dear Nigel,

Please come at once to the green saloon. I am in need of
your help and trust you will not fail me.

E.D.

When Emma fled the ballroom, she found the coachman
lounging against a column in the hall, half dozing. Emma
guessed that her ladyship had not yet felt well enough to
travel and was reclining on one of Lady Windolph's divans.
Emma had a sudden impulse to fly to every room in the
house until she had found Lord and Lady Chitting, throw
herself at their feet and beg them to permit their precious
Madelaine to explain. But a more sensible course, she
knew, was to have the coachman carry her home, then return for his employers. In that way, she could prepare herself to face them when they entered the house. She would
have time to ready her apologies and to make them with
some semblance of rationality.

A short time later, she was deposited in Green Street. As
she entered the house thoughtfully, she rehearsed explana-
tions in her mind. So engrossed was she that she did not notice the butler's gaping jaw at the sight of her shredded
bodice. "I shall be in the green saloon," she said. "Kindly
inform me the instant her ladyship returns."

"Miss Drenville!" the butler gulped, but Emma was too
preoccupied to notice. She hurried to the saloon, seated herself on a low stool, and reviewed what little she had to say
in her own defense, namely, that the entire calamity had

been an accident. Moreover, any scandal which resulted from the evening's events would shortly be extinguished when she and the captain were married. Hearing that last bit of news would cheer Lord and Lady Chitting. She hoped so, at any rate, because it pained her to distress two creatures who had showered her with nothing but kindness and affection.

She heard the noise of stirring in the hall. Immediately, she ran to the door and threw it open. Instead of Lord and Lady Chitting, however, she saw Captain Hale. He turned to look at her, saying nothing.

His unexpected appearance melted her with tenderness. Walking toward him slowly, she embraced him and laid her cheek against his chest. "I cannot tell you how grateful I am that you have come. Your presence by my side gives me the courage I was lacking to speak to Lady Chitting."

When he did not answer, she said, "I was wrong to run off without you, wrong to think I could meet her alone."

It was not very long before she became aware that he stood stiff and unmoving. Drawing back, she regarded him. "Nicholas?"

His eyes fell on her torn bodice. So stark was his look that she was impelled to look down. Conscious for the first time of her immodest appearance, she covered herself with her arms.

He looked away. "I believe there is something you neglected to tell me," he said, in much the same tone he might use to inquire about the weather.

"Yes, there is." She came close to him, putting her lips so near his that for an instant it seemed as if he would cover her mouth with kisses. But he held rigid. She said quietly, "I have neglected to tell you I love you."

Though his eyes burned, he made no response.

"I was certain you already knew. That is why I said nothing earlier. However, I was on the point of saying so when I was caught by the brooch."

He stepped back. "You know perfectly well you have more to say to me than that."

"No," she said simply. "There is nothing more. I love you with all my heart. That is everything. The remainder of my speeches must be devoted to explaining my behavior to Lady Chitting."

For a second, he studied the floor. It struck her that he appeared unnaturally pale.

"What is the matter, my love?" she asked.

He seized her roughly by the arms. "You know very well what the matter is. You lied to me."

He might as well have struck her with the full force of his open hand. Hotly, she cried, "I never lied! I told you from the first what I was."

"If it were not for your cousin George, I should never have known the truth."

Incensed, she cried, "If you needed George to tell you, it is only because you deliberately blinded yourself."

"You dare to lay the blame at my door?"

She reeled at the venom in his expression. However, she refused to wilt in the face of it, for she knew herself to be unjustly accused. Staunchly, she replied, "You did not see me as I was, only as you wished me to be."

He leveled a cynical smile. "I cannot quarrel with you there. I was besotted, so besotted, in fact, that I believed you to be unlike the generality of females. I looked into those blue eyes, saw that frank expression, and deluded myself that here at last was a woman capable of being both fair and true."

This was more than she could bear. "I told you the truth," she cried, "every jot of it. It is not my fault you would not listen. And as to liars, if there is one in this drafty hall, it is not I. You lied when you said it would not matter to you if I danced like a loppet. You lied when you said I could not possibly disgrace you. You lied when you said that no scandal could part us. Your coming here in such high dudgeon proves *you* to be the liar in the case."

"I meant every word I said to you, and you know it."

"I know only that we have a remarkable turnabout here. Now that I do not condemn myself for each and every misstep, now that I have come to see that one need not be hanged for being a loppet, now that I am able to love freely and to be loved, you have taken it into your head to change your mind. You have, on a whim apparently, decided to condemn what you formerly excused. If it were not so painful, it would be vastly amusing."

"A whim, you call it! I came after you tonight for one reason—to hear the truth. I wish to hear it from your own lips."

She backed away, defying him. "I do not think so. I think you are lying again. I think your intention is to be released from our engagement. You may as well confess it, Captain, for it is written plainly on your face. You are sorry you ever made me an offer."

"I am sorry I ever set eyes on you, or any member of your sex."

His corroboration sank her. She had hoped he would argue with her, protest that he still loved her and wanted her. Despondently, she said, "Consider it done. I release you. You are free, as free as your button is from my brooch."

Icily, he replied, "Had I given you a token of our betrothal, I should accept its return this instant. But as no such gift was made, I can do no more than bid you good night." He did not stay for a rely but flung from the house.

The slamming of the door caused Emma to fear that the knocker would fall from its hinges and the pretty glass window, like herself, would shatter to pieces.

To her surprise, she did not dissolve. Instead, with every appearance of calm, she instructed the butler to inform her ladyship, immediately upon her return, that Miss Drenville awaited her in the green saloon and begged to be allowed to speak with her. On that, she went into the saloon, where she sat once more on the low stool and contemplated all the twists and turns of the previous hours.

That Captain Hale should blame her for an accident which was as much his fault as hers, that he should be disgusted by her behavior at this juncture when he had not been before, that he should all at once be driven off by the stares and sniggers of gossips, and, finally, that he should accuse her of deceiving him—all of it seemed incredible. It was not what she had come to expect of him. She had believed utterly in his steadiness and loyalty. The man who had just left her was not the Captain Hale she knew.

She waited for emotion to overcome her. She ought to feel a sense of betrayal, outrage, sorrow. But she felt nothing. So numb was she, in fact, that she sat for a full half hour without a single tear. The chiming of the clock on the mantel roused her at last. She stood and went into the hall, where she found the servant locking the door for the night.

"Has Lady Chitting returned?" she asked.

"Yes, miss."

"Did you not tell her I wished to speak with her?"

"I told her, miss."

"She refused to speak with me then."

The man reported sorrowfully, "Her ladyship begged me to say that she did not wish to speak with you ever again."

"I see. Thank you, Brill. Will you wait a moment before you retire? I wish to send a note to Mr. Nigel Chitting."

"I expect he is asleep, miss."

"I expect you are right. I am afraid you must wake him. I shall just go into the saloon and write out the note. I shall not be long."

Within minutes, she had delivered the note into the butler's hand. Again, she went into the green saloon to sit and wait. This time, she did not sit on the low stool. The time for abjectness had passed. It was time for action, and that required all her determination and confidence. Her numbness would help immensely. She prayed that she would remain numb long enough to do all that was necessary, before the full impact of her loss hit her.

Nigel entered rubbing his eyes. He wore a dressing gown, as did his brothers, who followed him into the saloon, yawning and blinking, except for Frank, who demanded to know whether there was to be a prank or some such fun. They stood before Emma in a row, too sleepy to fall over one another's legs.

She rose from the sofa. "I wish to return to Southampton," she said. "To do so, I shall require your assistance."

A wail of protest went up. "Have we offended you in some manner?"

Patiently, she replied, "I fear I have made Lord and Lady Chitting unhappy."

"That is nothing!" they assured her. "We are always making them unhappy. But they never send us packing to Southampton, or any other place. They are too goodhearted for that."

"I am afraid they are deeply displeased with me, and it is best I go away, at least until they have had a little time to consider whether they might hear my explanation."

"Oh, do not leave us. We shall miss you dreadfully."

"I shall miss you too, but it is time I returned to my family. It occurs to me that I belong with them, and I very much wish to be in their midst as soon as I may."

The boys toed the carpet and sighed. It was impossible not to sympathize with a young lady who was homesick, especially such an agreeable young lady as Miss Drenville.

"How may we assist you?" Nigel asked.

"I have no means of transportation."

Frank was seized with an inspiration. "I have it! We shall take Father's carriage, and in less than a day, we shall carry you back to repose in the bosom of your family."

Emma smiled at this bravado. "I have disappointed his lordship enough for one day. I should not like to steal his carriage into the bargain. Nor should I like to be the cause of your being in his bad graces."

"Oh, that is nothing! We are always in his bad graces."

"I thought perhaps you might assist me in hiring a private conveyance to take me as far as the Maidenhair Tree, where I might wait for the stagecoach to Southampton."

Nigel nodded. "I believe we shall be able to do as you ask."

"No, we shan't!" Frank said.

They all blinked at him.

"Are we men or a collection of milksops? Are we too chicken-hearted to rescue a damsel in distress? Shall we permit her to travel alone on the stage, while we, sniveling fellows that we are, lie sleeping in our beds, all because we fear a little frowning from our father?"

"I shall not travel alone," Emma said. "I shall have Mary, my lady's maid."

"Faugh!" said Frank in contempt. "As if a girl of her size could protect you from highwaymen!"

Emma blanched. "Highwaymen?"

"Have you never heard of Gallows Jack?" Cecil asked.

"It is said his dagger left a scar across a lady's cheek this long," added Cyril, holding his hands several inches apart.

"But not before he assaulted her person in every vile way imaginable," Frank said with relish.

Putting up her hands, Emma said, "I am too weary to argue further. If you tell me I must take his lordship's carriage, I shall do as you say."

"And we shall ride with you," Frank said.

"Oh, no! I could not ask you to ride so far."

"You did not ask," Nigel pointed out. "Frank offered. Besides, it would be best if we were along, just to keep a lookout for Father's horses."

Emma glanced from one to the other, and as she did, she smiled. "You are very dear, all of you." One by one, she kissed their cheeks.

This show of affection inspired them to race to the door. Each wished to be the first dressed and ready to hand Miss Drenville into the carriage which would take her from London and its many vexations.

The following afternoon, tired but relieved, Emma and her escorts were received at Cracklethorne. They were ushered into the deer parlor, where the Admiral was seated with Lady Landsdowne.

Her ladyship rose. The unannounced arrival of Miss

Drenville in the company of her nephews boded ill, it seemed to her. As soon as introductions were performed and Emma had kissed her grandfather, the lady demanded, "Nigel, Cecil, Cyril, Frank, what do you mean by coming here?"

"We have rescued Miss Drenville, Aunt."

This did not bode any better. "Why, pray tell, did Miss Drenville require rescuing?"

"She has put Mother and Father in a snit."

Lady Landsdowne questioned Emma with her eyes.

With a sigh, Emma confessed that it was so.

Her ladyship sank down onto the sofa again. "Gracious, you must have been very bad indeed if you have contrived to put my sister in a snit. She is the most forgiving creature alive. She has certainly had a great deal of practice!" This last sentence was accompanied by an ominous look at her nephews.

Blissfully unaware that he had just been given a setdown, Frank agreed with his aunt. "She is right as a fiddle, our mother is."

"Is it true, dear Emma?" the Admiral said softly, taking her hand. "Has there been some difficulty?"

"I am afraid so, Grandpapa. I have made a muddle." At that, the emotion that had refused to come earlier now rushed forth. She shook. A sob escaped her, then a torrent.

As there was nothing he could do, either to reverse the misfortune or to make it go away, the Admiral folded her in his arms and held her. "I am glad you have come back," he whispered. "Very glad."

As Lady Landsdowne was not the least bit glad, she made her excuses and took her leave. "You shall accompany me," she announced to the boys. "I shall have you washed and fed and sent back to my poor sister. I declare, I do not know how she has contrived to endure you all these years."

Drying her tears, Emma took leave of the boys. Nigel assured her that he was completely at her service any time she might require rescuing. Cecil and Cyril wished her a speedy return to London, and Frank once more offered himself up as a prospective husband.

"I shall come into my money in six years," he said. "And if you have not already been shackled to some lucky dog by then, I shall present myself to you."

"Your mother will not like it."

"Oh, Mother will change her mind. She always does." They followed their aunt from the parlor, slapping each other's shoulders and mussing each other's hair. Her ladyship scolded them in vain.

When they were alone, the admiral said, "Emma, my dear, have you quarreled with Captain Hale?"

She gazed at him in amazement.

"He wrote to me asking permission to pay his addresses. Naturally, I wished him good sailing. But now you come home unhappy, and with no announcement to make. I surmise that either you do not like Captain Hale or you have quarreled with him."

"I do like him, Grandpapa. Indeed, I am in love with him. But he no longer wishes to marry me."

"Why?"

She could not explain without alluding to the Drenvilles, their reputation, and her own folly, all of which were too painful to contemplate at the moment. Happily, she was not obliged to answer. Angus entered with Fanny and Harriet and a hullaballoo went up as they greeted their dear Emma with hugs and expressions of delight.

"Why have you come back so soon?" Angus asked.

Emma smiled to see that his bluntness had not abated one iota. "I have behaved dreadfully," she said.

"What did she say?" Harriet shouted.

As Fanny repeated the words at top volume, Angus laughed. "You have behaved like a Dreadful, my little flutterbelle! We are prodigiously proud of you."

At first she colored. Then, she nodded. Finally, she laughed. Her heart might be breaking, but she could not be blind to the absurdity which met her everywhere, and so she laughed, even while she wept.

"Did you come back married?" Angus asked.

"What did he say?"

"He asked if Emma has come back married."

"Oh. Well, has she?"

"Stop shouting, woman and put that trumpet to your ear. What good is a trumpet if you will not apply it?"

"What did Emma say?"

"She said nothing. You interrupted her, you nodcock. For pity's sake, give the girl a chance to answer before you begin barking at her."

In the course of this exchange, Emma tiptoed to the door unnoticed. She was tired, had not slept at all that night, and wished nothing more than to crawl into her own bed. She was home, for better or worse, and as the loud voices of her relations followed her out of the parlor and down the corridor, she calculated that, taken all in all, it was probably for the better.

CHAPTER SIXTEEN

Invitation to a Wedding

My dear Miss Drenville,

I have had a letter from my sister, who informs me that your late adventure in Lady Windolph's pagoda interested the gossips for scarcely a week. It appears that Mrs. Leigh's elopement to Gretna Green with Lord Stonewood's son has been on everybody's tongue, to the exclusion of all else. I hope this news brings you some solace and that, as promised, you will send me the receipt for the excellent macaroon cakes in Italian cream which I praised last night at the Admiral's table. I am obliged to add that I suspect my sister's distress at your conduct has affected her mind. She writes that she and his lordship miss their precious Madelaine excessively and wish to embrace her once more. I have never heard of this Madelaine creature. Can you enlighten me as to her identity? If not, then it appears my sister's mental incapacity may prevent any likelihood of your ever being restored to her good graces.

Yours etc.,

D. Landsdowne

Five days after Emma's return to Southampton, George entered the door at Cracklethorne. "I could not stay in Town without Emma," he explained to his family, which gathered round him in the deer parlor and welcomed him in their inimitably noisy manner.

"What did you pay for that watch fob?" Angus demanded. "I trust it was not a great deal, for it looks a shabby thing."

"What did he say?" Harriet inquired.

"It is good you have come home, my boy," the Admiral

welcomed him. "Perhaps you will cheer your cousin. She has been dreadfully cast down of late."

George kissed Emma's cheek, saying, "You ought not to have gone from London without me. If anybody was to steal his lordship's carriage and bring you to Southampton, it ought to have been me. I have been chastising myself these several days for putting you at the mercy of the boys. They are excessively goodhearted, but they are always getting into scrapes."

"As you see," she said with a smile, "I have arrived safely. Were the boys very much scolded for taking the carriage?"

"To tell the truth, nobody at Chitting House seemed up to doing very much scolding, or anything else for that matter. They were too gloomy. The place was a veritable tomb."

With a sigh, Emma said, "I am sorry to hear it."

She could not indulge sorrow long, however. The reunion of his beloved family had put her grandfather in a celebratory mood. There must be a dinner to welcome his grandchildren home, he said. Lord and Lady Landsdowne must be invited, along with Mrs. George Austen and her daughters. And Emma must fashion one of her very finest desserts—macaroons in Italian cream, if she would be so kind.

On the next day, Emma sought to speak with her cousin in private. She invited him to walk out with her to the wooded stream where she customarily gathered watercress. Though the season for cress had passed, she was anxious to see whether she might find any late-blooming Jack by the Hedge for the salad at her grandfather's dinner.

As they entered the wood, she inquired, "Do you think I might write to Lord and Lady Chitting? Do you think they would read my letter? Would they go so far, do you think as to answer it?"

George sighed. "I do not know, Emma. Truthfully, I do not know anything!"

This confession, spoken with considerable vehemence, did not sound like the opinionated George Drenville she knew. "I have never heard you talk so," she said.

"My acquaintance with Lady Stonewood has opened my

eyes. She made an ass of me. That is to say, she permitted me
to make an ass of myself."

She put her hand soothingly on his arm.

"She used me, not merely to flatter her vanity with my
fawning attentions, but to arouse the jealousy of her husband
toward Mrs. Leigh. And what did I reap as my reward for
being so prodigiously useful? The opportunity to give her pre-
sents and lend her money! I declare, Emma, I am thoroughly
ashamed of myself."

"You are not to blame. The Stonewoods are a remarkably
attractive family. Consequently, one wishes to believe what
they say. How could you possibly know that they are not to
be trusted?" Her words revived a number of painful reflections, so that she was obliged to stop speaking.

"There was ample evidence," George said. "I simply refused to see it. I was even warned, by Captain Hale, and still I
refused to listen."

She wet her lips before saying, in as light a voice as she
could manage, "There are some gentlemen, it seems, who believe only what they wish to believe."

"It is plain as a pikestaff that I am one of them, but who are
the others, pray tell? I should take comfort in knowing that I
am not alone in being a puddinghead."

Rather than answer, Emma stooped to inspect a Jack by the
Hedge growing in a damp spot near a beech. Its leaves were
still ripe for picking and so she proceeded to fill her basket.
The flowers, which were dried and pale, fell onto her skirt,
staining it with petal dust.

"I shall tell you something else," George continued. "It will
astound you, and you will give me a wigging when you hear
it, but, Emma, this entire visit to London has taught me to appreciate what I have in the Drenvilles."

Emma looked tenderly at her cousin. "Far be it from me
to give you a wigging. I have reached the very same con-
clusion. There is nobody one may rely upon so completely
as Grandpapa and our uncle and aunts, despite their oddities. They do not care whether we have made cakes of
ourselves or what gossips may say of us. They adore us

and are more than delighted to take us in under any circumstances."

"Precisely. And knowing that, I am quite ready to be a Drenville. Our family may have its deficiencies, but at least we are not wanting in character and principle. I much prefer those who shout and babble to those who exploit and scheme."

Impulsively, she kissed George's cheek.

Blushing, he said, "I have more to tell you, and I am afraid that this time, you really shall give me a wigging, for I must confess, these past days I have doubted you."

"Ummm," she replied, inspecting a bird cherry tree. Taking stock of the number of blooms, she estimated the amount of fruit she might expect to harvest that summer for jamming.

"That is to say, I doubted whether you really wished to marry me."

She turned and regarded him. "Marry you? Whatever gave you the notion that I wished to marry you?"

"Blast it, Emma, it was not two months ago we stood near this very spot and you accepted me."

"George, I never did any such thing."

"You did! At least, I thought you did. You said you wished to see me happy."

"Yes, I did. I still do. But what has that to do with marriage?"

"Well, we had been talking of marriage and then you said you wished to see me happy, and so I naturally assumed. . . . Blast it, Emma, if you did not mean to have me, why did you give me this ring?" From his pocket, he took the trinket and held it up to view so that a beam of sunlight through the trees made it sparkle.

"The ring is a token of my love for you, George. I love you as I would a brother."

He slapped himself on the forehead and groaned. "Tell me, did you or did you not engage yourself to Captain Hale?"

Reluctantly, she confessed, "I did."

George shook his head. "Now I comprehend why he was in such a state."

Emma stiffened. She recollected the captain's "state" very
well. Even now she could hear his unjust accusations and his
repeated use of the word liar. As a rush of mortification
seized her, she replied, "Perhaps you comprehend his being in
a state, George, but I assure you, I do not."

"I expect he was not very pleased to hear that you were engaged to me as well as to him."

She stared. "What?"

"I believed you were engaged to me. Otherwise, I never
should have mentioned it to him. He said you could not be
engaged to me as you were engaged to him, whereupon I said
you could not be engaged to him as you were engaged to me.
We went round like that for a time until I produced your ring.
The sight of it put him in an uproar, I can tell you. Oh, Emma,
it is all such a blasted muddle."

Emma paid scant heed to the rest of this speech. What interested her was the fact that George had told Captain Hale
that she was already engaged. The words he had flung at her
in the hall of Chitting House took on a very different con-
struction now. They had had nothing to do with any awkward
conduct on her part, she saw; they had stemmed from the lie
he had heard.

She put her hand to her eyes and wondered whether she
was on the point of laughing or crying. In the end, she did a
little of both.

George patted her shoulder gingerly, and said, "I wish you
every happiness, Emma. I like Captain Hale and I think the
two of you will suit better than you and I would have done."

That was when she wept. "We are no longer engaged," she
said when she could command her voice again. "He has broken with me."

"Oh," said George bleakly. "Well, if you still wish to be
married, and if do not mind very much that we do not love
each other, and if you fancy being shackled to a puddinghead,
and if you wish your children to be blessed with a double
dose of Drenville blood, then consider this—I am still at liberty!" He grinned at her fondly.

That was when she laughed.

* * *

Captain Hale was determined to lose no time in forgetting his unfortunate acquaintance with Miss Emma Drenville. He showed himself at a number of routs, where he danced and flirted relentlessly, frequented a number of gaming houses, where he played for high stakes, often in the company of his mother, and cheered from the sidelines at boxing matches and horse races, where he poured as much champagne over the heads of his companions as he did down his own throat. His escapade in the pagoda had given him a reputation among the gentlemen of the Town as a blade. The gentle sex regarded him as a rogue who thought nothing of endangering a lady's reputation, and in consequence, they found him devilishly attractive. Taken all in all, Captain Hale had never enjoyed such popularity.

His reckless pursuit of amusement came to an abrupt end late one afternoon, when he was awakened by Mr. Ponce and informed that a lady had come to see him and now waited in his sitting room. Ordinarily, Captain Hale would have dismissed the information with a wave of his hand, rolled over, and gone back to nuzzling his pillow. However, when he learned that the visitor was Lady Chitting, he allowed Ponce to help him into his dressing gown and make him as presentable as possible for entertaining.

In the sitting room, the captain found a distraught Lady Chitting. He urged her to sit and brought her a glass of wine to calm her.

"Oh, Nikky, you poor boy," she lamented, "I am so sorry. I hope you are not entirely overset by the news."

"What news?"

"Good heavens, where have you been? Everybody is talking of it."

"I have been sleeping off the effects of a week's amusement. What is everybody talking of?"

"Your brother Stonewood. He has run off with Mrs. Leigh. They have eloped."

He took a moment to absorb this news. The irony of it got the better of him and he laughed.

This response astonished her ladyship. "I made sure you

would be perfectly dismal. After all, your brother is the heir to the title, and he has gone off and married a female of little fortune, scant blood, and no morals. What is to become of your family?"

"We shall do as we always do, which is to say, we shall do as we please without a thought to anybody else."

"You did not used to be bitter, Nikky."

"Well, I have changed, thanks to your Miss Drenville."

At the mention of the name, Lady Chitting let forth a stream of tears. "His lordship is quite low, now she is gone," she sniffed. "And the boys haven't the heart to do mischief any longer. She used to permit me to dress her hair, you know. I very much liked arranging her curls. One cannot dress a boy's hair. They will not sit still for it."

Having no wish to recollect Miss Drenville's hair or any of her ravishing qualities, he turned the subject. "It was good of you to come, but as you see, I am bearing up nobly under the scandalous news."

"And she cooked the most excellent dishes. Even Madame DePois misses her."

"I shall visit my mother and father to see how they do."

"She was our precious Madelaine."

Irritably, the captain said, "Lady Chitting, if what you wish to do is reconcile with Miss Drenville, then I beg you to do so and leave me in peace. She was not to blame for the events in the pagoda. I was. I kissed her so violently that her brooch became fastened to my button. It was a thoroughgoing piece of foolery and not worth the dust it has kicked up."

"It was *your* fault?"

"Yes, I do not see why everybody is always so ready in such cases to condemn the young lady and excuse the gentleman. Miss Drenville may be censurable for some things, but not this."

"Oh, Nikky, I have been wrong, very wrong. I thought only of the scandal. I did not think of what poor Madelaine might be suffering."

"You meant well. We all did, excepting some of us."

"Oh, thank you, dear boy. You have opened my eyes."

"If you wish to thank me, then make it up with your precious Madelaine, which, if I make my guess, is what you intended to do all along, but spare me any further mention of her name."

She clapped her hands. "Yes! I shall write to my sister to drop the proper hints. And when Madelaine writes to me, I shall forgive her with all my heart. I only hope she will forgive me!"

He opened the door so that the lady might make her exit before she made too many more allusions to Miss Drenville.

When at last she was gone, Captain Hale endeavored to rouse himself from the previous week's debauchery and, despite a reeling headache, contrived to dress. He breakfasted on coffee and biscuit, which he congratulated himself on being able to keep down, and took himself off to pay a visit in Portman Square.

His mother sat at her dressing table, preparing for a night of cards. She betrayed no great anguish over the marriage of her eldest son to her husband's mistress. "It serves them all right" was her succinct summation.

The pater was equally dispassionate. He smoothed the folds of his cravat and remarked, "Mrs. Leigh is not the wife I would have chosen for my heir, but I suppose she is not very much worse than your Miss Dreadful."

No sooner did he take leave of his parents than Captain Hale paid a call on an old acquaintance, an admiral of the Red Fleet. He spent an hour with the gentleman and came away with every assurance that the *Ambuscade* would be ready to sail in short order. When he returned to Fladong's, he retired to his rooms, and, sitting in a clawfooted chair, prepared his mental log.

His first entry concerned his recent devotion to bacchanalia, which had succeeded in giving him an acute sense of emptiness and ennui, but had not succeeded in obliterating the memory of Miss Drenville. Amusement, he concluded, was not at all amusing.

His next entry concerned Miss Drenville. As he remembered his last encounter with her, he saw her standing before him in her torn and disheveled condition, lying and denying. It had taken every ounce of discipline in him to master the impulse to reach for her, to keep from throwing reason overboard just so that he might touch her bare shoulder and taste her ear.

This recollection rendered him mighty uneasy, not to mention warm about the collar. Thus, he concluded it was folly to look back. He must look ahead, toward the horizon. He must chart his course and weigh anchor as soon as his ship was ready. He must drown all thoughts of Miss Drenville in a long voyage, a dangerous one if it could be arranged. The admiral had promised to do what he could on his behalf. Very soon, within a matter of weeks, perhaps, he would receive his orders.

But what the devil, he wondered, was he to do with himself in the meanwhile?

The answer was delivered to him by a servant, who carried it in on a salver. It consisted of a letter, which he tore open and read with interest:

My dear Hale,

I, who have never believed in anything so sentimental and ridiculous as miracles, must now write to you with the announcement of one. The miracle is this—Miss Merkle has accepted my hand and heart in marriage. The deed is to be done Tuesday next. Will you come? Although I am able to walk to the altar under my own power, I do not think I can bear up under all my good fortune without my old friend to see me through. Nothing would give me greater pleasure than the company of the man who saved my life as I take to wife the woman who has made it worth living.

Until I may shake your hand, I sign myself yours,

Dib

The letter placed Captain Hale in a dilemma. There was nothing he required so much at the moment as a diversion, and his friend's wedding seemed to answer that need perfectly. In addition, it promised to be a genuinely delightful occasion, for Lieutenant Dibdin Bentworthy was an excellent fellow and deserved every happiness. But the marriage was to take place in Southampton, the city to which Miss Drenville had fled. It was the last place he wished to go. As soon as he stepped foot in the Dolphin, inconvenient recollections would seize him. When he walked down the High Street and passed by the china shop, he would be done for. No, he could not possibly go to Southampton.

Taking up pen and paper, he prepared to write his regrets to his friend.

It struck him, however, that to avoid Southampton on Emma's account was to give that treacherous young lady far more power than he wished her to have. Though it might cost him a pang to tread the same streets she trod, though he might easily imagine he saw her on every corner and in every shop, he would be a paltry fellow indeed if he permitted such considerations to keep him from his duty to his friend. Surely, he could enter Southampton, a city of eight thousand, without encountering Miss Drenville. And if he did encounter her, surely he could do so without wringing her neck. Surely, a captain of his own ship, a man who had fought at Trafalgar, a man who had saved another man's life, captured enemy frigates and privateers, amassed a considerable fortune, and gained an estimable reputation, could come face-to-face with Miss Drenville and survive. Surely, these things were possible. Surely.

Like Captain Hale, Emma received a letter which caused her to deliberate at length. She was sitting with her grandfather, showing him the great progress she had made on her cookery book, when Lady Landsdowne's letter was brought to her. The Admiral urged her not to mind him but to read it immediately, for he was engrossed in her description of a mincemeat of lemon and did not wish to be interrupted.

Pacing the parlor, Emma read. To her joy, she learned that

Lady Chitting missed her. It appeared that the time had come at last when she might write to her ladyship and make amends.

But the same letter also brought troubling news. It reported that Lord Stonewood's son had eloped with Mrs. Leigh. She could not help fearing that the son was Captain Hale. His anger at her was so great that he might easily have done something rash. His disillusion at what he imagined was her betrayal might well have propelled him into the arms of another. A portentous feeling overcame her that she had lost him forever.

Her sighs caught the Admiral's attention. He begged her to be quiet, as he was reading her description of Jerusalem soup and his mouth was watering. "Will it be very long until tea?" he asked.

Curbing her sighs, Emma resumed her pacing and thinking. She would write at once to Lady Chitting. She would lay all the truth before her and trust that good creature's heart to know how to respond. Once she had patched it up with Lord and Lady Chitting, she would ask them to assist her in telling Captain Hale the truth. If by good luck he was still unmarried, and if he had not conceived a complete aversion to her, he might, in thirty or forty years, be brought to believe her.

Captain Hale saw the bride and groom married off, as was fitting, in the "sailor's church"—Holyrood Church on the High Street. He saw them carried off, as was fitting, in a coach bound for a honeymoon by the seaside. He saw the coach disappear round a corner and, at the same moment, heard a familiar voice call out his name.

"Ahoy there, Captain Hale! Draw up along side."

He turned to see sundry Drenvilles approaching, led by the Admiral, who clapped him warmly on the shoulder. "Well, Captain, what news of Bonaparte? When do you think he means to launch his attack?"

Angus chortled, "Well, it is Captain Hale!"

To which Harriet replied, "It is not. It is Captain Hale!"

"That is what I said, you nodcock. Why do you carry that infernal trumpet if you do not mean to put it to your ear?"

The clamor of their conversation attracted the stares of passersby. However, Captain Hale did not notice. He was aware only that one Drenville was missing—Emma.

"I daresay, Captain, you are here to visit your bird," Angus said to him with a wink.

Too busy wondering where Emma was, he did not reply.

"Your bird, your bird," Angus repeated. "Did you not say, when we were introduced at the Dolphin assembly, that you kept a bird in Southampton?"

At this juncture, George caught up with them. "This is good luck indeed, Captain," he said. "I thought I should never set eyes on you again, and here you are!"

"Yes, here I am. Tell me, Mr. Drenville, am I to wish you joy?"

Initially, George was baffled. Then as the captain's meaning dawned on him, he grinned. "No, sir, I am not married. Nor am I to be married. I fear I was misinformed on that head."

"The lady has jilted you, I collect. I am not surprised." He betrayed more bitterness in his tone than he intended.

"Oh, Emma would never jilt a fellow. It was all my own doing. I thought we were engaged, but it appears she never had any such intention."

Having been too credulous in the past, the captain was skeptical. "But she gave you a ring," he said.

"Yes, but she never gave me her heart. That she has given to another. A sailor, I believe."

Captain Hale inspected the young man's grin with narrow eyes. "What proof do I have that this time you are telling the truth?"

"None, only Emma's confession to me. But as I am her cousin and dearest friend in all the world, I know she was telling the truth."

The captain thought for some time, wishing to credit what he had heard but unwilling to be wrenched apart again.

"By the by, she has gone to the North West Tower,"

George said. "If you join her there, you may ask her your-self."

On that, the captain bowed smartly and made at a good pace for the Bargate.

The air was soft and mild, with enough salt to make it agreeable to sightseers on the tower, of whom, at the moment, there were only two—Emma and her Aunt Fanny. Leaning side by side on the stone rim, they gazed out to sea.

"Gracious," Fanny cried, "I forgot to buy suet for the canary's cage! I went to the tobacconist and found Angus's snuff, and then to the linen draper's, where I purchased yarn for Harriet's shawl, and then I stopped at the confectioner's for a taste of angelica, but I never thought to buy suet. I must go to the High Street at once. Emma, you will excuse me, I know."

Fanny was gone before Emma could offer to accompany her. Slowly, she turned back to the ocean waves. Their slow breaking and receding sent up a rhythm which, to Emma's ears, sounded mournful.

Hearing someone approach, she looked round. To her astonishment, she saw Captain Hale. So many possible words and actions leaped to her imagination that she could not move.

He studied her with a hard expression.

Taking a breath for courage, she said, "Have you married Mrs. Leigh?"

"Does it matter?"

"Yes. If you intended to make an imprudent match, I hoped you would make it with me."

After a pause, he said stiffly, "I am not married, and Mr. Drenville says you were never engaged to him."

She did not know how on earth George had contrived to communicate the truth to him, but she was profoundly grateful that he had. "I have been engaged to only one man in my life," she said. "Unfortunately, it was not for very long."

"It appears I accused you falsely," he said.

He came so close that she might have touched his brow, if she dared.

"And I accused you falsely."

"Did you?"

"Yes, you took your oath you did not stick at allying yourself to a Dreadful, and it appears you meant it."

He smiled a little. "Will you permit me to apologize, or will you run shrieking from my presence to the safety of a kitchen?"

"I shall not run from you again."

"Emma, you must understand that I do not trust easily." He took her hand and looked down at it. "My family—I need not tell you what they are—have taught me to be wary. I do not know whether I can unlearn the habit of a lifetime."

"If you will allow me, I shall spend a lifetime helping you unlearn it."

He glanced at her with a raised eyebrow. "Are you making me an offer of marriage, Miss Drenville?"

"That depends on whether you can abide being shouted at, treated to endless itineraries, and warned repeatedly of Bonaparte's imminent invasion."

"I think I could abide anything, if you were there."

"I should like to be there."

"Brewing beer, stirring lavender water, preparing fricassee, and putting it all down in your cookery book." He drew her to him and brushed her lips with his. Although he did not speak, the intensity of his embrace was eloquent.

"You must never doubt me again," she whispered between kisses.

"Yes, but I probably shall." He caressed her head so that it rested on his breast. Nuzzling his chin in her hair, he closed his eyes.

"Why should you doubt me?" she asked.

"As I have said before, no family is perfect. We shall certainly not be perfect. I am afraid, Emma, that we shall merely be happy."

She looked up at him. "I do love you."

Unaccustomed as he was to such declarations, hers moved

him profoundly. He kissed her again, this time with the full force of his need.

The sound of the Admiral calling their names roused them. "Ahoy there, Emma! Ahoy, Captain! Come aboard!"

Emma disengaged herself reluctantly and adjusted her person.

They looked over the tower rim to see the Admiral and his family on the street below, waving and shouting to them.

"Remember, my little goosechild, you are no spring chicken," Angus called. "You had better take the captain while you may!"

"But only if you like him!" Harriet yelled.

The captain and Emma exchanged a smile.

"Come," he said, taking her hand. "Let us go down and permit ourselves to be petted and adored."

As they descended the steps, he stopped her. "Do you suppose," he asked, "that you could contrive to stumble and fall so that I might catch you?"

"I have never contrived such a thing before. It has always come quite naturally."

"It does not matter to me how you do it, so long as you end up in my arms."

A stumble ensued, followed by a timely catch and a number of kisses. They then went down to the street, where they were embraced by a party of noisy, inquisitive, joyful Drenvilles.